FLAMES
OF ANARCHY

Also by Leslie Scase

Fortuna's Deadly Shadow
Fatal Solution
Sabrina's Teardrop

FLAMES
OF ANARCHY

LESLIE SCASE

SEREN

Seren is the book imprint of
Poetry Wales Press Ltd
Suite 6, 4 Derwen Road, Bridgend,
Wales, CF31 1LH

www.serenbooks.com
Follow us on social media @SerenBooks

ISBN: 978-1-78172-762-1
Ebook: 978-1-78172-763-8

A CIP record for this title is available from the British Library.

The publisher acknowledges the financial assistance of the
Books Council of Wales.

The maps of Pontypridd from the 1890s are adaptations of
OS maps kindly provided by Pontypridd Library

To my wonderful family and friends

Pontypridd Town Centre c.1896

Pontypridd Station, Graig and Tumble Area

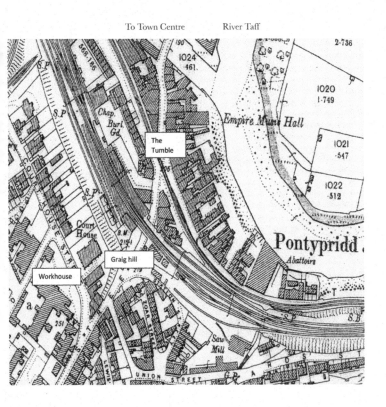

FOREWORD

(i)

This is a novel of the late nineteenth century. For authenticity, some characters may reflect attitudes of misogyny and other social prejudices prevalent at the time.

(ii)

Throughout the reign of Queen Victoria, the Establishment was always under threat. Originally from Chartists wanting electoral reform and Irish Republicans, but as social turmoil tore through Europe, there were even more radical elements – anarchists and nihilists who were prepared to go to desperate measures to achieve their aims. From Fenian bombs exploding in Glasgow to anarchist cells not only in the large cities but also in smaller towns such as Walsall, government agents sought to protect British society. Some extremists were to use methods later employed by the suffragette movement, such as breaking windows and setting fire to postboxes. Others would go further... *much* further.

The following prologue is based closely on the real events of September 1896.

PROLOGUE

Boulogne, September 1896

'No. I would never object to using it. I believe in dynamite as a weapon of war, and we Irish Nationalists are at war with Great Britain.'

The speaker, well-dressed and clean-shaven apart from a small, neatly trimmed moustache, spoke with an educated Irish accent.

'Waiter! Another glass of champagne, and one for my fellow countryman here, *s'il vous plaît.*'

'*Oui, Monsieur Gordon,*' replied the passing waiter, eager to please the large-tipping guest.

'There's no need, Patrick. I'm fine with the one I have,' said Gordon's companion. 'It's been good to run into you. How many years has it been?'

'Too many, but you know why I had to go to America, and I won't be going back to the old country until we've ousted those English bastards.'

'You need to watch what you're saying, Patrick, even here.'

Gordon waved a hand dismissively. 'The Frenchies dislike them as much as I do. It's quite safe.' Pausing to take a fresh glass of champagne from the waiter's tray, he gave a smile as he continued, 'If I had my way, I'd lease a building close to Marlborough House, dig a tunnel until I was right underneath it, stuff as much dynamite as possible in there, then wait until the Prince of Wales was in residence—'

'Say no more!' hushed his acquaintance.

'Fear not, my friend. Now is not the time for such a thing. I will be crossing secretly to England in the morning on a private matter, but Marlborough house is perfectly safe… for the time being.'

'I still think you need to be more discreet. You don't know who might be listening.'

Gordon finished his champagne, then frowned at his acquaintance. 'You haven't been drinking yours.'

'I've had enough and it's late. It's been good to see you, but please take care!'

'I'll bid you goodnight then, but for me the night is still young. I'm off to the casino,' announced Gordon, signalling to the waiter for the bill.

***

Three hours later, Gordon walked onto the quay and looked across at one of the South-Eastern Railway Company's steamers, which was berthed on the far side of the harbour.

'I'll be on you tomorrow morning, then it's a quick bit of business in England and back to the States,' he muttered to himself.

Tapping his jacket pocket to ensure he hadn't lost his wallet, full as it was with his winnings from the roulette table, he entered the quayside hotel.

'*Chambre* 201,' he demanded, as the bleary-eyed night clerk shook himself awake.

Taking the proffered key, Gordon went up to his room, locked the door and sat on the edge of the bed in the darkness. It felt too much of an effort to get undressed and, as the night's excess of alcohol started to finally take an effect, he started to doze.

***

Barely thirty minutes later, he awoke with a start, shaken by a loud bang as the door of the hotel room burst open, sending splinters flying across the room.

'What the hell…?' he exclaimed, trying to stand.

'Sit back down, you Fenian bastard,' shouted a voice from the darkness.

Gordon sensed there were several intruders in the room and he could hear one of them scrambling around, trying to light an oil lamp.

There was an exclamation of '*Voilà!*' as the light flickered and the room's occupants could finally see each other clearly.

'What's the meaning of this?' demanded the Irishman.

'Patrick Tynan, I have a warrant for your arrest in connection with the murder of Lord Cavendish fourteen years ago, and for being involved in the manufacture of dynamite bombs for use in England.'

'I don't know what you're talking about, man. My name is Gordon, not Tynan, and I'm not staying here to be falsely accused. I shall take myself elsewhere!' Getting to his feet, the Irishman took in the roomful of French police with the hard-faced Englishman at their head, and made to push through them, towards the broken door.

He stopped when he felt the cold metal of a gun barrel against his temple.

'*Non, Monsieur Walsh! Non!*' interrupted the panicked local Police Commissioner, before switching to heavily accented English.

'Remember that you are on French soil, Inspector.'

Walsh kept the gun pressed against the captive's head. 'Tynan, we know it's you. Your intentions were discovered weeks ago when you were still in America. You've been closely followed since you landed in Genoa. Everyone you subsequently met in Turin and Paris has been identified and will be rounded up in due course. Our Continental colleagues will take care of your foreign co-conspirators, but you and your three countrymen will come with us.'

'Three countrymen?' the Irishman asked innocently.

Walsh smiled. 'We took Bell back in Glasgow last night. Haines and Kearney will be taken at dawn. You may as well admit to your involvement.'

'It seems you have the better of me for the moment. Yes, I am Patrick Tynan of the Irish Invincibles.'

'Then come with me quietly or I'll have no alternative other than to put a bullet in you,' said Walsh calmly. 'We can take the next ferry back to England.'

'I think you are mistaken, Inspector. Your warrant is useless,' scoffed Tynan, his head clearing from the night's earlier excesses.

'I don't think so. You're coming with me.'

'What you seem to be unaware of, is that although I am proud of my heritage, I applied for and obtained American citizenship. Whereas I am sure the commissioner here would be quite happy to let you take a fellow Briton back across the channel, I doubt he would be prepared to risk an international incident. If he lets you take me, the American consul will no doubt raise the matter with President Faure himself.'

'If this is so, then he is right. I am sorry, Inspector, but this will have to go before the public prosecutor,' explained the French police commissioner.

'Quite right too!' added Tynan. 'Seeing as I have not committed any offence on French soil and have merely been a sightseer.'

Inspector Walsh's facial muscles tightened as he kept the muzzle of his pistol pointed at Tynan's head; then with a sigh of exasperation, he eventually lowered it, his eyes glowering at the Irishman.

'At least we've stopped your plans. The Czar of Russia can now visit England safely and your fellow Fenians will hang. Hopefully, in time, so will you.'

Tynan smiled as he held out his hands for the French police to handcuff him and take him away.

Berchem, Antwerp

'Get ready, men!'

The Englishman who spoke was tall, grim-faced and wore a long black overcoat with black leather gloves. The policemen he addressed were local Belgians, except for two London detectives. Technically he had no direct authority over them, holding no official post in either service, but the political persuasion of his masters had been all that was required.

'Third house from the left. Two of you with sledgehammers first, then all in as fast as we can. Do not let any of the occupants get away. Is that understood?'

A Belgian police inspector repeated the instructions to those of his men who did not speak English, then gave a nod of confirmation.

'Very well, let's waste no more time,' said the man in charge, indicating with his arm that the raid should begin.

The policemen advanced quickly with the two bearing sledge-hammers leading the way. The door of the property was securely locked, but after four tremendous blows the timber frame splintered, the door falling back on its hinges. A great commotion ensued as the police poured in, rousing the occupants from their slumber. Two men, quicker to respond than the rest, ran towards a door at the back of the property.

'Get them!' shouted one of the London detectives, trying to aim his pistol.

Despite their head start, the Belgian police were hot on their heels, and neither of the two fugitives made it beyond the garden wall. They were hauled none too gently back into the house to face the black-clad man, who stood with a satisfied expression.

'It's Haines and Kearney,' he confirmed to the detectives. 'Take them to the local cells with the other prisoners and I'll interrogate them later.'

Walking into an adjoining room, he looked for, and found, a door which led to a cellar. 'Bring a lamp!' he ordered. A few minutes later, two Belgian policemen and one of the detectives followed him as he descended the wooden steps.

In the cellar they were presented with the sight of two workbenches on which stood a number of ceramic utensils and clay moulds. The Belgians remained at the bottom of the stairs as the Englishmen walked into the centre of the room

'It's a complete dynamite factory, Inspector Harris,' explained the man in black to his fellow countryman.

'So it seems,' replied the detective. He didn't know his temporary colleague's name, but was aware of his influence and authority. 'What's that in the corner?'

Harris stepped across to a metal bucket in which was a leaden container that had been packed in ice.

'Don't touch it!' shouted his companion.

The warning came too late as the lid of the container was removed and a noxious vapour nearly overcame the detective before he was able to close it again.

'It's called a receiver and there's a mixture of acids inside used to make nitroglycerine,' advised the man in black, as Harris coughed into a handkerchief. 'The ice is to keep the contents below zero degrees. Let's see what else we've got.'

'Look over here,' spluttered the detective. 'There's an old pair of trousers that's been burnt by acid, hanging on the back of this chair. It's a dangerous business.'

'There's another three containers of acid over here. Good God! I've just found phials of nitroglycerine. There's enough here to blow up the whole street. Keep that lamp away, just in case.'

'They've left a drawer open in this cupboard. There are papers inside, and they're in English,' said the detective.

'Let me see!' Striding across the room, the other man snatched the papers, took the lamp and began to read. After ten minutes of reading in silence, he stuffed the papers inside his coat and led the way back upstairs.

'*Monsieur*, we found the owner of the house trying to burn these…' said a police sergeant, handing over an assortment of charred documents.

The sergeant looked in anticipation as the mysterious Englishman turned the papers over in his gloved hands, trying to decipher the contents.

'*Merci*, Sergeant. These are most valuable. It seems the danger is not over. Take the prisoners to your cells and my colleague will interrogate them later. I need to return to London immediately. If prompt action isn't taken, there's going to be a catastrophe!'

ONE

'That's our man. Bring him to me!' The gloved hand indicated a man in his mid-thirties, with neatly-trimmed sideburns and moustache, heading towards Shrewsbury station. Slightly stocky and not markedly tall, he carried a small suitcase in one hand whilst the other held the lead of a Staffordshire bull terrier that padded obediently alongside.

Unaware he was being observed, Thomas Chard entered the station and waited on the busy platform for the train which would take him back to South Wales.

The impending journey weighed heavily on his mind. He knew that he should feel elated about returning to his recently adopted town of Pontypridd; instead he had a feeling of apprehension which he just couldn't shift.

Caught up in a scandal eighteen months earlier, Chard had left Shrewsbury and started a new life as a police inspector in South Wales. Just a matter of weeks ago, he'd been accused of a double murder back in Shrewsbury and sent to the feared Dana prison. He had escaped from his cell, uncovered the true killer and cleared his name, but there had been casualties. Two people he cared for had come from Pontypridd to help his endeavours, and both had suffered as a result. Facing them would be difficult but necessary.

'I don't suppose you're in the least concerned about going to your new home, are you boy?' Chard asked of his recently acquired dog.

In response, it just lay down on the platform, totally ignoring its master.

'Mr Thomas Chard?'

'Yes?' responded the inspector, turning to face a tall, stern-faced man.

'Come with me please, Mr Chard. I'm afraid you'll have to miss your train.' The man spoke quietly, so as not to be overheard by other travellers.

'I beg your pardon?'

'This is a matter of the utmost importance. My instructions are to take you to my superior. He's waiting outside the station.'

'Then he can bloody well wait a long time. And it's Inspector Chard by the way.'

'We know exactly who you are. My instructions are to bring you willingly, if possible.'

'Is that some kind of threat?' demanded Chard, feeling his temper rise.

'Just lower your voice and do as I ask please, sir.' The stranger discreetly opened his coat to reveal a pistol holster strapped to his belt. 'This is a matter of national importance and I'm sure Superintendent Jones would rather have his inspector oblige us.'

Chard was taken off guard. Whoever seemed to be intent on meeting him clearly knew he was an inspector and the name of his senior officer. After a moment's hesitation he nodded an assent.

'You can oblige me by carrying my case. I'll keep the dog.'

The stranger's face remained expressionless as he picked up the case and indicated with a nod of his head that Chard should head for the exit. Their departure was accompanied by a loud rumble as the train for South Wales came into the station.

'You'll be on the next one, don't fret yourself, sir,' said the stranger as Chard gave the train a wistful look over his shoulder.

Outside, they headed towards a two-horse carriage and as they approached, the door was opened and a black leather-gloved hand beckoned Chard inside. The inspector handed the dog lead over to the man carrying his case, warning him as he did so, 'Be careful what you say in front of the dog. If you accidentally say the attack command, Barney will rip your foot off.' A glance at the man's discomfited face looking at the dog's powerful jaws made it necessary for Chard to suppress a smile. The docile animal gave a yawn and sat on the stranger's foot.

'Welcome, Inspector Chard. Take a seat, please,' said the person inside the carriage.

'I hope you've got a damn good explanation for this,' said Chard, taking in the man's appearance. He was craggy-faced and bore the same stern expression as his subordinate. The most striking thing about his appearance, though, was his dress. He was attired completely in black, even his shirt. Chard didn't know it was possible to get starched black shirt collars, but evidently this man had his especially made.

'Indeed I do, Inspector. Though I have probably spent too much time on your involvement than is really justified. It may turn out to be unnecessary, but there is too much at risk not to cover all eventualities. Hopefully, this will be the only time we shall meet. I have more pressing business elsewhere.'

'Perhaps we can begin by you telling me who you are?' suggested Chard.

'My name is Farrington. Here is my card, and this document will verify my authority.'

Chard took the card, which had the man's name on it, a London address and a telephone number. The document held more interest, and the inspector raised an eyebrow when he saw the signature.

'Sir Matthew White Ridley, the Home Secretary,' Chard read aloud.

Farrington took the document back, but indicated that Chard should keep the card. 'I'll get right to the point, Inspector. I am aware you have been somewhat preoccupied recently. However, I must ask if you have read anything about the arrest of Patrick Tynan?'

'The papers have been full of the attempts to get him extradited, but I'm afraid my understanding of the whole business is rather cloudy,' admitted Chard, curious as to why the affair had anything to do with him.

'I'll be as brief as possible. Our contacts in the American police uncovered a devilish plot involving Tynan. He was already wanted by us as the sole survivor of the so called 'Irish Invincibles', who planned and executed the murder of Lord Cavendish in Dublin some years ago. However, that deed would have paled into insignificance in comparison with their new plan, if they had managed to carry it out. It involved an unholy alliance with Russian nihilists, facilitated by Belgian anarchists; the target being the Czar and Czarina of Russia.'

'Good Lord!' exclaimed Chard.

'The intention had been to blow up the Czar on his way back from Balmoral after his meeting with the Queen. There were four Irishmen involved. Two of them went to Antwerp to liaise with the bomb makers. Another went to Scotland to make preparations, whilst Tynan travelled to the continent to oversee arrangements and meet with the Russian malcontents. Having caught wind of the plan reasonably early, we worked with our overseas counterparts and tracked their operation through America, Italy, Belgium and France. The intention was to catch everyone involved.'

'I understand you were successful,' ventured Chard, noticing that Farrington had an expression of discontent. 'Apart from Tynan, that is.'

Farrington shrugged. 'Forget him. He's out of the picture. The French won't give him to us so he'll return to America as a hero to his Fenian friends. The fact that he failed won't matter. He'll write a book no doubt, and live on the fame for the rest of his life. However, he may yet have something additional to crow about, and that's the problem.'

'May I stop you there?' interrupted Chard. 'There's something I don't understand. Why on earth should those Irishmen want to kill the Czar of Russia? What's in it for them?'

Farrington gave a sardonic laugh. 'You are indeed an intelligent fellow, aren't you? That is exactly the point. When we searched the bomb factory in Antwerp, we found a number of papers, and they gave us most of the answer. It was a case of quid pro quo. Killing the Czar requires more than one assassin, since he's so careful with his security. The Russian secret police know everyone back in their own country and he cannot be targeted. The nihilists realised he would be an easier target on his visit to Queen Victoria, but a group of Russian peasants suddenly appearing in Scotland would be extremely noticeable. As I said, one man wouldn't be enough.'

'Hence the reason why they enlisted the Irish. Because they could move around England and Scotland with relative ease,' said Chard 'They are also experienced in the use of explosives, and it would take a bomb to guarantee a kill. But where is the quid pro quo?'

'We're not entirely sure,' sighed Farrington. 'We found a certain name which is very unsettling. Someone who at some time was called Lucheni, but that doesn't get us very far, other than we know he's an assassin and he has killed at least half a dozen people. On this occasion he's been hired by the nihilists to pay their debt to the Irish. We were able to ascertain from the papers found that he's been settled over here for up to a year, planning his kill.'

'Who is his intended target?' asked Chard.

'I regret to say we don't know Lucheni's current name, his nationality, where he is, or his intended target. The only clues we have are a charred piece of paper with the name Lucheni, a missing burnt section, then a name Edward. We also have a list of anarchist sympathisers and locations which we presume is where we might find our man.'

'Could the target be the Prince of Wales? His middle name being Edward,' suggested Chard.

'That's a possibility. Heaven knows he's difficult to keep protected, but it could just relate to Lucheni's alias. The Czar and Czarina are enjoying themselves in Balmoral at the moment and are due to leave soon, but the royal residence will soon be used for a meeting of the Privy Council. Plenty of targets there, of course. As for the Prince of Wales, he will be in County Durham visiting Wynyard Park in the near future.'

'So, you have an assassin on the loose that you can't identify or locate, who is planning to kill an unknown target, at a location you can only guess at. Quite a pickle.' Chard frowned. 'But what on earth has all this got to do with me?'

'Patience, Inspector; all will become clear. I mentioned we found a list of anarchist sympathisers. They are our only lead to finding the assassin. Nearly all of the names were already known to us and our agents have infiltrated several of their groups. They are located mainly in London, Glasgow and the major cities in the North of England. All of them are under surveillance, but we aren't going to rush in without having identified Lucheni first. The only name not known to us was one Sean Padraig MacLiam.' Farrington noticed the recognition in Chard's eyes as he continued. 'We subsequently found a police record for him in Manchester. Further investigations revealed he'd been a student at the university until he was thrown out. Apparently, he'd been more or less friendless there, with one exception.'

'Myself,' volunteered Chard.

'Exactly! The chancellor of the university mentioned you had joined the Manchester police force as a detective. They referred us to Shrewsbury where we've heard all about your recent exploits. You're quite a resourceful character, Inspector.'

'That's as may be, Mr Farrington, but I've not seen Sean for years, and I'm on my way back to South Wales to resume my duties there.'

'So we understand. The fact of the matter is that the location alongside MacLiam's name reads Glamorganshire. No doubt he is using a different name, but at least you should be able to recognise him.'

Chard frowned. 'Where in Glamorganshire? It's a big place.'

'Wherever he's most likely to find people he can infect with his anarchist views. The coalfields of the Rhondda, the docks of Cardiff; we just don't know. Realistically, it's unlikely that the assassin will have gone to him. It is far more likely Lucheni has gone to one of the anarchist groups in the north, near to where we assume he'll strike. Nevertheless, it's incumbent on me to try and cover all possibilities. Therefore it's imperative that you make every effort to locate MacLiam and establish whether he is aiding the assassin.'

'My duty is to my superior, Superintendent Jones,' replied Chard. 'I'll take the matter up with him.'

'No,' said Farrington firmly. 'Discretion is all. We don't want anyone involved in this delicate affair who doesn't need to be. This is a matter of national security and the fewer people who know about this the better. You are now under direct orders from the Home Office.'

'Even if I agree, the restrictions of my duties would prevent me from searching for MacLiam unless I had permission from my superintendent.'

'I will take steps to ensure you will have sufficient freedom to do what I ask; but the essential details of the matter must remain secret. If you are successful then you will be rewarded,' stated Farrington with what passed for a smile.

'And if I refuse…?'

'The last man to refuse me was called Caldwell. Do you know what happened to him?'

'No,' admitted Chard.

'Neither does anyone else. You have my card, Inspector. Call me if you find out anything. I understand you will be reporting for duty at Pontypridd tomorrow. When you get there, you'll find that certain changes will have taken place. I suggest you take time to consider my proposal in the station's waiting room. It will help to pass the time until the next train arrives. Do enjoy your journey.' With that, Farrington made it clear the conversation was concluded.

Feeling confused, intrigued and angry at the same time, Chard left the carriage, retrieving his case and canine companion from the man waiting outside.

'Why me?' he asked the heavens as he headed for the station once more.

TWO

It seemed like an age since Chard had last been in the town of Pontypridd, even though it had only been a matter of weeks. As he went to insert the key in his front door, he was taken aback as it swung open.

'Oh! Mr Chard, I'm so pleased to see you!' exclaimed Lucy, his young housemaid.

The inspector couldn't help but smile in response to the warm welcome. 'Lucy! I hadn't expected you to be here at this time of day.'

The maid blushed. 'I'm afraid I have something to confess, sir.'

'Take the dog through to the back yard and then you can tell me when we are settled inside,' said Chard, aware that Lucy was clearly troubled about something.

'Is he yours, sir?' she asked, taking the lead.

'Unfortunately, I've acquired him. He's called Barney and he's a Staffordshire bull terrier,' answered the inspector, curious as to why Lucy was calling him sir, which she rarely did unless she had done something wrong.

'My uncle used to have a Staffie, so I know what they're like. I'll take him out, then make you a cup of tea, sir.'

As the docile Barney let himself be led away, Chard walked into his sitting room and gave a sigh as he relaxed into his favourite armchair. Moments later the maid re-appeared and stood before him, averting her eyes.

'Well, spit it out, Lucy. I know something is troubling you.'

'It's like this, sir. I haven't been paid by you these last few weeks and when word got round that you were imprisoned, my mam told me to leave this house and get my old job back at the pub. I told her that you couldn't have done what they said, but she wouldn't listen. It was either get my old job back or she would rent my room out to a lodger for some income. The problem was that the pub wouldn't take me back, so I was stuck. True to her word my mam threw me out, so I've been staying here and eating what was in the pantry.'

Chard frowned. 'Staying here?'

'Not in your room, mind, sir. I've made myself a bed out of some spare blankets and been sleeping in the spare room at the back. I hope you aren't too angry.'

'It's my fault,' sighed Chard. 'I should have sent you some money somehow. I'll see to it this very afternoon. As for having a maid living here, I suppose I can put up with it. It is quite a normal thing after all, but given it's such a small house, you're so young, and the things which have probably been said about me…'

'Oh!' interrupted Lucy. 'You mean that you're a womaniser, an adulterer, and—.'

'Yes, that's enough, thank you…'

'Don't you worry, Mr Chard. If anyone says anything untoward then I'll give them a piece of my mind.'

The inspector looked at the fierce expression on the girl's face and found it hard to suppress a smile. She was young, inexperienced in her duties and had a tendency to speak out of turn, but he trusted her. It would be a small sacrifice to give up a little privacy for her loyalty.

'Very well, I'll employ you full time and pay you accordingly for the next month. We can review matters then. Now, I'll have that cup of tea you mentioned and a bit of a rest before going to visit someone rather important.'

***

It was only a short omnibus journey to the mining village of Hopkinstown. There, in the middle of a terrace, Chard found the home of Constable Morgan.

'I'm sorry to disturb you,' Chard apologised, as Idris Morgan opened the door. For a moment there was an uncomfortable silence as if neither man knew the right words to say. Constable Morgan was a solidly built young man of medium height who, although in his early twenties, looked much older due to his mutton-chop whiskers. The other noticeable thing about the police officer was the absence of his left ear, the skin in that area being puckered from extensive stitching.

'You'd better come in,' said Morgan after an awkward pause.

Chard followed the younger man into a small living room where a newly lit fire crackled as the kindling caught the sticks of firewood in the grate.

'How are your injuries?' asked Chard.

'Healing well, all things considered,' Morgan answered, indicating that the inspector should take a seat.

Chard took one of the two chairs which stood either side of the fireplace, as Morgan remained standing.

'I spoke to the superintendent today,' Morgan continued, 'and I'll be returning to duty next week. Just on light duties though. My ribs aren't fully mended yet, Inspector.'

'You needn't call me by my rank. Not after all we went through.'

'I'd rather keep to things as they were before I came up to Shrewsbury, if you don't mind.'

'If you insist,' agreed Chard, feeling slightly uncomfortable. 'I assume you'll feel glad to return to duty?'

'It'll be good to be with the lads again, but the demotion hurts.'

'Demotion?' exclaimed Chard in astonishment.

'Reduced from constable first class to constable second class,' Morgan answered grimly.

'Why? What reason could there possibly be?' demanded the inspector.

'Word got around about how I helped you in your escape from prison, and then aided you in evading the Shrewsbury police, when in theory I was supposed to be up there helping them.'

'But I was innocent and without your help I might not have been able to clear my name!'

'Conduct unbecoming of a law officer, Superintendent Jones called it,' said Morgan, finally taking the other seat.

Chard's heart sank. 'I will do everything I can to rectify matters. I'll speak to the superintendent first thing in the morning.'

'I don't think that'll do any good. From what I've heard you'll have enough to deal with on your return to duty, sir. You're hardly in the superintendent's good books.'

Both men fell into silence, the crackling of the fire sounding unnaturally loud. Eventually it was Chard who spoke. 'Before coming here, I went to May's house. Her father said she's gone away.'

'So I heard.'

'The last time I spoke with May she said that she intended to accept your proposal of marriage. Her parents may have arranged for her to go to Bristol, but she's twenty-one and can make her own decisions. You can still marry her, you know,' advised Chard with a friendly smile.

Morgan gave a little cough and looked uncomfortable. 'When May got back from Shrewsbury, she asked me to repeat my proposal.'

'And…?'

'I refused.'

Chard felt his jaw drop open in shock. 'But you've been chasing her for ages.'

'When we were in Shrewsbury, you said I didn't know the real May Roper, and after what happened to me, I realised you were right. She had become so headstrong and reckless. May was no longer the person I really wanted to share my life with.'

Chard nodded his understanding. The young woman had been seriously injured by a killer about eighteen months earlier, and her feisty character had been subdued for months as she coped with the trauma. It was the quiet, vulnerable May who Morgan had fallen for, and when the adventures in Shrewsbury had re-awakened her true personality, it had come as a shock to the young constable.

'I am then to blame for your injuries, your demotion and also the loss of your relationship.'

Morgan shook his head. 'No, Inspector. If anything, you saved me from a life of matrimonial unhappiness. My injuries were caused by May's reckless actions and my demotion was my own bloody fault for deciding to get involved in the first place. Wait there a moment.'

The constable got up from his chair and went out of the room, only to return shortly with a bottle of ale and two glasses.

'Let's drink to the hope that things can only get better!'

***

Ada Quill wrapped her shawl tightly around her shoulders and walked out of her house, onto the street. She gave a sigh as she anticipated what would happen at the meeting. Men! Bloody stupid men! It would be yet another quarrelsome gathering. Why couldn't there be more women? There were some who contributed to the cause, even from amongst the better-off, but no others who would share in the leadership or take practical action. I suppose I can't blame them, Ada told herself. What would happen to their children if they were arrested and sent to gaol? Who would raise the little ones? Not the husbands, that's for sure. Most working men just wouldn't have the time or patience.

'Damn you!' she shouted at the driver of a cart which had sped through a puddle, causing mud to splash against her skirt.

Not all husbands were the same, she corrected herself. Her Billy would have found time, had she been arrested, and if they had been blessed with children. But now he was gone, and she had nothing much to lose. Fortune had been kind, to an extent. She owned her own little house and managed a living as a seamstress. Although she missed her husband deeply, another man had shown her affection recently, despite her fading looks.

An omnibus stopped just ahead, but determined to save her precious pennies, Ada walked past regardless. 'I hope we make some progress this time,' she muttered to herself. Wilson was right about doing too much too soon, but they surely needed to move their efforts away from Cardiff and up into the valleys. There were tales of people starving in some parts, with unaccompanied children as young as five or six turning up at the workhouse door, asking for food. Things had to change. Her Billy had wanted change, to make things safer in the quarry, but what happened? The owner didn't want to slow production so they hadn't had time to ensure the blasting would be safe. The rich make their profits and the poor die. Damn society! Damn it all to hell! She cursed as she hurried to the rendezvous.

***

'Come now, everybody, let us not bicker!'

'It's Ted's fault, he started it!' grumbled Charlie Janssen.

'He was just saying what most of us think!' argued Frank Edwards.

'I said stop this bickering!' demanded the man seated at the head of a long wooden table, which had seen better days.

Sean Padraig MacLiam, or John Wilson as he now called himself, waited as the squabbling slowly subsided. 'That's better,' he declared, as everyone finally came to order. Sometimes the behaviour of the group troubled him. Their activities would at some point lead to at least some of them being arrested, that was inevitable, but imprudent action by some of the hotheads in the group would no doubt bring the day closer than it need be. The Irishman looked around the room. It was a disused workshop, damp and dusty with an unpleasant odour of decay, but it was safe from prying eyes and large enough for the core members of his following to meet. Slightly built, with fair hair and a pallid complexion, he hardly had the appearance of a leader of anarchists. In truth he preferred his own company and being responsible for his individual actions, but when he'd been asked to lead this disparate group, he'd understood the sense of it.

It was ironic in its way. They were all anarchists, deploring the corruption and inequality of governments, believing that the people should organise their lives as they saw fit, yet they were unable to organise themselves without someone telling them how to do it. It was partly to do with their backgrounds and personalities. Victor Blandford, a young bespectacled man, had, like himself, been thrown out of university for his ideological beliefs and actions. James Eden had expressed an interest in helping those less fortunate, whose lives were ruined by an oppressive government. Ted Schwartz had been raised in the London slums, where he had experienced extreme poverty. Frank Edwards had come from North Wales where he had seen his family's health ruined by the business practices of the hated Lord Penrhyn. Ada Quill was the only woman present. Taller than most men and fierce in her passion for change, she had lost her husband in a quarrying accident only two years earlier. Of the remaining members of the group, Charlie Janssen worked at the docks whilst Eddie Ward had a small business in Cardiff. The latter was a printer whose commitment was perhaps a little suspect, but he did make money printing their pamphlets, and was by now implicated in all their actions. Finally, there was Willy Rabinovitz, not really part of the group as such, but a bedraggled waif of a man, less than five feet tall, who they'd adopted after finding him homeless.

'Do you all know the parts you need to play for our plan to be a success?'

'Yes John,' answered Ted, 'we've all got our own target.'

There was a murmur of agreement from the others.

'But we need to be doing more than this.' Frank spoke out. 'A damn sight more.'

'And we shall,' Wilson said, his tone placatory. 'More active recruits are needed and we must take our campaigns beyond this town. In our discussion last week, it was agreed we will start by moving our protests north to Pontypridd and Merthyr. Ted and Victor have already given us some ideas and we'll discuss them at our next meeting. First things first though, let's concentrate on what we have to do here in Cardiff. Work in pairs. Victor and James; Frank and Ada; Ted with Charlie…' Wilson hesitated as he noticed the pasty, fat-lipped Eddie Ward slowly shaking his head. 'And finally, I'll take Willy with me,' he decided, glancing at the sad, scruffy figure who gave a hesitant nod. 'Any more questions?'

'No. We know what we're doing,' responded Ada, her face a mask of grim determination.

'Good. In which case a drink is in order,' declared Wilson, gesturing with his arm.

Willy fetched a bottle from a table at the back of the room and placed a glass in front of everybody, into which he poured a shot of cheap whisky.

'A toast then,' announced Wilson. 'To anarchy, and may fire always be our friend.'

THREE

Chard looked at his reflection in the mirror and adjusted his uniform jacket. He gave a grunt of satisfaction and then put on the matching cap with polished silver badge. Once he was convinced that his appearance was absolutely immaculate, the inspector left his bedroom and went downstairs to the hallway, where Lucy was waiting to see him off.

'You do look dashing, if I might say so, Mr Chard,' she said as she opened the door.

Chard warmed to the compliment, aware that the military cut of the navy-blue, black-braided uniform did help to present a particularly smart image.

'Thank you, Lucy. I hope the superintendent thinks so. By the way, remind me to order you a proper bed for your room. I'll get one delivered by Monday at the latest.'

Lucy beamed a smile as the inspector went into the street, not noticing the worried expression on his face. His main concern was how Superintendent Jones would react. Chard knew him to be a good, honest man, who cared about his officers. He did however, have very high standards. That was why Chard had taken so much care over his appearance. In Superintendent Jones's opinion an inspector should be a paragon of virtue, someone the men could look up to as an exemplar of strong leadership, model appearance and impeccable morals. Before coming to Pontypridd, Chard had been a detective, first in Manchester and then in Shrewsbury, and had only worn a uniform on ceremonial occasions. The superintendent, however, had different ideas. The Glamorgan County Constabulary had yet to set up a detective department and in Jones's opinion an inspector was employed to inspect the work of those beneath him. The role of inspector was one of leadership and dealing with the higher levels of society encountered during their investigations. That meant a smart uniformed appearance and it was something that Chard had been forced to accept. Today there would be no problems on that score, he told himself. The difficulty was that by now the superintendent would have heard more or less everything that had happened over the past few weeks, and some of it would hardly show him in the best light.

***

'Good morning, Inspector,' said the sergeant at the front desk of the station. There was no warmth in the words, nor did Chard expect there to be.

'Good morning, Sergeant Jackson,' replied Chard with no warmth in his voice either. Jackson was a despicable individual, the one rotten apple amongst the station's complement. 'I assume the superintendent is expecting me?'

'He said to instruct you to go directly to his office,' answered the sergeant with a smirk.

Chard went past the desk and into the main body of the station. As he entered, he was aware of heads turning and the whispering of comments amongst the few constables present. Paying them no attention, Chard went straight to the door of the superintendent's office and knocked. His knuckles barely had time to leave the woodwork before Superintendent Jones acknowledged his arrival with a barked order to enter.

'You wanted to see me immediately, sir,' said Chard, removing his cap and standing to attention. Their previous discussions were not usually so formal, but this was not going to be a normal conversation.

Superintendent Constantine Jones sat behind his great oak desk looking at his inspector like a lion staring at a tethered goat. Chard tried to see any signs of emotion in the superintendent's granite face, framed by his bushy moustache and large sideburns. There were none.

Eventually the superintendent spoke. 'I do not know what to make of you, Inspector Chard. Truly I do not. When you first came here to this station, after having been found brawling in the street, I thought I had made a great mistake in accepting you into my command. Then, after you showed great resolve and considerable ability in bringing a number of miscreants to justice, I changed my opinion. I thought I had unearthed someone with real talent who just needed a little guidance in order to achieve their full potential. You appeared to have the right kind of moral fibre to make the common man look up to you.'

Chard stared at a point just over the superintendent's head, deliberately avoiding direct eye contact. It was an approach taught to him by an old soldier, and he had found it useful when trying to withstand a severe reprimand. The inspector knew what was coming next and he waited for the storm to break.

'How dare you misrepresent yourself to me!' admonished the superintendent, raising his voice and allowing his native Welsh accent to come through, which it rarely did. 'It has become common knowledge that you are a libertine and adulterer. If that was not bad enough, you took it upon yourself to break out of a prison whilst on remand.'

'Only to clear my name, sir, and I did bring a murderer to justice…' said Chard, failing to keep to his intention of letting the superintendent's temper blow itself out without interruption.

'That's as maybe, but it showed a lack of confidence in the judicial system which you are meant to uphold. All of this, however, is nothing compared to what has really disappointed me.'

Chard raised an eyebrow, wondering what was coming next.

'I am of course referring to Constable Morgan,' continued the superintendent. 'A fine young man with excellent prospects of advancement, yet due to your actions he has returned maimed.'

'I saw him last night, sir. He said that he's been demoted to constable second class.'

'I had no choice other than to take disciplinary action.' The superintendent shook his head in disappointment. 'He went to Shrewsbury with the best of intentions, sent by myself to find out what possible cause there could be behind your arrest. Then, when you escaped from prison, he was meant to be helping the Shrewsbury police to locate you, for your own good. Instead, he was aiding and abetting your actions, and I blame you for that.'

'I can assure you that I didn't want him to become involved. When Morgan turned up on the night of my escape, I was astonished. Nevertheless, I accept the responsibility,' said Chard.

'Which is as it should be. It had been my intention to ask for your resignation, but it seems I am unable to do so.'

Chard felt puzzled by the odd statement. Superintendent Jones was also the Deputy Chief Constable and there was very little beyond his authority. He waited in silence for the superintendent to continue.

'Yesterday afternoon I received a telephone call from the Chief Constable,' continued Jones, with a grim expression on his face. 'Apparently, for some reason or another, the Home Office has taken an interest in our constabulary. They appear concerned that we do not have a detective department.'

Chard could feel the superintendent's eyes scanning his face for any flicker of reaction.

'As you are aware, Inspector, you and I have had a number of conversations on this point. Indeed, you had already swayed me to a certain extent. I had told you earlier this year that I would try to gain funding for an additional inspector post, which would allow you to indulge yourself.'

The superintendent paused, still looking for some sort of reaction.

'The Chief Constable was told,' continued Jones, 'that we must look into the practicalities of following many other forces in introducing detectives into our ranks. The Home Office made it known they were aware that we already had an inspector with sound experience; a certain Thomas Chard. Now how would they know that?'

Chard kept his face expressionless and gave a slight shrug.

'I have been directed. *Directed*, mark you, to put you in charge of looking into the matter. You will be excused your regular duties for the time being and the Home Office will look at additional funding depending on the outcome of your report. Were you aware of this?'

'No sir,' answered Chard honestly. 'I am as surprised as you are.'

Superintendent Jones continued staring at Chard's face for a number of moments. Then looked away.

'I have already made arrangements to convert one of the refurbished rooms on the first floor into an office for you. In the meantime, you will have to share your old office with Inspector Hulme. He's been your temporary replacement and is retiring in a few weeks.'

'I must emphasise once again, Superintendent, that I have not instigated any of this,' said Chard.

Jones gave a dismissive snort. 'In respect of your new temporary role as a detective, you will be excused uniform. However, you must ensure you are properly attired as befits a senior police officer when there are civic occasions. Do I make myself clear?'

'Understood, sir.'

'Good. I also want to ensure you are doing something useful whilst also compiling your report. Inspector Hulme is busy enough, so if anything new comes in, then you can deal with it. You have a lot of work to do in order to win back my trust. Do you understand?'

'Perfectly, sir,' said Chard.

'Then get about your business, Inspector.'

The superintendent dismissed Chard with a wave of his hand, without looking up.

Once outside his superior's office, the inspector let out an audible sigh, relieved his admonishment was over, for the time being at least. The dressing down had hurt, not least because much of what had been said was true. He had let everyone down, and now he needed to salvage his reputation amongst his colleagues. At the same time, he also had to process his change in circumstance. Getting Superintendent Jones to accept the need for a formal detective post had been what he'd been working towards for months, but having the role imposed on the station from above was not what he'd envisaged or wanted. Obviously, the mysterious Farrington had been behind it, though it was still difficult to take the man's far-fetched notions seriously. If the assassin's target was probably at the other end of the country, then why would he be lying low in South Wales? Perhaps to wrong-foot the authorities until nearer the time? But then, why go to a group led by Sean MacLiam? At university he was known to be a bit hot-headed, but would he actually become involved in a plot to kill someone? No, surely not.

Chard went straight to his old office and entered without knocking. Inspector Hulme, sat behind the desk, looked up and smiled warmly. He was an elderly man with deep worry lines around the eyes, but of cheerful countenance.

'Chard! Nice to see you back. I'm told we are to share the room for the rest of the week. God knows how!' he exclaimed, waving at the piles of paperwork on the desk. 'I'm afraid Superintendent Jones wasn't very clear on the matter.'

Chard had met Hulme twice previously at social events arranged by the Chief Constable and had found him to be good company. 'I don't appear to be in his good books at the moment. How did he persuade your superintendent to release you from Aberdare station?'

'I'm retiring in a few weeks and they already had an experienced replacement lined up, so they got him in earlier than planned. I had no objection because I intend moving down here after retirement in any case,' replied Hulme.

'I've been tasked with writing a report on the possibility of setting up a detective section for the county,' said Chard. 'I can make a start by visiting the other stations. That'll keep me out of your way for a few days and you can have the office to yourself.'

'Most obliging of you. I don't suppose you can lend a hand with some of this paperwork next week, could you?'

'I'll make sure to give you some help next Monday when I get back,' agreed Chard. 'There is something you might be able to help me with actually. I don't suppose you've had any problems with anarchists in Aberdare, have you?'

Hulme looked puzzled. 'Anarchists? Heavens no!' he laughed. 'Why do you ask?'

'No reason,' lied Chard.

Inwardly he sighed. If Hulme had said yes, it would at least have given him a starting point. Finding Sean MacLiam would be a difficult and probably pointless task. Hiding his mission would also be problematic despite the cover of writing the report; on top of all this, there was still the debt to be repaid to Constable Morgan. Something told him that there would be troubling times ahead.

FOUR

It had been a busy week, thought Chard, reflecting on the past few days as he walked to the north end of town. Visiting the stations in the west of the county, at Neath, Gowerton and Bridgend, had allowed him to make a start on compiling his report, as well as providing an excuse to discreetly enquire into any anarchist activity. As expected, there had been none. Swansea was a problem, because although it was in the county, it had its own police force. With its port and heavy industry, it could be a breeding ground for anarchists, but without revealing his true purpose, Chard could find no excuse for going there. A sudden breeze made him pause and adjust the collar of his overcoat to protect against the evening chill. Standing on the New Bridge, after which the town had formerly been named, he reflected on how quiet it was for a Saturday night. At the southern end of town, the junction known locally as the Tumble would be raucous, with drunks already being turned out onto the street. But here, close to the bridges, Old and New, which crossed the River Taff, the pubs were frequented by less troublesome clientele. On the far side of the river stood the Maltsters Arms and just beyond that lay his intended destination, the Ivor Arms.

On reaching the door of the pub, Chard tapped his walking cane against the pavement in thought as he envisaged the possible reception. From his first week in Pontypridd, it had become his place of refuge when he wanted to escape from the pressures of his work. There he could relax with a pint of ale and have convivial discussions with a number of the local patrons, without thought of his position as a police inspector. Although the superintendent was unaware of his choice of drinking establishment (and would have been displeased at the choice of some of Chard's companions), the rest of the station knew to keep clear of the premises and only to interrupt the inspector in cases of dire emergency.

Taking a deep breath, he leant on the door, which always stuck in its frame, and gave it a shove. As expected for a Saturday night, it was very busy and he found it difficult to push his way through to the bar. When he got there, he had a shock.

'Good Lord! Sergeant Humphreys! What are you doing here?'

The man serving behind the bar gave a grin, which due to his front teeth being missing, looked rather grotesque. Thinning hair and a broken nose added to his disconcerting appearance.

'You'll need to call me Bert from now on, Inspector,' he replied. 'My wife didn't want me around the house all the time now I'm retired, so I do a few evenings here to top up my pension.'

Chard smiled. 'In which case, call me Thomas and I'll have a pint of porter.'

'Right you are,' said Bert. 'One pint coming up.'

Once served, Chard made his way through to the far corner of the room, where he hoped to find his three former drinking companions. As anticipated, they were huddled together in deep conversation, as was often the case on a Saturday night.

'*Shwmae*, gentlemen,' he said warmly as he approached, using the local Welsh greeting.

The three men stopped talking and turned to stare. One was bespectacled, with dark hair turning grey at the sides, another was stoutly built with black receding hair, wearing a coachman's long coat and the third had an enormous bulbous nose, drooping black moustache and shifty eyes.

'Oh, it's *shwmae* is it, Mr Chard?' answered the coachman, known as Will Horses.

It wasn't the formal address which put the inspector on his guard, because despite telling them to address him as Thomas, they had always insisted on calling him Mr Chard. It was the tone Will used which was worrying.

'Yes, indeed!' added the shifty-eyed Dic Jenkins. 'We've got a bone to pick with you. Haven't we?' He nudged his bespectacled friend.

'Aye, I suppose so,' said the former librarian known as Dai Books.

'Being so quiet about your past, and all that,' said Will.

'Having been married, divorced and then getting caught up in a wild orgy with the wife of the Mayor of Shrewsbury; *chwarae teg*, fair play to you, mun. But why didn't you tell us?' demanded Dic.

'Wait a minute!' exclaimed Chard, holding up his arms in denial. 'I wasn't at a wild orgy, I've never met the mayor's wife and I was never divorced. You've been listening to Chinese whispers.'

'*Duw*, mun, I'm sure that Shrewsbury policeman who came down here sniffing for information, after you killed that prison guard to escape, said something like that,' replied Dic.

'I didn't kill a prison guard! Where do you get these daft ideas from?'

'Hang on a minute,' interjected Dai Books. 'Did you say you were never divorced?'

'You heard correctly.' Chard nodded.

'But you were walking out with Mrs Murray recently. Serious it was getting too, so I understand.'

Chard sighed. Was there nothing that could be kept private in this town? 'It's complicated.'

'In which case, Mr Chard, get in a round of drinks and tell us the full story of how you escaped from prison and cleared your name. That'll make it up to us,' said Will.

'Aye, the full story,' added Dic. 'Leave nothing out!'

'*Ych a fi*, disgusting. I don't want to hear it,' said Dai Books dismissively. 'If you were married and then were still "carrying on" with other women, then you deserved all your troubles.' Saying that, he downed his pint of beer and made to leave.

'Don't be like that, Dai!' snapped Will. 'We know you've got things on your mind, mun. How about you meet us here Monday night and tell us how it went. Dic and I will come out especially.'

Dai waved an arm in acknowledgement as he made his way through to the door, leaving Chard looking puzzled and a little disappointed.

'I thought he might have waited so I could explain. What's the matter with him? He looked down in the dumps when I got here.'

Dic made to reply, but before he could say a word Chard was distracted by a hand falling heavily on his shoulder and spinning him around.

'What the…'

'Thomas! Let me give you a *cwtch*.'

With no chance to react, Chard suddenly found himself enveloped by the mighty arms of Gwen, the pub's owner, as he was crushed against her enormous bosom. A kind, generous woman, the landlady was of a stature best described as very substantial.

'Yes… quite… that'll do now, Gwen,' gasped Chard as Will picked up the inspector's hat, which had fallen to the floor during the embrace.

'I'm sorry, Thomas,' said Gwen, releasing her grip. 'It's just that I've been so worried about you. Then there's been so much gossip about what's been going on.' She stopped to glare at Will and Dic who looked away shamefacedly.

'Not all of it's true, but I confess there were some things which did me no credit,' admitted the inspector.

Gwen gave him a guarded look. 'In which case, the next round of drinks is free and you can tell us all about it. The whole truth, mind!' she warned.

Chard crossed his fingers behind his back. 'I'll do my best, but some things are restricted as part of the court case.'

It was three pints of beer later by the time Chard had finished the tale of his adventures in England and answered, or avoided, all of their probing questions.

Eventually, Gwen returned to the bar to help out a beleaguered Bert, who was struggling to manage the number of customers demanding their drinks, leaving Chard alone with Dic and Will.

'Now, where were we before Gwen turned up?' asked Chard. 'I remember, you were going to tell me about Dai.'

Dic frowned. 'He's not been himself since he took up the teaching job at the new school.'

'I know he was reluctant about taking it, but I'm sure he'll settle,' said Chard.

Will shook his head. 'I'm not so sure. He liked being a librarian for Lady Llanover and translating the old Welsh documents. When she died and he was dismissed, it hit him hard.'

'Well paid it was,' interjected Dic, 'and now he's got money problems. It also kept him away from his wife for a few nights when he was staying away. Terrible nag she is.'

'Be fair,' said Will, 'you know why she's like that.'

'All right, all right,' said Dic. 'You see Mr Chard, they had two children, twins in fact.'

'I never knew.'

'The young ones died of the typhoid. Dic and his wife took it hard, but her especially. Their marriage has been a cold one ever since.'

Chard nodded his understanding. 'So that's why he sometimes seems a bit morose.'

'Truth to tell, he's also been drinking like a fish and getting very moody about all sorts of things. Gwen has threatened to bar him twice,' confided Will. 'Then, there's been the latest incident at school.'

'What's happened?' asked Chard, frowning.

'He came across a boy being punished for speaking Welsh in class and he intervened. The teacher in question told him to mind his own business and threatened to report him.'

'Aye, he's going to have it out with the headmaster,' added Dic. 'We've warned him not to, but I think the loss of his old job and the problems with his wife have built him into a right old temper. This business has been the last straw and driven him over the edge. Will and I are going to meet with him on Monday night just to find out what happens.'

'I'm afraid I won't be able to join you,' said Chard apologetically. 'I've got important work to be getting on with, so I'll need to keep my head clear at the start of the week. I wouldn't worry about Dai, though. He's an intelligent man, and I can't see him doing anything stupid.'

***

Standing in the doorway of a shop in St Mary Street, Cardiff, Ada Quill gave Frank Edwards a nudge.

'The coast is clear, Frank. No, wait!' she suddenly cautioned.

Usually thronged with people during daylight hours, the street in the centre of Cardiff town was largely deserted. It was well-lit in parts, although some of the streetlights were broken, giving cover to a handful of vagrants who cowered from the cold beneath layers of old blankets and newspaper that would need to be removed before the constables walked their morning beats. Yet, even at this late hour, well after the pubs had closed, there was still the odd hansom cab carrying a fare back from the illegal gambling dens and brothels which pervaded society.

One such cab rumbled down the street causing Ada and Frank to draw back.

'Bloody stupid, this is,' complained Frank. 'We should be doing something worthwhile, not pissing about. I'd rather be back in Merthyr, not having to spend the night bunked up at your place.'

'At least we're taking some action,' snapped Ada. 'And we wouldn't have to do it on a Saturday night if it wasn't for the likes of you having to work every morning bar a Sunday.'

'Still, we should be doing something big,' replied Frank. 'I've got something in mind, you wait and see.'

'Alright then, I'll support you. I want revenge for what happened to my husband. Talking of which, when we get back, you can tell me about what happened to your wife and family. You've never explained properly about them or your life before coming down here.'

'I don't want to talk about it,' replied Frank harshly. 'Quick! It's clear now. You go first with the bottle. I'll give you a few minutes to get away and then I'll go and light it. I'm too big not to be noticed, so I'll have to run like hell afterwards.'

Ada nodded. 'I'll see you back at my place,' she answered, setting off hastily.

A few streets away, close to the town hall, Victor Blandford and James Eden were having a disagreement.

'You realise we could go to prison for this,' said James.

Victor gave an exasperated sigh. James was, like himself, in his early twenties, but at times behaved with an appalling naivety.

'What the hell did you think you were getting into, James? Remember it was you who introduced me to Wilson. It isn't some stupid boys' club that we've joined. This is serious and it will get even more serious if I get my way. With Frank being in Merthyr, and the two of us from Pontypridd, we can spread our movement. This is just one small step.'

'Very well then, I'll keep watch, but you can do the deed,' said James determinedly.

Victor and James were not the only couple arguing. Charlie Janssen was in deep discussion with Ted Schwartz.

'Look, I'm not saying we shouldn't be doing this. I'm all in favour, but what happens after is something we've got to talk about.'

'Slit a few throats me old mucker,' snarled Ted in his strange accent that seemed to be an amalgamation of German and Cockney.

'That's going too far!' said Charlie. The handsome, tanned dock worker liked to give himself the image of a lover rather than a fighter. His strong political beliefs and chequered past were something he preferred to hide. 'Doing something that stupid will only draw attention to ourselves. I'll hear no more of such talk. Just give me the stuff and keep watch. I'll do the business and then we can get the hell out of here!'

The final pair of anarchists stood in the shadows of the outer wall of Cardiff Castle.

'There's not a soul in sight,' exclaimed Wilson delightedly. 'Just keep watch for me, Willy, and thank you for coming. I know you didn't really want to be here.'

The small, pathetic figure mumbled something and handed over the bottle of paraffin that he'd been cradling in his arms.

Wilson smiled and dashed across the road. His heart racing with excitement, he poured out the bottle's contents into the postbox, lit a match and threw it in to ignite the paraffin.

'One small stab at the authority that must be brought down,' he muttered to himself as the flames flickered into life.

FIVE

Chard felt ill at ease as he stood in the hallway, waiting to leave. 'Move, you stupid animal!' he snapped at Barney who, as was often the case, had dropped his heavily muscled body onto his master's foot, refusing to move.

Lucy found it hard to suppress a giggle as she pulled hard on the Staffie's collar and dragged him away. 'He misses you when you're out of the house.'

The inspector glanced at the dog, which sat wide-eyed with its tongue lolling out, and grunted. 'I took him for a walk yesterday. He should be grateful I haven't given him away.'

'I take him twice a day, in between my jobs. He's lovely.' Seeing Chard's scowl, Lucy quickly changed tack. 'I haven't said thank you properly for my new bed.'

The inspector's scowl disappeared. 'I've left some money out for you to get anything else you need. Just write down what you spend.'

'Thank you, Mr Chard.' Lucy was aware that his ill-humour was to do with something concerning his work, but he was not someone who shared his thoughts. Barney probably learned more on his walk the previous day than she would find out in a month of Sundays.

It was ironic, thought Chard as he crossed the main road and headed for the police station. After months of resenting having to wear a full inspector's uniform since arriving in Pontypridd the previous year, he now felt unsettled wearing civilian dress as a detective.

He knew he cut a fine figure in his dark grey suit, black woollen overcoat and stylish bowler hat, together with his ebony walking cane, but it would also mark him out as different from the rest of the station. Normally, that wouldn't be a problem, but now things had changed. They would no doubt have believed in his innocence when he had been arrested and taken to Shropshire; well, perhaps not Sergeant Jackson. However, by now everybody would be aware that Constable Morgan had become involved in the fight to clear his name, and the poor chap had returned missing an ear and facing demotion. There was no doubt the blame had fallen squarely at one person's door. That much had been obvious on Chard's first day back. Luckily the reasonable excuse of needing to visit the stations in the west of the county had kept him away for the rest of the week, but it was important to be back this Monday morning, as he had promised Inspector Hulme.

'Good morning, Sergeant,' said Chard, pleased to see it was the massive frame of Sergeant Morris behind the front desk and not Sergeant Jackson.

'Good morning, Inspector Chard.' The big man hesitated as if he wanted to say something, but then looked away.

'Is there anything you wanted to tell me, Sergeant?'

Morris looked as if he was going to shake his head, but then spoke up. 'It isn't really my place to say, sir. But it's about the lads.'

'Go on,' encouraged Chard.

'Just give them time, sir. They are very protective of their own, and Constable Morgan was in a bit of a state when he returned from Shrewsbury. I'm sure you understand, sir.'

'I do, Sergeant. Indeed, I do,' answered Chard truthfully.

Rather than go straight to his new office on the first floor, the inspector went directly to his old room, where he found Hulme already laying out piles of paperwork.

'How's it going?' asked Chard.

'Slowly,' answered the older man, 'but I'm getting on top of it. Could do with a hand though,' he added meaningfully. 'It's all straight-forward stuff. Just a lot of it.'

Chard was about to respond when his attention was distracted by a none too polite cough which came from behind him.

'Ah, Inspector Chard. I've been wondering where you'd got to,' barked Superintendent Jones.

'I've been working on my report, sir.'

'And dressed for the part too, I see.' The words expressed disdain for Chard's civilian attire.

'I assumed that as I was looking into the practicalities of introducing detectives into our constabulary, it would be best if I dressed according-ly, as we agreed, sir,' Chard said, testily.

'What exactly have you achieved so far?'

'I've visited our principal stations in the west of the county and made notes of the existing complements, taking particular note of their experience. I've also compiled notes of all serious cases over the last twelve months where the culprits were not obvious, and how long the cases have taken to be solved. Some remain unsolved. My aim is to repeat the exercise at each divisional headquarters and provide you with a full report and recommendations in the next three weeks.'

Superintendent Jones was taken aback at the speed and efficiency of the reply; for a moment he struggled to find a response. 'What about…' he eventually garbled, nodding his head towards Hulme's paperwork.

'I'll take half of it up to my office and sort out the wheat from the chaff. Any complicated issues I'll work on during today. May I suggest that as Constable Morgan is returning on light duties, he might be able to lend Inspector Hulme a hand? I would like to be free to visit the other stations in the county over the next week or so.'

The superintendent grunted. 'I suppose that would be in order. Alright with you Inspector Hulme?'

'I think Inspector Chard's suggestion is reasonable,' replied Hulme.

'In which case, I'll leave you to it,' snapped Jones. 'I don't think your report will come to anything, mind you, Inspector Chard. The best you can expect is for you to be appointed as a token detective for the force, and for funding to be provided for a uniformed inspector to replace you once Hulme here retires.'

With that confident prediction, Superintendent Jones turned on his heel and left.

Shortly afterwards, having taken his leave of Inspector Hulme, Chard followed the superintendent out into the main body of the station, where several constables were crowded around the familiar figure of Constable Morgan. No one seemed to notice the inspector pass by as they welcomed the return of the popular constable. Taking the stairs to the first floor, Chard found which room had been cleared for use as his office and gave it a cursory inspection. There was a battered unvarnished desk which looked as if it had been picked up at a furniture sale, with two chairs, one of which was decidedly rickety. A large cupboard was against the wall, which looked suitable for storage but was found to have damaged hinges. The sturdiest piece of furniture seemed to be the hatstand on which he hung his bowler.

'It looks like I'm back to square one at this station,' Chard muttered, relieved that at least he would be able to get away for the rest of the week. The task of searching for anarchists was, he felt, a complete waste of time and just an excuse to get himself out of the office until the atmosphere in the station settled a little. On the other hand, if he could really produce a report which resulted in funding for more posts, it might put him back in favour with the superintendent. The anarchist question couldn't be completely ignored though, so the hunt must continue. Scratching his sideburns in thought, Chard resolved he would have to head for the docks first thing in the morning.

***

The battered, broken remains of an old piano had lain unwanted on a piece of waste ground for weeks. Not entirely unwanted perhaps, for someone had a use for part of it. It took just a bit of work with a pair of pliers and a good length of piano wire was quickly obtained. The owner of the pliers took it back to his lodgings and put it to one side whilst he made himself a cheese sandwich. Returning with his food, he went to a cupboard and took out the two pieces of wood, each about four inches long, which he had cut to size earlier. Humming to himself, in between mouthfuls of his sandwich, he took a sharp knife and made a notched channel around the centre of each piece of wood. Once complete, he put the wood down and sat back to admire his handiwork.

'It has to be done and I'm damned anyway,' he declared to the empty room.

Getting up from his chair, the man took the piano wire and began to wind each end around the wooden handles he'd made. After several turns, he twisted the wire around itself until it was firmly held in place. Finally, he took one of the wooden grips in each hand and gave a sharp tug, until the piano wire joining them was pulled taut.

A nice garrotte, even if I say so myself, he thought. Time to put it to good use.

***

It was usually quiet in the Ivor Arms on a Monday night, and this was no exception. A young man in his twenties sat reading a newspaper in the corner of the room closest to the door; an elderly couple sat nearby, the husband with a half pint of stout, whilst his wife sipped gin; and one of the town's lamplighters quietly enjoyed a pint of porter at the bar. These were the regular Monday night patrons, Gwen had explained to Bert on his first night behind the bar. Anyone else was a bonus.

This night the 'anyone else' didn't feel like a bonus, thought Bert; and Gwen wasn't around to appreciate his point of view.

'I'll have another,' demanded Dai Books, slapping a hand on the counter at the far end of the bar.

'It'll be your last, David Meredith,' replied Bert sternly as he moved across to take the empty glass from Dai Books's other hand.

Dai shrugged and resumed the conversation he was having with Dic Jenkins and Will Horses.

'So, I told him, didn't I? I went right up to his face and put it to him straight!'

'Yes,' sighed Will. 'You've told us half a dozen times.'

'I wasn't having it,' slurred Dai. 'I wasn't having it at all! You can't treat children like that, as much as I dislike the little bastards. They've got the right to speak their own language.'

'Quite right too,' agreed Dic.

'Do you know what the headmaster said? Do you know what he said?' repeated Dai, his voice raised an octave higher.

'Yes,' answered Dic and Will in unison. 'He said you're fired.'

'He said... he actually said... you won't believe this now... but he said that I was fired!' replied Dai, his face a picture of amazement, as he staggered against the bar. 'Can you believe it?'

Will and Dic looked at each other, then back at Dai, and nodded.

'Exactly! It's unbelievable!' continued Dai, not registering his friends' reaction. 'And there's the problem. People like that in charge, firing whoever they want. It's the same everywhere. Those who have no common sense lording it over us. Poverty and destitution for all working men. That's what they want! Have you seen...?' he asked, elbow slipping off the bar, causing him to steady himself. 'Have you seen the newspaper reports of the poverty further up the valleys?

Families unable to feed their children…' he continued, voice rising to a higher pitch.

'Yes, *bach*. We understand, but keep it down a bit,' suggested Dic.

'Revolution!' shouted Dai. 'That's what we need. Sort them all out!'

'Oi!' yelled Bert, dashing from the other side of the bar. 'You've said quite enough! Get yourself gone.'

'Best take yourself home, Dai. You've had a bad day,' added Will gently.

Dai Books looked thoughtfully into the remains of his beer, then swigged it back in one go, before placing the empty glass back on the bar.

'I'll be off,' he said quietly as he made his way towards the door.

On reaching it, he turned and spoke loudly. 'It's all wrong. The whole world is wrong and needs to be changed, and I'm going to do something about it.' He waved his fist. 'You'll see if I don't.'

'Poor Dai, he hasn't been the same since he lost his old job. He thinks the world is against him,' sympathised Dic, as their friend staggered out through the door.

'He'll come round and get back to his old self eventually,' said Will.

As they talked, neither man noticed someone get up and follow Dai out of the door.

***

Once outside in the fresh air, Dai Books decided to cross back into the town over the Old Bridge, rather than the New Bridge. It was higher, narrower, and suitable only for pedestrians. Once recognised as a wonder of engineering, being the longest single span stone bridge in Europe, it was in reality too steep and narrow for vehicles and was rarely used. At the bridge's apex, Dai bent over the parapet and gazed down into the black waters beneath. He didn't hear the footsteps approach and was surprised when a voice spoke close to his ear.

'Not thinking of jumping, are you?' The voice was jocular, and it initially sparked annoyance.

'Who the hell are you?' asked Dai, turning to see who had the nerve to disturb his thoughts. It was a young man who stood close by, and his sudden appearance confused the recently-fired teacher.

'I'm sorry. I didn't mean to interrupt your thoughts; I was just making a friendly remark.'

Dai stared at him through an alcoholic haze. The young man had an amiable, excitable smile and with his studious appearance looked like a youthful, happier version of himself.

'You shouldn't go creeping up on people. I could have fallen over the edge,' complained Dai.

'I apologise for alarming you. To tell the truth, I couldn't help but overhear what you were saying in the pub just now. I could see you were upset when you left and I was concerned for your wellbeing.'

'Upset! Yes, of course I'm upset, but no-one seems to understand.'

'You spoke admirably in the pub and I sympathise with everything you said. The world is wrong and it does need to be changed.'

'Damn right it does! I want to do something about it. I need to do something… anything,' said Dai, miserably.

'There are a number of us, freethinkers, who want to take action. I wonder if you would like to talk with us one evening. My name is Victor Blandford by the way.'

Dai shook the proffered hand. 'David Meredith, but friends call me Dai Books.'

'Would you like to go to another pub and talk more?'

Dai shook his head. 'My wife's going to play merry hell with me as it is,' he replied, his voice slurring. 'I'd better be on my way home. It's the other side of town.'

'Then I'll walk with you. Might I ask if you are free on Saturday evening?'

'Why?'

'I have some friends who I'd like you to meet. They think the same as you and me, and I think you would enjoy some time with like-minded people. It would mean going down to Cardiff, but it's only just over half an hour on the train. They run until late, so there'd be no problem getting home.'

Dai frowned. 'I'm not sure. Cardiff doesn't appeal to me,' he slurred.

'Trust me. I'm sure you're just the man we're looking for,' cajoled Victor. 'You'll get on famously with us. Wait a moment,' he said, putting a hand on Dai's shoulder. Reaching into his pocket, Victor took out a pencil and a scrap of paper and scribbled a few words. Putting the note into Dai's top pocket, he gave an enthusiastic smile. 'Meet me at the Hayes in Cardiff at seven p.m. on Saturday. I live here in Ponty and would travel down with you, but there's business that I need to attend to first.'

'You think it's possible to make things better…?' asked Dai, his vision blurring at the edges.

'I'm sure of it, and after Saturday, you'll be one of us!'

SIX

The morning sun was trying to break through the blanket of grey cloud, but it was a losing battle. It made the whole docks area feel dismal and depressing, and it wasn't helping Inspector Chard's mood. The journey from Pontypridd down to the coast should not have been overlong, but there had been a fault with the train causing an hour's delay. Then, having reached his destination, Chard was dismayed to discover that the paperwork he needed to look at was in a shocking state.

The police station of the Glamorgan County Constabulary at Barry Docks was not particularly impressive, but it served its purpose. Barry Dock Number One had been completed less than a decade earlier, built in response to the stranglehold which the Cardiff Docks, and the Taff Vale Railway Company, had over the coal trade. With a quarter of the world's industrial fuel coming through this single port, the coal exporters could be held to ransom. The response was to build a new port a few miles down the coast near the town of Barry. Fed by a new railway to rival the existing Taff Vale Railway, the enterprise was booming. The Barry Railway Company, which now owned both docks and railway line, had started to build Dock Number Two which was halfway to completion, evidenced by the loud din which irritated Chard as he tried to make sense of the figures before him.

'How're you getting along?' asked Superintendent Bowden, the senior officer at the station.

'I'm trying to tie up the dates of offences over the last year with the dates of arrest, but some of them don't seem to make any sense, sir.'

Bowden shrugged. 'I'll get constable Richards to come and give you a hand. Most of the paperwork gets done by him. He's walking his beat at the moment, so you'll have to wait an hour or two until he gets back.'

'If you don't mind my suggestion, I'd rather take some air and track him down now. It would save me a lot of time, as I can't go much further until I've got an explanation for these anomalies,' said Chard.

The superintendent consulted his pocket watch, then snapped the lid shut. 'If you're quick you should catch him before he goes up into Barry town. He's the only one of my constables with grey hair, so you'll spot him easily enough.'

***

Eager to find his man, Chard had grabbed his hat and rushed outside, heading away from the docks towards the town. After walking briskly towards a policeman in the distance, only to find that the uniform was worn by a young, freckle-faced officer, he decided to double back towards Dock Number One. The dock itself swarmed with stevedores and sailors of many nationalities, speaking half a dozen different languages amidst the clatter and confusion befitting a major commercial port. Yet, only a few dozen paces away, there was a little oasis of calm. With the permission of the port authorities, a small covered stall had been set up, providing mugs of tea, filled rolls and shellfish to whoever was fortunate to be on a break.

Out of instinct, paired with a knowledge of a police constable's inclinations, Chard made his way towards the stall. Initially he was disappointed to find that around the far side there was only one customer, a swarthy docker with coal-stained arms, but then he noticed there was a low wall adjacent to the main dock. As soon as he got close to the wall, he could hear voices coming from beyond it.

'So, I tells 'im to put it down or I'll stuff my truncheon right up his arse.'

'Only way to treat 'em. I'll be sorry to see you go. When's your last shift?'

'I'm switching to evening duty for the next few nights, then I finish on Sunday. I'm looking forward to walking into the station on Monday morning and handing my stuff in....'

The conversation halted as Chard walked in front of the two uniformed men, who were seated on a low bench, out of sight to general passers-by.

'Constable Richards?'

'Who wants to know?' asked the larger of the two men. He had a prominent, heavily-veined nose, heavy-lidded eyes and a thick grey moustache. In his hand he held a nearly empty container of cockles, which made Chard's nose wrinkle with disgust.

'I'm Inspector Chard from Pontypridd. Your superintendent told me you were on your beat. I understand you're on your way to Barry town.'

Richards dropped his container of cockles, sprang to his feet and stood to attention, gazing into the distance. 'Sorry sir. On my way I was sir, until I saw good Constable Jones here from the Barry Railway Company Police, and we started to liaise, like.'

'I'll be off then,' said Richard's companion, hastily putting on his cap and leaving.

Chard found it hard to contain a smile. 'Walk with me, Constable Richards. Just around the dock here for a few minutes. You can catch up on your beat later.'

'Yes, Inspector. Anything you say, sir.'

The two men set off on a slow stroll around the side of the dock, Chard finding he enjoyed the salt in the air, the slightly sweet, decaying smell which pervaded working ships, and the bustling atmosphere as the vessels were loaded with their cargo.

'I've been going through the division's records of cases and arrests and I'm having difficulty tying up a number of the dates. I've scribbled a couple of examples down here,' explained Chard, taking out a notepad.

Richards took the pad and squinted as he stared at the couple of cases listed.

After a few moments, he smiled in recognition. 'Ah! There you have it! It's because the victims or culprits were either seamen or dockers. The cases would have been reported at first to the Barry Railway Company Police. Then, if it became clear that the matter was more serious than at first thought, they would pass it to us. The Company Police only deal with dockers' fights, minor thefts, drunkenness and the like. Sometimes the dates get muddled. Also, we might have a case where we've charged someone, but the victim doesn't want to press charges, so we return it to the Company Police who might just issue a fine to the relevant ship's captain.'

'That might explain it,' answered Chard, aware of similar relation-ships between the County Constabulary and other commercial police forces such as the Glamorganshire Canal Police.

'I'll take a fresh look at them when I get back to the station and if I've still got questions, I'll talk to you when you've finished your beat.'

'Gangway! Mind yer backs!' yelled a stevedore, causing the policemen to move to one side as a cart with coils of rope was pushed past them.

'I overheard you're retiring,' said the inspector, continuing the conversation.

'Yes, sir,' answered Richards. 'I'll be at home with the missus this time next week.'

'You must have done some time in the force. I'm surprised you haven't reached the rank of sergeant.'

'Three times, sir,' answered Richards with a rueful grin. 'I'm afraid I've fallen short of expectations a few times and dropped back to constable. I tend to like the bottle a bit too much, but there's nobody that's perfect.'

'Quite true,' agreed Chard. 'You must have a lot of local knowledge, or so I would assume.'

'You get to know a lot, working these docks,' agreed Richards, nodding.

'This might seem an odd question, but have you heard of any anarchists in these parts?'

Richards stopped walking and raised an eyebrow in surprise. 'What? You mean those fellas who blow up things with bombs and whatnot?' He shook his head. 'No, nothing like that. It's mainly fights, the occasional stabbing and theft around the docks; up in the town itself we get the same as what you probably get in Ponty.'

'What about in Cardiff town?'

'It's not our patch of course, but I do hear things. Nothing like bombs going off though. You'd have read about it in the papers if anything like that had happened.'

'Nothing political then? People talking about bringing down the government. That sort of thing.'

Constable Richards rubbed his chin. 'When I've been in Cardiff on my days off there's always people in the pubs moaning about how bad things are for the working man ... and there's been those pamphlets that come out every so often...'

'Pamphlets?' asked Chard.

'They're headed The Fix. Usually saying how we shouldn't have to pay our rates and such like. Then at the last council elections they said it was all rigged and votes hadn't been properly counted. All sorts of nonsense like that.'

'Do people believe the pamphlets?'

'Most don't, but some do,' replied Richards.

'Anything else?'

'There have been a few small fires over the past year. Just the odd public vehicle. They might not be connected, but the pamphlets have mentioned them, praising whoever was responsible. Then of course there was what happened last Saturday night.'

'What do you mean?' asked Chard.

'Don't you read the Cardiff Times? There were four postboxes, packed with overnight mail, set on fire at about the same time. There were ructions about it. The Cardiff Borough Police have been getting it in the neck for not catching the culprits.'

'Thank you, Constable. You've been most helpful.'

Leaving the constable to his beat, Chard walked back in the direction of the police station. At least I have a potential lead, he thought. It'll be worth going to Cardiff on Saturday night to see what I can dig up.

***

Later that evening, the atmosphere in the disused workshop was fractious.

'Come, now!' admonished John Wilson, shaking his head in disappointment at the eight others in the room. 'There is no need for such disagreement. Our plans on Saturday worked perfectly well. It's a cause for celebration, not discord.'

'All we did was set a few postboxes on fire,' scoffed Ted Schwartz. 'It means nothing. We should be setting buildings on fire at the very least.'

'I agree,' said Ada Quill emphatically.

'I don't!' countered Eddie Ward. 'The police haven't put much effort into tracing our pamphlets, but if we go too far there'll be hell to play, and they might end up at the door of my printing shop.

'Settle yourselves down, everyone!' insisted Wilson. 'Our aim is to damage the reputation of the authorities which exploit the common man. We need to show them to be weak and unable to control our society. To that end, the disruption of the Royal Mail is a valid target.'

'But it's not enough,' argued Frank Edwards. 'I intend returning to North Wales soon to what little family I have left. I wanted to do something that would make a real impact down here first, before I go back.'

'I agree that we need to expand our efforts,' placated Wilson. 'As I mentioned previously, we must look to spread our influence. Apart from my own private funds, we have had a number of contributions from sympathisers to our cause.'

'Yes,' said the docker, Charlie Janssen. 'Sympathisers who don't want to get their hands dirty.'

'Maybe so,' said Wilson, 'but we welcome their money nevertheless.' Hitting the table before him with his fist, he spoke with fervour. 'Our great advantage is that the railway network allows any of us to travel from here into the heart of the valleys and back, inside a single evening. If we are firm in our resolve and can attract more good people to our cause, then there'll be no stopping us. Yes, we've started slowly, but we will grow.' Wilson gestured to Victor Blandford. 'Tell everyone of your progress.'

Getting to his feet, Victor gave his usual enthusiastic smile and pointed at Ted Schwartz. 'Ted suggested we should go ahead and start trying to find new sympathisers straight away. Perhaps trying out one at a time, to see if we've recruited the right sort of person, because the last thing we want to do is to get several in one go and end up with one of them being a traitor in our midst. Ted was going to join Frank up in Merthyr one night next week, but in the meantime, I decided to try my luck in Pontypridd.' Victor paused to gesture apologetically towards James Eden. 'Sorry James, I should have involved you, but I went out on the spur of the moment. As it happens, I think I've been successful. I found someone who may be useful to us. With everyone's agreement, I'll bring him here on Saturday.'

There were a few uncertain murmurs, but the excitement in Victor's face swayed the majority.

'As you wish. Just ensure he's blindfolded on the way here,' cautioned Wilson. 'Now, on to more pressing matters. I think we should mark the expansion of our activities by taking some small action in both Pontypridd and Merthyr.'

'About time,' interjected Frank.

Wilson ignored the interruption and continued. 'I would like the honour of striking the first blow at Pontypridd. I won't need any help, unless Willy would like to come along?'

The little man looked reluctant but eventually nodded.

Noticing the unhappy expression on Frank Edwards's face, Wilson added, 'I think we should hit Merthyr this week as well. With regards to that, I've got a little task for you as well, Frank.'

Noticing the big man's expression relax a little at the thought of being given a new mission, Wilson continued, 'If you stay behind, together with James, I'll give you your instructions. As for everyone else, we'll meet again on Saturday when we'll see who Victor has brought us.'

SEVEN

Chard groaned at the sight of the paperwork before him. Another day and another station. This time Ton Pentre division. Only two more to go, he consoled himself. Aberdare the following day and the hell-hole of Merthyr on Monday.

'Cup of tea, Inspector?' offered a cheery constable.

I'd rather have a whiskey, thought Chard, before accepting the mug of hot, brown liquid that looked more suitable for staining wood. He felt unsettled, as he had explained to Barney whilst walking the dog the previous evening. There were conflicting priorities and it was difficult to foresee how things were going to resolve themselves. The main concern was getting things back to how they were before he went away. Surely the situation would settle down at Pontypridd? Had it been a mistake to go off visiting these other stations instead of staying put and trying to mend fences straight away? Barney had no answer. He'd just stopped to relieve himself against a lamp post, before pulling on the lead as he set off again. Bloody dog, absolutely useless!

The visits around the county were necessary, though. After all, he'd promised Superintendent Jones that his report would be completed as a matter of urgency, and getting on his superior's good side was essential. Not for himself as such, but in order to try and make things right for Constable Morgan. There were two matters to consider in relation to the report. The first was whether he could make an efficient, comprehensive job of it and present it in good time. The methodology Chard was working to was sound, and he was sure he could make the case for the recruitment of detectives a convincing one. It just needed a lot of hard work in extracting the key information from the stations' records, then compiling the details in a concise, readable manner.

The inspector grimaced as he swallowed a mouthful of the tea. Barely suitable for human consumption, he thought.

The second aspect of the report to consider was whether the whole exercise was a complete waste of time. Money for extra officers had always been hard to come by. The realistic outcome was likely to be a pat on the back, and an apologetic explanation that the report's recommendations may be implemented at some time in the future. Meaning never.

After another mouthful of tea, Chard got up from the desk and put his jacket and hat on.

'Finished already, sir?' asked the local constable, as the inspector headed for the door.

'Just going for some fresh air, Constable,' he replied.

Once outside, Chard took a deep breath and set off on a stroll down the street. There was one more thing on his mind, Sean Padraig MacLiam. The whole thing described by the man Farrington seemed ridiculous. First of all, the idea that there was some assassin on the loose. Yet, such things were not unknown, and hadn't there been treasonous acts by Fenians not that long ago? The Phoenix Park assassination for one, the blowing up of the Glasgow gasworks for another. He'd also read about anarchist bomb plots having been foiled in London. But here, in South Wales? It just didn't ring true.

'Oi! Mind where you're going!' admonished a matronly lady as Chard absent-mindedly walked into her.

Tipping his hat, Chard apologised profusely before crossing the road, narrowly avoiding being run over by a builder's cart.

Once on the other pavement, his mind turned once again to Sean MacLiam. Even if there was an assassin, it seemed impossible to believe his former fellow student would be complicit in concealing a murderer. Sean had been a lonely figure in his university days. His father had been forced to leave Ireland as a boy due to the Great Famine, but had made his fortune in the goldfields of California. Returning to Britain, he had married an heiress, but never forgot his roots. As Sean grew up, his father filled his head with tales of the famine; how the protestant English had preferred to profit by keeping food prices high, allowing a million Irish to die of starvation and disease. They were views Sean had felt free to express at university debates at every possible opportunity. Unfortunately, there were some students who took exception, and rather than reason with him, they preferred to bully the young Irishman. That was when Chard was persuaded to befriend him. Sean was a little odd at times and clearly didn't fit in, but seeing him taunted every day was unpleasant to witness. Only once did the bullies look to physically assault Sean, but when they did, it was Chard who stepped in to thrash his assailant, a student called Brown.

Nevertheless, the taunts and jibes continued, Sean responding each time by becoming more and more outspoken. Eventually he had over-stepped the mark by criticising the government and the Queen herself, in such a manner that the University felt forced to send him down. The night after he was expelled, the rooms of the bully called Brown were set alight. Sean was arrested at a hotel in Manchester and held awaiting trial. However, with no real evidence he was released from custody and subsequently disappeared.

Did Sean start the fire? Probably yes, but he would have known Brown was out that evening. Every discussion Chard had ever had with Sean indicated that he would never actually harm anyone.

Getting to the end of the street, Chard turned to walk back towards the station. Perhaps the information from Constable Richards does need to be followed up, he thought. But not before I've got this bloody report well in hand!

***

Cornelius Jeavons checked his pocket watch. Pursed his lips, then after a moment's indecision, got up from his armchair.

'I'm going out, Flora dear,' he announced to his wife. He tutted to himself as he left the warm fireside and went out into the hallway. A damn ridiculous decision to obey the note's instruction, he thought; but perhaps worth the discomfort. Not bothering to use the bell pull to call a servant to assist him, Jeavons put on his warmest coat and took his top hat from the hatstand. Pausing for a moment before the selection of walking canes kept close to the front door, he finally selected a thick, rather inelegant one weighted with lead. 'Best be on the safe side,' he muttered.

Stepping outside, he felt the cold breeze against his cheeks and he wished that he'd bothered to pick up a scarf on his way out. Too late now, he told himself, as he strode downhill towards the centre of Merthyr Tydfil town.

Jeavons was tall, elderly and some would call him frail, cursed as he was with a persistent cough which had dogged him for months. That said, he was a man of ambition, who valued his position as a county councillor beyond all else. It had given him social contacts, advancement, and the power to shape so many decisions which affected people's lives. The awarding of contracts, planning permission, public nominations – all subject to his influence – at the right price.

A figure stood in the shadows across the street, making Jeavons increase the grip on his cane. He knew he should have arranged for a cab to pick him up, but the last-minute decision to make the rendezvous meant he couldn't wait around for his servant to run on into town and order one.

As the councillor walked forward, he could make out that the figure in the shadows was just an old woman, clutching a bottle of what was probably gin. He gave an inaudible sigh of relief and resolved to ensure more street lamps were provided for this stretch of road.

Bloody Mordecai Thorpe! If that shit hadn't have come along with his pathetic bleating about the state of the poor, all would be satisfactory. Yet, the man had the impudence to contest his seat at the next election. His ideas were a danger to civilized society, but some fools were starting to agree with him. There was actually a chance he might win, and that would mean ruin. I treated him fairly, thought Jeavons. I offered him a fair inducement to stand down, but the beggar had the cheek to turn me down and call me corrupt.

A stray mongrel made the mistake of advancing towards the angry man and start sniffing at his feet.

'Bastard!' swore Jeavons, bringing his lead weighted cane down with some force on the unfortunate animal's skull.

Ten minutes later, Jeavons reached the town centre and stood beneath a street lamp. Using a clean handkerchief, he wiped the head of his walking cane clean before discarding the stained piece of cotton onto the pavement. Reaching into the inside pocket of his jacket, he took out an envelope and read once again the note which had persuaded him to come out on this chilly night.

'*I have the means to bring down Thorpe. If you want the information then bring this note with you to the Beehive in Castle Street at ten tonight. Come alone.*' It was signed '*A well-wisher*'.

Jeavons grunted. He knew the pub and was loath to patronise it, but needs must, he told himself.

'Damn!' cursed the councillor as he felt the spasm in his chest which would inevitably result in one of his coughing fits. After hacking up gobbets of phlegm for a couple of minutes, he set off once more for the rendezvous at the Beehive Inn.

Entering the pub, his senses were hit by the stench of cheap tobacco which filled the room. Tempted as he was to immediately turn on his heel and walk out, Jeavons went to the bar and looked for a bottle of spirits that might sport a name he recognised. There was none, so instead he glanced around until he saw someone holding a pint of beer that didn't look fuggy, and pointed to it.

'I'll have a half pint of whatever that is,' he told the barman, who, surprised at seeing a wealthy gentleman asking to be served, dropped his stained bar towel and immediately reached for a glass.

Once served, Jeavons went to a small table close to the door and sat down. No sooner had he done so than a hand fell on his shoulder and gave a slight squeeze. Turning around in a mixture of surprise and indignation, he found himself looking at a young man in workmen's clothes. He had a round, pleasant-looking face with wavy blond hair showing beneath his flat cap.

'Don't get up,' he said softly, before taking a seat opposite the councillor. 'I think we have business to discuss.'

***

Half an hour later, Jeavons walked out of the Beehive smiling broadly. Even another bout of coughing couldn't dampen his spirits. His heart felt lighter, as did his wallet, for the information did not come cheap; but it was worth every penny. It appeared that Thorpe was a sodomite, regularly paying young men to defile them. Furthermore, the informant had provided names and places. Thorpe would be forced to stand down from the election and could be blackmailed into paying a regular sum to ensure the revelations would never come to light.

'I must have something to celebrate!' Jeavons said aloud. There was a pub in Glebeland Street where he was well known and which stocked a particularly fine malt whisky, and that would be his next destination.

He would have to be quick though, or he wouldn't get his order in before closing time.

***

It was gone eleven when Jeavons stepped out of the pub on Glebeland Street. He had been hailed when entering the bar and ordering a round of drinks for everyone present. More votes for the upstanding Councillor Jeavons, he thought. There had only been time for a couple of double whiskies, but they were sufficient to warm his insides, ready for what would be a chilly walk home. He had intended taking a cab, but it was too late for one now. The other pub patrons had left, disappearing towards their own homes, and the street seemed deserted.

It was a hundred paces later when the whistling started, a soft mournful melody. Jeavons stopped and looked around, but could see no one. The sound stopped, so he walked on. Then he heard it again, and instinctively started to walk faster. The whistling stopped once more, and Jeavons slowed his pace, but his heart was beating a little faster. Why were there no police walking a night-time beat? Why were the streets not better lit? He would bring it up with the town clerk. Suddenly, there was the pain in his chest again, the one that heralded another coughing fit. He stopped. He had to. The first hacking cough made his body convulse and he leant against a wall, dropping his cane as he did so.

Mid-way through bringing up a bolus of phlegm, he heard a movement behind him and felt something being placed around his neck. It hurt.

Desperately, he tried to put his fingers beneath the wire biting into his throat and claw it away, but at the same time his body was still trying to cough. His chest was burning with the effort, whilst his throat was feeling the agony of the garrotte's constriction. He gagged as he started to choke, the pain of every desperate attempt at breath competing with the agonies of his other torments. His eyes bulged, looking desperately into the night for the sight of a saviour. Eventually, his body convulsed, before becoming still.

Releasing the garrotte from around the councillor's neck, his killer let the body slump to the ground.

'Mustn't let you be found until the morning,' he muttered, grabbing the corpse by the legs and dragging it into the shadows of a nearby alley. Taking a cursory glance down the street to ensure no one had observed the killing, the murderer retrieved Jeavons' cane from the pavement and placed it next to the body.

Just one more touch. The important one, thought the killer. He put a hand into his jacket and took out a piece of paper. Folding it neatly, he placed it inside the councillor's coat pocket then, whistling once more, he disappeared into the night.

EIGHT

The morning sunlight filtered through the partly drawn curtains of the Whitehall office, illuminating the documents over which the man behind a grand oak desk pondered.

Sir Matthew White Ridley, Home Secretary, pursed his lips as he read the report once more. In his mid-fifties, he cut an elegant figure, looking younger and fitter than many of his contemporaries. Having gained a senior cabinet position in Salisbury's government, his future prospects seemed excellent, but it would only take one disaster to bring everything tumbling down. He glanced at his diary and then at the clock which hung on the far wall of the large, high-ceilinged room.

There was a knock on the door and a small, bespectacled man entered nervously.

'Send him in!' barked Sir Matthew, before the clerk could open his mouth to speak.

Nervously, the little man backed out, to be replaced moments later by a tall, confident figure dressed completely in black.

'I see you are as punctual as ever, Farrington. Take a seat,' instructed Sir Matthew.

Inwardly, the Home Secretary felt irritated. Damned pretentious fellow, he thought. Looks like a bloody undertaker. No breeding, just a mongrel from the gutter who's got above himself.

'I've just reread your report, Farrington. I am not pleased.'

'In what way, Sir Matthew?' answered the man in black, calmly.

The Home Secretary raised a questioning eyebrow. 'You still believe this assassin, Lucheni or whatever he now calls himself, is at large?'

'I do, Sir Matthew.'

'Even though Tynan failed in his part of the bargain? The Czar is now safely in Paris meeting the President of France.'

'I'm afraid that isn't how these people do business, Sir Michael. Once someone like Lucheni is contracted to kill, then they will endeavour to fulfil their assignment. Whilst he is at large, he remains a danger.'

'You still don't know who the target is?'

'We can't be certain,' replied Farrington. 'The obvious targets still appear to be members of the Privy Council at the meeting with Her Majesty at Balmoral, or His Royal Highness the Prince of Wales.'

'Your report indicates you have extra men allocated to protect them.'

'Balmoral is as secure as it can possibly be. Unfortunately, the Prince of Wales can be, if I might say so, rather difficult.'

The Home Secretary frowned. 'I think everyone is aware of His Royal Highness's occasional free manner. Would I be correct in thinking that he declines to stick rigidly to a formal calendar?'

Farrington nodded. 'Last-minute attendance at parties or shooting weekends, I'm afraid. It makes it difficult to keep abreast of his movements and make the necessary arrangements to protect him.'

Sir Michael slammed a hand down on his desk as he considered the potential damage to his career if a member of the Royal Family were to be killed. 'Damn it, Farrington! Why can't you find this assassin? Surely you've got people who can seek him out?'

'As my report says, it is probable he has inserted himself into a group of like-minded people, though he may not have informed them of his true identity or his mission. Thankfully, there are not that many anarchist sympathisers in the country, and they are nearly all known to us. I have allocated men to keep watch on every one of them and we have even managed to infiltrate groups in Glasgow, Newcastle and, of course, London.

'Yet there is no sign of the man we're after,' accused Sir Michael.

'Not yet, but we'll find him.'

'You said you know nearly all the anarchist groups. What about the ones you don't?'

'To our knowledge, there is only one other. We have the name of the leader of the group, but cannot trace him. I wouldn't be too concerned though, Sir Michael. The group seems to be inactive. Nothing of any consequence has reached our ears, and it is located in South Wales, far away from the likely targets.'

'You are aware that it doesn't take long to travel from one end of the country to the other on the rail network?' asked the Home Secretary sarcastically. 'Have you done nothing about South Wales?'

'The possibility has been covered,' answered Farrington. 'I excluded the detail from my report as I considered it to be inconsequential. I located someone, a police inspector, who can identify the group leader. I took the liberty of involving the Under-Secretary in making arrangements which will allow him the scope to work for us unofficially.'

'What's the man's name?'

'Chard. Inspector Thomas Chard. He seems intelligent and resourceful.'

'He'd better be, or I swear I'll have his hide!' declared the Home Secretary, thumping his fist on the desk.

***

It was nine o'clock in the evening when John Wilson arrived in Pontypridd with his reluctant accomplice in tow. Willy Rabinovitz carried a metal container and a canvas bag, whilst Wilson, eyes wild with excitement, strode on, empty-handed.

'Come on. Keep up,' he encouraged, as his companion tried to keep in the shadows, with his cap pulled down over his face.

Wilson had chosen the evening well, because Thursday was always a quiet night, before the hell-raising which regularly happened on weekends. Avoiding the high street, he led the way around the western edge of the town, heading for the police station.

'It's important to let the people know we have come to free them,' said Wilson, slowing his pace so Willy could catch up.

'No!' said the small man urgently when he recognised where they were heading.

'Don't worry my friend.' Wilson's gentle Irish was accentuated by his enthusiasm. 'We're not going to target the police.'

Reluctantly, the Irishman's helper agreed to carry on beyond the police station, where Sergeant Jackson played cards with a constable, oblivious to the ill-intentioned men passing outside.

'Give me the stuff,' said Wilson once they had gone further ahead and reached the outer wall of St Catherine's Church, which faced onto the normally busy Gelliwastad Road.

'You go on ahead to where the road rises slightly,' he continued.

'It'll give you a good view in both directions. Just whistle if you see something and I'll stop what I'm doing.'

'Someone'll see you,' grumbled Willy.

'It's poorly lit on this section next to the church, and no one will notice my handiwork until daylight,' replied Wilson. 'Now go.'

Clearly not happy, Willy went about thirty yards away, which allowed him to see the length of Gelliwastad Road, and immediately gave a low whistle which alerted Wilson that a vehicle was on its way.

The Irishman waited for a four-horse carriage and a gig to pass, before reaching for the bag and container left by his accomplice.

What better way to announce our arrival than one of our most famous slogans? Wilson thought as he opened the tin of red paint and inserted a wide stiff-bristled paintbrush.

***

Chard had spent all day at Aberdare, collecting the information he needed for his report. Then he had spent some hours, either side of his evening meal, preparing early drafts which could be finalised after the following week's visit to Merthyr. Eventually, having finished his paperwork, he felt able to relax.

The inspector was sitting in front of the fire, sipping a glass of Jameson whiskey with Barney curled up at his feet, when he heard the police whistle. Gelliwastad Road was a quiet part of town and being so close to the police station, there was rarely any rowdiness to disturb an evening. Curious as to what might be going on, Chard got to his feet and went to the window. To his alarm, he saw the distinctive outline of Constable Davies running past, still blowing his whistle. His concern was not for the potential crime being committed. Rather, it was for the health of the constable. Of all the officers in the station, Davies, who was eighteen stone if he was an ounce, was not one you wanted to see trying to move at speed.

'Bugger!' cursed Chard. Not stopping to reach for a jacket, the inspector ran to the front door in his shirtsleeves just as Lucy came down the stairs from her room.

'What's going on?' she asked.

'Trouble!' replied Chard, rushing out of the door.

By the time he caught up with Constable Davies, the officer was bent double and wheezing heavily.

'They... got... away,' he gasped.

Chard shook his head in compassion as he helped the overweight, red-faced officer upright.

'Don't worry about it. Unless they've committed murder that is,' he said with a reassuring smile. 'Look, young Constable Connelly has heard your whistle, so he can have a look for whoever you were chasing.'

Feeling embarrassed at his lack of fitness, Davies grimaced when he saw his colleague running up from the police station. 'They were just too fast,' he explained to Chard before Connelly reached them. 'A slim man in a flat cap was who I was after... he joined up with someone short ...could have been a lad I suppose...They ran in that direction,' he gasped, pointing ahead.

'Two rogues, one slim the other short, running to the top of town. Get after them, Connelly!' shouted Chard to the arriving constable.

The officer ran on, reaching for his truncheon as he did so, leaving Chard with Davies.

'Now then, what did they do?' asked the inspector. 'But catch your breath properly first.'

It was a minute or two before Davies was able to compose himself, but finally he was able to talk without wheezing.

'The slim one was painting something on the church wall. I don't know what it was, but I interrupted him. It was the small man who yelled an alarm when I appeared unexpectedly up from Church Street.'

'Take yourself off back to the station and have a sit down. I'll get a lamp from my house and take a look at the damage. Hopefully, Connelly will catch them. Either way, we can sort it out properly in the morning.'

'Thank you, sir,' said Davies.

Chard let the constable wander back to the station whilst he returned to his house, put on a jacket and then took a small oil lamp across the road and down to the outer church wall.

On the pavement was a pot of paint, spilling its contents into the gutter, and a bag containing a couple of paintbrushes.

The writing on the wall had been done in red paint which, due to the poor light, was difficult to see against the dark stonework. Lifting the lamp to read what had been daubed, he saw the words NO GOD followed by a scribble where another letter had been started but not finished. It would have to stay there until it could be cleaned off in the morning, but what the superintendent would say, he dreaded to think.

NINE

The next morning, Chard made sure to arrive at the police station in good time. He had passed the declaration of NO GOD which remained brazenly daubed on the church wall, and noted the stares of the passengers on the morning omnibuses as they travelled by.

On entering the station, he realised Superintendent Jones had arrived even earlier, as indicated by the bellowing coming from his office.

'It is bad enough, Sergeant Jackson, that some atheist has defiled the wall of the churchyard. It is even worse that the swine's handiwork can be seen by every bit of traffic going down Gelliwastad Road. However, what makes it so bloody shameful is that it happened within fifty yards of the station. It makes us look like a laughing stock. You were on duty overnight, so you are to blame. That's why I ordered you fetched back from your bed.'

Chard found it hard to contain a smile. Sergeant Jackson was a bully, a schemer and a liar; as far as the inspector was concerned, he deserved everything that came his way.

'It wasn't my fault, sir,' Jackson could be heard saying. He had only come off duty two hours earlier and had been comfortably settled in his bed when a constable had thumped on his door to tell him that the superintendent demanded his immediate return. 'It was Constable Davies who was at fault. He should have caught the culprit but failed.'

'Your men, your fault!' accused the superintendent scornfully. 'Now get out of my sight!'

Chard stood by as Jackson left the superintendent's office hurriedly and bustled his way towards the station's exit.

I think I'd better get up to my room, thought Chard as he turned away.

'Inspector Chard!'

The superintendent appeared at his office door, and as the inspector turned to face him, he beckoned with his finger. 'Come here, if you please.'

Chard joined his superior in his office and did his best to adopt a pleasant, calming demeanour.

'How can I be of help, sir?'

The superintendent looked disdainfully at Chard's civilian attire, a tweed three-piece suit, bowler hat, and ebony cane.

'How is your report progressing?'

'Splendidly, sir. I've just got Merthyr station to visit and then I can start pulling all the details together.'

'Good, because the sooner you finish this nonsense and get back to doing some proper police work, the better.'

'I haven't had chance to speak to Inspector Hulme yet, sir. I assume he has everything in hand?' asked Chard.

Jones nodded. 'More or less.'

'Has Constable Morgan been helpful in assisting the inspector?'

The superintendent gave a grunt of affirmation.

'He is a very fine constable, wouldn't you agree, sir?' continued Chard.

'Don't push things too far, Inspector Chard. I believe in discipline and I won't have that undermined.'

'Quite so sir.' Chard knew that at heart Superintendent Jones was a fair man who cared for his men, but sometimes he was overly influenced by an inbuilt need for strict discipline. The inspector felt Jones was already regretting the decision to demote Morgan, but didn't want to admit it.

The superintendent gave a sudden careworn sigh. 'I am afraid this business with the wall outside has put me into rather a bad mood, Inspector. I take it that you've seen it.'

'I have sir, but I'm sure it can be scrubbed off easily enough.'

'Not before members of the town council have been told about it. I've no doubt that I'll have Colonel Grover the town clerk down here before the morning's out.'

'I'm sure you'll be able to placate him, sir.'

The superintendent, still uncertain of his feelings towards his inspector, was aware that Chard had previously had a good rapport with the rest of the station, and knew the rank and file probably better than he did himself.

'I may have been rather hard on Sergeant Jackson before you came in,' Jones confessed.

'I'm certain you would have been fair, sir,' said Chard, smiling inwardly.

'Perhaps so, but he blamed Constable Davies for not catching the culprit. I do wonder whether he is suitably fit to carry out his duties.'

'I have concerns about Sergeant Jackson myself. Perhaps if he went back to being a constable?' suggested Chard, wickedly twisting the superintendent's words.

'No, Chard. I mean Davies. He's the size of a house and is ponderous at best. I shall have to speak to Inspector Hulme and the sergeants about it, but wanted your opinion first.'

Chard scratched one of his neatly-trimmed sideburns in thought. 'He's a good man. Useful in controlling a crowd and hard to knock over in a fight. It's the fast work which lets him down. I think I have an idea though. It was something I saw when I was in Shrewsbury and perhaps you might allow me the chance to give it a trial. Please don't mention anything to the others yet, if you don't mind, sir. I'll hope to sort things out next week.'

The superintendent gave him a look that bordered between curiosity and apprehension. 'I have a feeling I will regret this, but you have my agreement. Do what you think is best and I'll leave speaking to the others until next Friday.' Jones waved a hand in dismissal. 'Carry on, Inspector. I sense that I need to prepare for a meeting with the town clerk.'

On leaving the superintendent's office, Chard noticed that Inspector Hulme had arrived.

'Have you seen what's been painted—' Hulme began.

'Yes,' Chard interrupted. 'The superintendent is furious. No doubt he'll be having a word with you presently.'

Hulme looked worried, even for a man close to his retirement. 'I wish I'd stayed in Aberdare,' he confided.

'May I suggest you get Constable Morgan in here straight away and tell him to go around the town's chapels as well as St Catherine's. If there is some atheist lunatic going around, he may have been causing problems for the vicar or one of the ministers. As Morgan is only on light duties for the next couple of weeks it should be just up his street. When the superintendent comes around you can tell him the investigation is in hand.'

Hulme's face brightened. 'Why, thank you. I'll do just that. If ever I can return the favour, just ask.'

'There is just one thing,' replied Chard with a smile. 'Once Morgan has finished his task, I'd like to borrow him. I've got something special in mind.'

***

It was dusk when James Eden got off the train at Merthyr Station. A bag, carried over his shoulder, contained twenty posters declaring the future council elections to be rigged. They also encouraged all those eligible to vote to burn their ballot papers outside the doors of the council offices.

Exiting the station, Eden noticed the burly frame of Frank Edwards waiting impatiently near a streetlight.

'What took you? I was expecting you on an earlier train.'

'I did the best I could,' said the younger man. 'I might live just down in Ponty, but can't you see from my clothes that I've come straight from work? I say straight, but of course I had to pick up the posters from Eddie's print shop first.'

Frank scowled in disdain at the sombrely dressed young man with the permanently naïve expression. 'Follow me, Jimmy boy!' he ordered, turning and walking away.

'It's not Jimmy, it's James. Where are we going?'

'For a drink, jug-ears. I'll explain when we get there,' came the terse reply.

Holding back his annoyance at the insult regarding his prominent ears, Eden followed Edwards down several streets and into the back room of an unsavoury pub which smelled of stale tobacco and mould.

'We're safe here, and the beer doesn't taste of cats' piss,' said Edwards.

'When can we get this done? You don't seem to have any paste or brushes with you. My last train is ten o'clock and I don't want to have to rent a room.'

Edwards shook his head in exasperation. 'It's off. Didn't you notice anything after we left the station? The streets are crawling with peelers. There was a killing the other night and it's stirred up a hornets' nest. It's not worth the risk, Jimmy boy.'

'Stop calling me that. My name's James and I'm twenty-two, not ten years old,' snapped Eden. 'I suppose I'm not surprised you've called it off. Victor said you're all mouth.'

'Speak to me like that again and I'll put my fist down your throat. Go and get us two pints,' Edwards ordered, handing over a shilling. 'And make sure you get the right change.'

The younger man made as if to argue, but then averted his gaze and reluctantly took the money.

Edwards smirked as he watched him go. Eden was a strapping lad, though not as big as himself, but he had the face of a milksop and clearly knew better than to risk a fight.

When Eden returned with two murky brown pints and sat down opposite him, Edwards wagged his finger as he gave his point of view.

'You're too young to understand, and you'll get into trouble if you're not careful. The likes of John Wilson and Charlie are just playing at this. We should be taking real action. It'll take some real damage, and aye, maybe some killings, for our voices to be heard. That's something to risk arrest for, rather than putting up some poxy posters.'

'John gets us the money we need to pay our train fares though, and more besides,' Eden protested.

'He's just pissing about. He says he listens to us and that he's taken ideas from Ted and Victor, but has he? This posters idea will have come from Eddie and he never wants to get his fingers dirty. He'll make a couple of bob for doing the posters, then let us get arrested for achieving sod all. If he wants to put the bloody things up, then why doesn't he do it? It's what, two hours at most from his shop to Merthyr by train? He could catch the ten o'clock home and be back by midnight or pay a few pennies for a night's digs.'

'I think you're being unfair.'

'At least I won't be around here much longer,' the older man continued. 'I'm heading north to see what can be done there.'

'To see what remains of your family? You've mentioned your background before, but not in any detail. What exactly happened?'

'It's not for discussion. Just finish your pint and you can get yourself home. I'll see you tomorrow night.' Finishing his pint in two large gulps, Edwards walked out without waiting for a response.

TEN

The man lay on his bed in his darkened room, thinking about the next step to take. There was a bright morning sun outside, but he kept the thick curtains drawn because the darkness helped him to think. Lazily, he reached out to the cupboard at the side of his bed, and opened a small drawer. Reaching inside, he brought out the home-made garrotte and played with it in his hands. No-one was expecting to see him this morning, so his time was his own.

Keeping the curtains drawn had another blessing. It meant that it hid the sight of the dilapidated room that he had been forced to rent. Stained wallpaper, a crack in the ceiling from which dust occasionally fell, and a window with a broken pane stuffed with old newspaper to keep out the draught. Still, it wouldn't be for long, the killer told himself. He started to whistle softly as he planned his next victim, though it was more the location that occupied his thoughts. There were certain logistics which had to be considered. He pulled hard on the handles of the garrotte, causing the wire to stretch taut, as if the action would somehow help in his deliberations. Illogically, it did. The place of execution was decided; the victim would be chosen by destiny.

***

It had been quite a pleasant afternoon, Chard thought. Having made the commitment to chase up the possibility of anarchist activity in Cardiff, he had decided to make a midday visit to the town. Often the best people to talk to if you want information about a place were not those who you came across at night. They tended to be guarded and suspicious. In Chard's experience you could get just as much infor-mation, if not more, by making the casual acquaintance of the older, wizened worthies who enjoyed a lunchtime tipple. The inspector had taken the decision not to use an elaborate disguise; he'd had enough of that whilst on the run in Shrewsbury just a few weeks ago. Instead, he wore his normal attire and pretended he was just visiting to see the town's impressive architecture. At the Rummer Tavern in Duke Street he'd been unable to find anyone keen on starting a conversation, but at the Bluebell in High Street, he'd struck lucky. A garrulous old soak, who no doubt regularly attached himself to strangers in the hope of cadging a free drink or two, had given him a possible lead. There was talk of regular coin collections that took place 'for those who would take action to help the common man' at a pub called the Golden Cross.

Pleased to have taken a break from the daily toil of compiling his report, Chard had treated himself to a pleasant meal in a café close to Cardiff Castle, before setting off to the pub in Hayes Bridge Road.

The Golden Cross was located on the street corner. The outside walls were ornately decorated with glazed ceramic tiles, and on the large panelled windows the local brewery's name had been emblazoned on individual glass panes. It no doubt attracted good business at night, but there were few customers when the inspector walked into the saloon bar. Two men, one with a tanned face and scornful expression, the other with close-cropped hair and angry demeanour, were clearly having a disagreement, whilst attempting to keep their voices low. Three Irishmen were toasting each other in Gaelic as they drank their whiskey, and an elderly man in a grease-stained bowler hat was talking to the barman in Welsh.

'*Peint, os gwelwch yn dda,*' said Chard as he approached the bar.

The barman nodded and poured a pint of Brains bitter.

'*Diolch,*' thanked the inspector, as he gave payment and took the beer.

'*Mae hi'n oer uffernol,*' said the elderly man, by way of conversation.

'*'Dwi ddim yn siarad Cymraeg yn dda,*' responded Chard.

The man raised his eyebrows in surprise. 'You speak it alright to me, butty. What I said was, "it's hellish cold".'

'I can speak about half a dozen phrases and a few words,' said Chard. 'I'm not from around here.'

'No, you're not. I can tell that, now you're speaking English. Where're you from? Bristol?'

'No. Shropshire.'

'*Duw, Duw.* An Englishman speaking Welsh. Whatever next? What brings you in here then?'

The question seemed innocent enough, so Chard gave his story about just being a visitor, before offering to buy the man a drink. The offer was keenly taken up and they began to talk. Several times Chard tried to steer the conversation towards general unrest about how the country was run, but without his elderly companion providing any information of interest. It was only when Chard mentioned he wouldn't mind contributing to a good cause, that he noticed a marked reaction. What he didn't notice was the way the barman's ears had pricked up, or the gesture he made towards the two men who had previously been arguing.

'Do you know of any good local causes? Perhaps there's one that this pub supports?' Chard suggested.

'Not as I know of,' replied the elderly man, averting his eyes. 'I need to be off...' he muttered, downing his drink and heading for the door.

The inspector shrugged in disappointment and finished his drink too, before making a visit to the gentlemen's convenience. Placing his walking cane against the wall, he went to the urinal, then started to turn his head as he heard someone else enter.

'Stay where you are,' demanded a voice as a hand grabbed him by the back of his jacket. Instinctively, Chard tried to elbow the man in the ribs, but to no avail. He was pushed firmly against the white-tiled urinal and was struggling to free himself from his assailant's hold.

'You don't belong here and you ask too many questions,' said Charlie Janssen coolly, maintaining his grip. Chard threw his head backwards, hoping to catch his attacker on the bridge of his nose, but the docker was ready for it.

'Stop struggling, or I'll have to hurt you.'

Ignoring the threat, Chard tried to reach behind for his opponent's right thigh in order to squeeze the nerve endings that he knew would cause extreme pain. Once again Janssen was quick to avoid the attempt and responded by grabbing Chard's left arm and twisting it up behind his back.

'I warned you,' snapped Janssen as he pushed his captive against the urinal with greater force. The inspector twisted his head to avoid a broken nose, but his skull hit the tiled wall heavily. Determined not to be beaten, he tried jabbing with his elbow once again, but the docker laughed.

'You won't learn, will you?' he said as he forced the helpless inspector hard against the wall one more time. The inspector's head collided with the wall once again, and this time he slipped to the floor, unconscious.

***

It was five minutes later when Chard eventually came to, lying on the floor of the toilet. Groggily getting to his feet, he went across to the far wall where his hat had fallen in the struggle. He bent down to pick it up, smelled it, and wrinkled his nose in disgust. Ruefully, he gathered up his walking cane with its weighty brass handle, and walked back into the bar. It had emptied of customers and only the barman stood there, polishing a beer glass.

Chard opened his mouth to say something, but thought better of it. Instead, rubbing his sore head, he left the pub without saying a word and went out into the fresh air. As a county policeman he had no authority in the borough of Cardiff, and if he called the local police, what could he say? The barman would claim he must have slipped and fallen and would deny anyone else had been in there. Also, the reason for his being in the town had to remain a secret if he was to be at all successful. No. It was time to go home and change his soiled clothes. If he felt up to it, he might go to the Ivor Arms, but perhaps even that would have to wait. He needed some time to himself to decide what to do next. There was a real possibility that an anarchist group was active in Cardiff, but to what extent? There didn't seem to have been any major crimes committed, other than his own unfortunate experience. However, it couldn't be ignored, and if such a group existed then there was a chance his old university acquaintance Sean MacLiam might be involved. Even if this was the case, it still seemed unlikely such a low-profile group would be involved in hiding an assassin in their midst. Perhaps it would be worth returning to the pub in disguise one evening in the week, Chard thought, but then dismissed the idea. There had to be a way to track down Sean, he reasoned as he headed for the railway station, but how?

***

Dai Books wondered if he was doing the right thing. At Pontypridd station he'd seen Thomas Chard getting off the northbound train as he was waiting for the train to Cardiff. The inspector looked a little bit the worse for wear, and hadn't noticed him as they passed each other. After that, Dai had spent the journey worrying, nearly getting off at one of the stations on the route, in order to return to Pontypridd. The problem was that he hadn't had the chance to talk to anyone. He couldn't face his friends at the Ivor Arms yet, not after the way he'd spoken to them. Talking to his wife was certainly out of the question. Indeed, after the state he'd arrived home in that night, she'd barely uttered a word to him. He hadn't even been able to tell her he'd been dismissed from his employment. Everything was such a complete and utter mess. Now he stood in the centre of Cardiff town, in the area known as the Hayes. Nearby, there was a stall selling tea and sandwiches, with some tables and chairs outside. Dai decided that perhaps he would just take a seat there for ten minutes, and if Victor did not show up in time, he would go home. Frowning as he pondered the wisdom of having turned up at all, he walked towards the stall, only to stop and turn as someone hailed him.

'Mr Meredith, or may I call you Dai? I'm so glad you decided to come.'

Dai gave Victor Blandford an uncertain smile as he approached. 'I'm not sure I should have.'

'Nonsense, nonsense. You've done the right thing. Come with me and you'll meet my friends. We all see the unfairness in our society, as you do. I'm certain you'll get along famously.'

As Blandford spoke, he waved a hand towards the driver of a hansom cab across the street, who responded with a tip of his hat.

'We can take this cab. The driver can be trusted,' said Blandford with a conspiratorial wink.

Such was the smiling enthusiasm of the young man that Dai felt almost obliged to go along with the suggestion. It was only once they were both seated, and the cab set off, that his concerns returned.

'I'm afraid you must put this on,' said Blandford earnestly. He passed Dai a black hood and, removing the former teacher's hat for him, slipped the hood over his head. 'There's no need to worry, but you must understand that we like to keep our business confidential. We aren't going far, but for the moment, it's best you don't know exactly where we meet.'

Dai, his stomach churning, and aware the cab was moving rather quickly, decided it would be advisable to comply.

The journey lasted fifteen minutes at the most. He was aware the cab had taken several turns, though whether or not they were necessary, or just a ruse to confuse him, he couldn't tell.

'We're going to get out here,' said Blandford as the cab came to a stop, 'but you'll need to keep the hood on for a little while. I'll help you out.'

Dai allowed himself to be led from the vehicle onto the street, then after perhaps twenty paces, he was taken through a doorway and down some steps.

'Here we are,' said Blandford.

Dai blinked as the hood was removed, and he found himself in what looked like some sort of workshop. The air felt musty and he wrinkled his nose at the odour. In front of him stood seven men and a woman, their expressions blank. One of them, a slim man with a pale complexion, stepped forward and gave a reassuring smile.

'Mr Meredith, I believe,' he said, holding out a hand.

Dai shook the hand and smiled back, but it betrayed his nervousness.

'My name is John Wilson,' said the man, speaking with a soothing Irish lilt. 'And this is our band of fellows,' he added, waving his hand towards the rest of the group, who made no acknowledgement other than to stare.

Dai looked at them, trying to ascertain what sort of people they were. One particularly large man stood out, then there was another who looked perhaps a little younger than Blandford, a tanned workman of sorts, another with close-cropped dark hair, a bedraggled short fellow, a fidgety man with ink stains on his clothes, and finally a tall, hatchet-faced woman.

'Victor explained your situation. He said you find yourself unemployed and unfairly treated,' said Wilson, his voice full of compassion. 'I understand you would like a fairer society and you're prepared to try and make change happen. Am I right?'

'You see, I lost my job when Lady Llanover died and the heirs to her estate no longer wanted me as a librarian and translator,' explained

Dai, eager to get his troubles off his chest, and also keen to not upset the people who were watching him as if in judgement.

'It's always the way with the rich and powerful families. They would discard the honest worker if it suited them, regardless of years of honest service.' Wilson shook his head in commiseration.

'Then,' continued Dai, 'unable to find employment as a librarian, I was forced to turn my hand to teaching.'

'A noble profession,' interjected Wilson, nodding sagely.

'But I couldn't just stand by and see the school drive the Welsh language out of the pupils by disciplining and bullying them. It isn't right!'

'Quite so,' agreed Wilson, putting a hand on Dai's shoulder. 'But of course, it isn't the school that is to blame.'

'Isn't it?' asked Dai, confused by the comment.

Wilson shook his head. 'No. Of course not. The headmaster will have been instructed by the local authorities, who in turn will have been instructed by parliament. It is those in power who define the limits on the lives of the individual. If the people were left to themselves then good practice would prevail. We must change things for the common good. It is our mission.'

'Do you mean to form a political party and put yourselves forward for elections?' asked Dai.

Wilson shook his head and gave a patronising smile as if correcting an innocent child. 'Of course not. The whole system is corrupted. Can everyone vote? No! Can anyone get elected? No! They need money. What are the chances of, say, a dock worker standing for parliament? None! Can anyone without "influence" become a magistrate? Of course not! What have we seen happen these last ten years or more? Wages cut, unemployment going up, more evictions and higher interest rates. The last one's important because it means those who are rich receive higher returns. The rich get richer and the poor get poorer.'

'But what can anyone do about it?' said Dai with a shrug.

'We can take action. Show the people they must look beyond what's directly in front of them. Explain it's the very fabric of society which needs to be brought down; the institutions that control us. Councils, banks, the police, the state. Only by destroying everything can we achieve true liberty.'

'What do you mean, destroy?' asked Dai, nervous once more.

Wilson patted him on the shoulder. 'Calm yourself. We mean no bodily harm. Our intentions are solely to point out to people the ineffectiveness of the authorities.' There was a snort of derision from someone in the group, which Wilson ignored. 'To free them from their fear of civil disobedience. The small acts we carry out may be mere pinpricks against the beast of authority, but once more people follow our example and take action, we will gradually change the way society controls us.'

'I agree things need to change, but I'm not sure...'

'I understand that as you are no longer in employment, you may be short of funds. You will find our supporters can sometimes help with that, and as for not being able to find a post as a librarian, let's just say I have certain contacts.'

Dai bit his lip in thought at the Irishman's words.

Wilson gave another smile as he saw Dai's thoughtful expression. 'Would you like to join our happy band? There is some small risk, I would agree, but do you have any better alternative? If you are prepared to join us, we would of course have to put you to the test. Well? What do you say? Will you join us?'

After what seemed an age, Dai stopped biting his lip, and slowly nodded. 'Yes,' he replied, and prayed he was doing the right thing.

***

It was after Dai Books had left that the arguments broke out.

'What do you think?' asked Wilson.

'Bloody dangerous. He's not the type of man we need,' said Ted scornfully. 'Never done a day's hard work in his life.'

'If you mean he hasn't had to lift timber or carry bricks for a living, then maybe you're right. But then again, neither have I,' responded Eden angrily. 'For that matter, nor have John, Victor or Eddie.'

'I bloody have,' objected Eddie. 'The printing business can be hard manual work at times.'

'Stop squabbling!' Wilson ordered, his Irish accent more pronounced as he shouted. 'We have all suffered in one way or another. I was forced to leave university, though I would have been a brilliant academic,' he boasted. 'Victor, the same. As you know, he was at Oxford and ended up leaving to spend five years on the continent, where his views could be freely expressed. James was disowned by his family, and Eddie's previous clashes with the authorities over some publications they found immoral are no secret.'

'Bloody right, they were disgusting,' whispered Ada to Frank.

'Getting back to the point,' interrupted Charlie Janssen. 'We shouldn't let anyone in to our group that we don't know. There was someone asking questions in the Golden Cross earlier. I had to sort him out.'

'What were you doing in there during the day?' asked Wilson.

'Ted wanted a word with me. He's got ideas, and tried to persuade me to back him up,' explained the docker.

'Ideas? What ideas?' demanded Wilson.

'It's time we stopped pissing about,' said Ted forcefully, the combination of cockney and German accent sounding aggressive. 'We need to do some real damage. Something which will really make people sit up and take notice. Set fire to the Town Hall or kill a police horse. Something! Anything!' he shouted, raising his arms in frustration.

'I'm not going to kill a horse,' objected Ada.

Wilson waved his arm, indicating that Ted should calm down. 'What we have been doing might appear to have little effect, but stop and think. We now get regular collections because people have heard of us and like our vision. They haven't been frightened off by us doing anything too extreme. The next step is to broaden our reputation by spreading our action to other towns. As we do so, we can recruit other active members like the one Victor has brought us. Once we've got half a dozen people in key towns, we can increase our activity and others will be flocking to join us. At that stage we can increase the scale of our demonstrations, setting fire to key buildings and such like. People will also start to take action to disrupt the authorities on their own. Then we will see real change beginning. It might take another five years, but it will happen. Don't you understand?'

'I do,' said James Eden, raising a hand in support.

Frank Edwards scoffed at James. 'Myself and Jimmy boy here might have got caught in Merthyr if I hadn't called things off. In front of the magistrate we would have been, and for what real purpose? I don't mind going to gaol for strangling someone like Lord Penrhyn, or blowing up a bank, but not for doing something as petty as putting up a few posters.'

'We'll be strangling no-one, nor blowing anything up,' snapped Wilson. 'The next task will be assigned to our prospective new member. It'll be something straightforward, just to test him. I've given the details to Victor, but actually I think James should go along to ensure Dai Meredith does what he's told.'

'A waste of time. I say we should cause a real outrage and start breaking heads,' insisted Ted. 'We all have an equal say here, don't we?'

'Of course we do,' conceded Wilson.

'Then I say it's time to ditch your plans, and to do something worthwhile which will put us on the front page of every newspaper. Who's with me?' demanded Ted.

'Very well,' said Wilson firmly. 'We'll have a vote. Who wants to go along with Ted's suggestion?'

Frank Edwards's arm was the first to shoot up. Ted turned to him and nodded his thanks. Then Ada Quill slowly raised her hand, looking at Wilson with an apologetic expression.

'You didn't convince me in the pub and you haven't done now either,' said Charlie Janssen, putting his hands in his pockets.

'Nor me,' added Eddie. 'Go too far and my business could be at risk.'

'What about you, James?' asked Ted, desperate for support.

The young man shook his head and stared at his feet.

'Three for the motion and four against,' said Wilson smugly.

'Wait! When Victor gets back, he'll be in favour. It's a tie,' responded Ted, pointing a finger aggressively.

'That's not enough to win,' said Wilson calmly. 'Anyway, there's still Willy. He hasn't voted yet.'

'You can't count him!'

'He's one of us. Every one of us has a say, remember? Well, Willy. What do you say?'

The scruffy little man didn't say a word, but slowly shuffled across the room and stood alongside the Irishman.

'There you are. I'm very sorry, Ted, but the motion fails. We keep to my plan.'

'Damn you Wilson! Damn you all!' shouted Ted, as he made for the door and slammed it behind him.

ELEVEN

After an indulgent laze in bed until nearly midday, Chard took Barney for a walk through Ynysangharad Fields on the east bank of the River Taff. It was a blustery Autumn morning and Barney had been let off his lead, only to bury himself in piles of fallen golden-brown leaves. Unfortunately, he had also spotted a rat and chased it down to the river's edge, to emerge moments later with muddy paws which subsequently stained Chard's trousers. Consequently, it was a slightly disgruntled inspector who returned to his house an hour later.

'Did you enjoy your walk, Mr Chard?' called Lucy from the kitchen, on hearing his return.

'This animal is filthy,' grumbled the inspector, carrying the solid lump of muscle through the hall and out to the back yard.

'I'll give him a bit of a clean after dinner,' said the maid, smiling to herself. She knew that however much her master grumbled about Barney, he was really quite attached to the dog.

Chard went upstairs to change his clothes, then returned to sit in his armchair and think about the week ahead. The following day he would be visiting Merthyr Tydfil police station. Given the town's history of industrial unrest, Chard realised he probably should have started his tour of the county with Merthyr, but there was one good reason for leaving it until last. The Chief Constable had chosen to base himself there, whilst the constabulary's administration headquarters on the out-skirts of Cardiff was being refurbished. No doubt he would want to question how on earth the request for Chard's report had originated. At least if he was interrogated at this stage, Chard would be able to provide the Chief Constable with sufficient facts and figures to justify his efforts.

Hopefully some good would eventually come out of his recommen-dations, but at heart he knew the whole exercise was just an invention by Farrington to give him an opportunity to investigate anarchists. At least there was some minor progress on that score, since he had discovered the possibility of an anarchist group in Cardiff. It still seemed dubious that Sean MacLiam could be involved, but he was duty bound to make an effort to find him. With a sigh, Chard reached for a newspaper resting on a side table close to his chair. Someone had left it on the train the previous day and he'd picked it up on his return journey from Cardiff.

Hoping for some sort of inspiration, Chard read the headlines. The main story was the plight of the miners who were having yet another cut in their wages. Beneath the article there was a report on the ongoing European tour of the Czar and Czarina. It was the next page which caught the eye. The trial of Bell, the accomplice of Tynan who had been caught in Glasgow. Whilst Tynan and the two men caught in Belgium were being returned to America, Bell was still trying to plead his case as an innocent American visitor in front of a Bow Street magistrate. Like the others, he'd been using a false name. That was the problem with names, you just couldn't trust them. Perhaps Sean MacLiam was using a false identity, thought Chard. Just another complication to add to it all.

'Dinner is ready, Mr Chard,' announced Lucy.

The inspector quickly thumbed through the rest of the newspaper before getting up, not expecting to discern anything of importance, but then he noticed an article that piqued his interest.

'Ha!' he exclaimed excitedly, getting to his feet.

'Mr Chard?' asked the maid.

'Nothing Lucy… nothing…'

***

It was a chilly evening and Constable Richards stamped his feet to get the circulation going in his legs. There were shouts in the distance as a ship in Number One Dock was making final preparations for its departure on the next high tide. Coal destined for Genoa; he could taste the dust in his mouth. Strange, but he would miss this, he thought. Yet he had a decent pension to look forward to, his own house and a good wife. Just one final shift and it would all be over. Then it would be a life of late mornings, afternoons spent in his armchair whilst his Elsie wittered away whilst doing her knitting, then evenings down the pub. He would even be able to take time to visit his four married daughters, all of whom had moved away.

Turning away from the dock, he stared into the distance and sighed. Barry town was a fair old walk away and was largely obscured by the sea fog which had started to roll in.

'Sod it!' he exclaimed. 'They can hardly sack me on my final shift.'

Instead of heading towards the town, the constable changed direction and walked slowly towards the partly built Number Two Dock. The construction workers were all safely at home or more likely in a pub. There was a full moon which might have been a concern, but with the fog becoming thicker, no-one would be likely to disturb him. Walking carefully, so as not to trip over any obstacle, he made his way down the quay, reaching into his pocket as he did so.

Suddenly, he stopped. He could have sworn he heard someone whistling. No, he must have been mistaken, he thought, shaking his head. There were often strange sounds at night around the docks, caused by the sea or wind. Sometimes even the smallest of sounds could travel from a hundred yards away. No, it was nothing, he decided.

Taking the hip flask he'd removed from his pocket, he unscrewed the fastening and put it to his lips. The fiery whisky it contained coated his tongue and he held it in his mouth, savouring the taste before swallowing.

'Ah! Bloody wonderful!' he exclaimed, with great satisfaction.

Moving towards the edge of the quay, he sat down on the cold stone, with his legs dangling over the side. Then, reaching into another pocket, he took out a pork pie.

'Come to me, my lovely!' declared Richards, biting through the thick pastry crust.

He had just begun to swallow his second mouthful, when he was aware of a noise behind him.

'Wha—?'

The constable's words were cut off as something was pulled across his throat. Immediately, due to the piece of pie at the back of his throat, he began to choke. In a panic Richards started to flail with his arms, caught between whether to try and free the pressure around his throat, or grab the leg of his assailant who was standing above and behind him. His left hand did manage to grab hold of an ankle, but then he realised his buttock was starting to slide off the edge of the quay. At the same time, there was a burning in his throat and he wanted to gag, but couldn't. His body's natural reaction made him let go of the ankle and use both hands to try and free himself from the garrotte. Then he felt himself on the verge of going right over the edge, so he used all his remaining strength to try and shuffle his weight backwards. It worked but the pressure on his throat didn't stop. Desperately, he tried to get a finger underneath the wire around his windpipe, but it was too little, too late. His eyes began to bulge and his tongue protruded from his mouth as he slowly lost the ability to breathe.

'That was more difficult than I thought it was going to be, old man,' said the killer softly.

Taking a grip of the constable's arms, he dragged the body into the centre of the quay, away from the edge.

'There you are. We don't want you getting wet, do we? Oh, just one more thing; I nearly forgot.'

Producing a folded piece of paper, the killer put it in the top pocket of the constable's uniform.

'All done,' he declared, as he turned and disappeared into the fog.

TWELVE

It was a wet, miserable morning and as far as Chard was concerned, it was a wet, miserable place. Rain hammered on the pavement as the inspector left the railway station and walked onto the streets of Merthyr Tydfil. Glad of his decision to choose an umbrella over his walking cane, having seen the foreboding grey clouds at Pontypridd, Chard headed in the direction of the police station. He had with him a briefcase containing his working notes for his report.

As he made his way through the town, Chard was aware of how much less prosperous it seemed than the other places he'd visited. There were more vagrants begging for the odd coin, fearful of being moved on by a patrolling constable, more shoeless children and more poor old souls with haggard, lined faces. Their images, together with the rain, made for a dismal atmosphere. The smoke that came from the nearby ironworks, resting heavy on the lungs, didn't help either.

On reaching the police station, the inspector introduced himself to the desk sergeant, a cheerful man with a florid complexion.

'This way, Inspector. Superintendent Hughes is expecting you.'

After the sergeant took charge of his wet umbrella, Chard was led through to an office occupied by a stern-faced individual with a tooth-brush moustache.

'Ah, Chard, is it?'

'Yes, sir.' The inspector noted there was no invitation for him to take a seat.

'The Chief Constable said he wanted to see you on arrival, but I'm afraid that will have to wait for another time.'

Chard looked puzzled, and waited for an explanation. None came. After a long pause, the superintendent continued.

'I understand the nature of your intended report, and support its aims. I believe a detective department for the county is long overdue. However, given the importance of this borough and the vast experience of our officers, I am somewhat surprised that the task of compiling the report has fallen to someone outside of this station.'

'I am as surprised as you are sir,' responded Chard, in an effort to placate the clearly irritated superintendent.

'I would normally introduce you to one of our inspectors but they have other matters to attend to. Instead, Sergeant Marsden will give you whatever you need.'

Chard felt summarily dismissed and left the office to find the desk sergeant waiting outside. 'The superintendent told me earlier on that I'd be assisting you, Inspector Chard. How can I be of service?'

'I need to see the register of cases, particularly those of a serious nature and which took longer than two weeks to solve, or which remain unsolved. Also, a full list of officers, giving their rank and years of experience. That will be a good start.'

The sergeant puffed out his cheeks and gave a sigh. 'Alright, Inspector. I'll find you a free desk, then I'll get the necessary records.'

It was after he'd been settled in an empty office and the sergeant had returned with a thick ledger that Chard decided to enquire about the chief constable's absence.

'It's all a bit strange, Inspector. He was in here early on, then took a telephone call. The next thing I knew, he was rushing past the front desk telling me to cancel any of his appointments for the day. Something about an urgent incident and having to go to Barry Docks.'

'I see,' said Chard. 'Never mind, I'm sure he would probably prefer to see me after I finish my report. There's no rush.'

It was hours later, by which time Chard was finishing his notes, when there was a sudden interruption as a tall, grim-faced man in an inspector's uniform burst into the office.

'Who…?'

Chard stood and held out his hand. 'Inspector Chard, Pontypridd. Would I be right in assuming this must be your office? Sergeant Marsden put me in here.'

'Oh, then I'm sorry for interrupting you. I'm Inspector Greene, and yes, this is my office.'

'I'll be finished in half an hour, but I'm happy to move elsewhere,' suggested Chard.

'No, you may as well stay. I need to speak to one of the constables in any case. I'll return in thirty minutes.'

As the man went, Chard noted Greene had not taken his proffered hand, and the 'thirty minutes' had been said with some emphasis.

Deciding it would be best to make every effort to placate his fellow officers, especially in the Chief Constable's home station, Chard pushed hard to complete his work.

He'd just put his pen down as the thirty minutes ran out and Greene walked in.

'I've just finished. Sorry if I've caused any inconvenience. The superintendent told me you were very busy at the moment.'

'Garrotting of a local councillor,' grunted Greene. 'It's got everyone in a flap and we were rushed off our feet to begin with.'

'Not due to problems with anything like anarchists?'

'Anarchists? What are you talking about, Inspector? We've not got those problems here, unless you know something different?'

'No, it was just that Merthyr has had its problems in the past; and in the current circumstances, with wages being cut in the area and unemployment going up, it would seem a natural breeding ground for sedition.'

'There has been some trouble with the labouring classes, that much I'll grant you, but God forbid that we should have anarchists as well. When I said we were rushed off our feet, it's because we're always rushed off our feet. Too few men and too many petty crimes.'

'Do you want me to mention this garrotting case to my superintendent? He might agree to release me to lend a hand,' offered Chard.

'We are quite capable of dealing with it,' snapped Greene, who then moderated his tone slightly as he went on to describe the case. 'It seemed motiveless at first, but this morning we discovered a witness who saw the victim on the night he was killed. The councillor had apparently passed money over to a young man who we believe to be the murderer.'

'The motive being...?'

'Blackmail. The young man in question is a known deviant. We haven't caught him yet, but we will, you can be sure of that,' said Greene, wagging his finger emphatically.

'I don't quite understand...'

'What don't you understand?'

Chard felt torn between wanting to be diplomatic, but also needing an explanation. 'Are you saying the victim was blackmailing the suspect? It's just that if he already has a reputation as a deviant then I wouldn't see the point.'

'No,' said Greene with a tinge of exasperation, 'we believe the suspect was blackmailing the victim. Clearly, despite the reputation he had for being an upstanding citizen, the councillor had been up to some unnatural business.'

'In which case, why would the suspect want to kill him? I could see the sense of it if he'd refused to pay up and was going to file a complaint, but you said yourself he'd already handed over money that evening,' Chard pointed out.

Inspector Greene's face coloured and his body noticeably tensed. 'I'll thank you not to interfere, Inspector Chard. I'm sure you'll want to be getting back to Pontypridd as soon as possible, so I'll bid you good day.'

Chard took the hint and left. On the way back to the railway station he congratulated himself on what had been a relatively successful day. He now had all the information he needed to complete his report, which should earn him a pat on the back from his superintendent, even if his recommendations came to nothing. A meeting with the Chief Constable had been avoided through sheer luck; and Inspector Greene had confirmed there had been no anarchist activity in Merthyr. He could at least report back to Farrington that the only major towns in Glamorgan he hadn't covered fully were Swansea and Cardiff. Both were outside his constabulary's jurisdiction, having their own police forces. Nevertheless, there were suspicions about activity in Cardiff and if Sean MacLiam was involved, he hoped to find him very soon.

***

'Here he is, Will. And there's us thinking he'd been sent to gaol in Shrewsbury again,' joked Dic Jenkins as Chard walked into the Ivor Arms.

Chard smiled. He probably should have stayed in yet again, in order to work on his recommendations; but he needed to put some problems to rest. The mission for Farrington and his report were one thing, but there were other things that still weighed heavily on his mind. In the past year there had been a wonderful romance which sadly failed and cost him a valuable friendship. Later on, he'd discovered the death of his estranged wife and been imprisoned. The disfigurement and demotion of Constable Morgan, together with May Roper having been dismissed from her employment, were not entirely his fault; but he knew he was hardly blameless. It was enough to make anyone feel depressed, he told himself; and the best treatment was to be with friends.

'A round of drinks, please, for myself and these reprobates,' Chard said to Gwen who stood, smiling broadly, behind her bar.

'I was beginning to think you'd forgotten all about me,' replied Gwen with a cheeky wink.

'It's only been work that's kept me away, otherwise I would have been here on the weekend,' explained Chard.

Once the drinks were poured, he handed Will Horses and Dic Jenkins their pints, which they raised to toast his generosity.

'I wasn't sure you'd be here on a Monday night, but as I decided to free myself from my papers, I took the chance.'

'You were lucky,' replied Dic. 'As you know, we are men of moderation,' he said with a twinkle in his eye, 'but we haven't seen Dai Books since he walked out. He often would come in on a Monday night, just for a swift one, so we'd hoped to catch him.'

'Aye, just to see he's alright, you know. What with his having lost his job and all that,' added Will.

'You haven't called at his house?' asked the inspector.

'*Duw*, no, mun. Have you met his missus?' Dic shuddered.

'I thought I saw him going into the railway station on Saturday, when I was waiting by my cab. I would have called out, but then a fare came up, so I had to be off,' said Will.

Chard sipped his pint and thought for a moment. 'Perhaps he was off looking for a job in Cardiff?' he suggested.

'Not likely on a Saturday though,' Dic replied.

Will, evidently feeling thirsty, drank half of his pint in one gulp. 'We shouldn't worry about him. He's got more brains than he knows what to do with. Our Dai will be alright.'

***

It was half past midnight and the centre of town seemed deathly silent to the two men hidden in the shadows of a shop doorway. One of them constantly adjusted his spectacles in nervous agitation, whilst the other, a well-built young man, prodded him in the back.

'The pubs are long since shut, there's no traffic and nobody is out on the street. So get on with it,' chided the young man.

'But if we're caught…?'

'We won't get caught because there's no-one around to see us,' snapped James Eden. 'I don't like being here any more than you do, but John wants you to prove yourself with this small act. If you come through, then you'll be one of us and we'll see you right. I've been given funds to pay you something to see you through the week, whilst John uses his connections to find you work.'

Dai thought about how useful the money would be. His savings couldn't last forever, nor could he hide things from his wife for much longer. Thankfully she wasn't speaking to him at the moment, which avoided difficult conversations, though after staying out so late this time, words would be said. If he could wave some money in front of her face, it would ease the storm.

'Why me, though? You can see I'm not sure about all this. Why are you so desperate to have me in particular?' asked Dai.

'Because I can see you have a good heart and want to make things change. I also know you're not the sort of hothead to do something stupid. I came to the area less than a year ago, having travelled aimlessly following a family argument. By chance I found our group. There were only six of us at first. Everyone had a say and John had a clear vision to build our actions slow and steady, but since then things have changed. Three more joined us and now we're split between those who want to continue with John's vision and those who want to commit terrible acts right now. You'll be on our side and will sway the vote.'

Dai nodded, accepting the reasoning. 'Then I'll do it,' he said finally.

After fiddling with his spectacles once more, Dai took matches and a bottle of paraffin from Eden and crept out of the shadows. His hands shook as he poured the paraffin into the post box, aware he was illuminated by a streetlight as he performed the act. As quickly as he could manage, he struck a match and threw it into the post box. Immediately, there was a burst of flame, and Dai ran in panic back towards his accomplice. No sooner had he done so, than a carriage appeared, coming from High Street. On seeing the flames, the driver pulled on the reins and it came to a sudden halt. Getting down from his seat, he peered around and then noticed some movement.

'Oi! Who's there? I can see you!' he shouted.

'Quick! Run for it!' exclaimed Eden.

Dai needed no encouragement and in a moment both men were running as if the devil was after them.

THIRTEEN

Chard took the piece of paper from his pocket and read it once again. It'll have to do, he told himself as he continued on his walk through the town. A Tuesday morning was always quiet in Pontypridd, particularly early on, and there were few vehicles travelling into the town centre. The following morning would be a contrast, as the mid-week market day would bring perhaps a hundred traders into the town, ready to set up their outdoor stalls in the streets surrounding the permanent indoor market.

Making his way towards the post office, the inspector wondered whether he was right to contact Farrington by telegram. The card given to him did provide a telephone number after all, but the only telephone he could access was in the police station, and the risk of being overheard was too great. The message he had drafted onto the piece of paper read: 'NO ACTIVITY FOUND STOP SWANSEA UNKNOWN STOP CARDIFF MAYBE STOP HOPE TO CONFIRM MORE SOON STOP'.

It was obscure enough to maintain secrecy, but sufficient to confirm he was actively doing something.

'What the hell…?' Chard stopped abruptly as he saw a tall, lanky constable standing by a smoke-blackened post box.

'Constable Temple, what's going on?' the inspector asked, as he approached.

'Good morning, sir. We had a bit of an incident last night. Someone set fire to last night's mail.'

'Any suspects? Young lads thinking it would be a prank, perhaps?' suggested Chard.

'A witness saw two men running away, so we can count that out,' answered the constable dismissively.

Chard knew Temple was a close friend of Idris Morgan and no doubt still held him responsible for Morgan's demotion, so he let the manner of the comment pass.

'Was there much in there overnight?' asked the inspector.

'We'll never know. Everything was reduced to ash.'

'In which case I'd better go and speak to the postmaster. You can come along and take any notes that might be required.'

'I've already taken notes, Inspector.'

'Then you can come and take some bloody more!'

***

No further notes needed to be taken. Temple was a good officer and had indeed written down anything worth recording, but Chard had wanted to assert his authority. After ten minutes he released the constable to continue the rest of his duties and then stayed behind to send the telegram. By the time he eventually made his way to the police station most of the constables were already out walking their beats. One of the exceptions was Idris Morgan who was behind the front desk.

'Good morning, Constable. I see you're still on reserved duties.'

Morgan looked decidedly unhappy. 'I think the ribs have healed enough, Inspector. I can't wait to get back on the streets.'

'Time enough for that. Which sergeant is on duty?'

'Sergeant Morris, sir.'

Chard's face relaxed into a smile, pleased it wasn't the odious Sergeant Jackson.

'I'll suggest he sends you up to the infirmary to get an opinion from Doctor Henderson. He might say you're sufficiently recovered. Where can I find the sergeant?'

It was Morgan's turn to smile. 'Out in the yard, sir. I carried out the errand you gave me and he's assisting Constable Davies.'

Chard walked through the station, taking care to sneak past the superintendent's door, then went into the yard. The sight which greeted him was something worth seeing.

Perched on a sturdy bicycle was the even sturdier frame of Constable Davies, who was being assisted by the huge Sergeant Morris, the only officer in the station capable of supporting Davies's weight. Chard had paid for the bicycle himself, in the hope it would help deflect pressure away from the constable. If Davies could master it, then perhaps the force would provide other bicycles, which would be a boon considering the distances the men had to cover on foot. For the moment however, the inspector was enthralled at the sight of the sergeant, struggling to run alongside Davies whilst helping to keep him on course. After ten minutes of watching, little tears of laughter were forming in the corners of his eyes. Chard was delighted to see Davies give a shout of elation as he eventually got the knack. Soon he was cycling around the yard unaided, to the applause of his sergeant.

'Well done!' shouted Chard, joining in with the applause.

'Inspector!' came a call from the station building.

Chard grimaced as he recognised his superintendent's voice. Slowly he turned and then followed the beckoning arm back into the building. Superintendent Jones turned his back, led the way to his office and then closed the door behind them.

'I understand it was all your idea,' said the superintendent.

'My idea, sir?'

'The bicycle, Inspector.'

'Yes, sir,' confirmed Chard, wondering what was to follow.

Superintendent Jones pursed his lips as if in disapproval. 'Damned undignified in my opinion. However, never let it be said that I am not progressive in outlook.'

Chard bit his lip as that was exactly what he would have said.

'I can see the benefit. If Constable Davies can master a bicycle, then I dare say other officers can. If we had a few more then we could lose one or two of our gigs which would mean reduced stabling costs. We could also attend the scene of a crime more quickly, and so on…'

'Thank you, sir. I had thought of putting something to that effect in my report,' Chard interjected.

'Good. I think there is more chance of achieving an increase in our budget for a few bicycles than there is for more officers,' scoffed the superintendent. 'When will the report be finished?'

'The end of the week, with any luck, sir.'

'I will look forward to seeing it, and I'll be even happier to see you doing something more useful. Where were you earlier, Inspector?'

'At the post office, sir. Someone set fire to last night's mail in the postbox. Unfortunately, we've got very little to go on.'

'I don't know what the world's coming to, Inspector. At least we haven't had an incident as serious as that which happened in Barry.'

The superintendent shook his head sadly.

Chard raised an eyebrow. 'I was in Merthyr yesterday and apparently the Chief Constable had rushed down there early in the morning.'

'One of our officers was murdered at the docks. He was on his last shift before retiring.'

'Really? I was talking to a constable down there last week. Constable Richards as I recall, and he was due to retire soon.'

'The same man. He was garrotted.'

'That's a coincidence. There was a similar murder in Merthyr recently. A local councillor was killed in the street. They've got a lead on a young man known around the town as being of dubious character.'

'Hardly a connection, Inspector. Though I suppose their suspect could have been looking for a ship in order to flee arrest. I'm just on my way out, so whilst I'm gone you can use my telephone to find out if A Division have caught their man. After which, you can assist Inspector Hulme with sorting out the duty rosters for the next month. That should keep you busy.'

'More bloody paperwork,' Chard muttered under his breath as Superintendent Jones left the room.

***

It was early evening, but Dai Meredith was already on his fourth pint of ale. He sat alone in the back room of the Llanover Arms, with a demeanour that signalled he was in no mood for company.

'Mind if I join you?'

Dai looked up at the cause of the unwelcome interruption. 'Go away!'

'Don't be like that,' said Victor Blandford. 'I spoke to James earlier and he said you did a grand job the other night.'

'I shouldn't have done it,' Dai groaned.

'James said you had some regrets, but there's no need. You were right to join us.'

'I shouldn't have let him persuade me. Anyway, he only wants me in your group to vote against the more radical members.'

Victor's ever-present smile faded. 'Is that what he said?'

'It doesn't matter now. Nothing matters. I was hoping to impress my wife with the money James gave me. It meant nothing, because she found out second-hand that I'd been dismissed from my post at the school. She was furious. I tried explaining that I'd been looking for a way to tell her, but it was all just too late.' Dai took another gulp of his drink before continuing. 'I realise now I should have told her from the start. Getting involved with you lot was just a way of losing myself and trying to avoid reality. Now I'm a criminal. But I won't do anything like that again. I'm through with it. I'm through with everything. So sod off!'

Victor said nothing in reply. He just turned and departed, leaving Dai alone. The former schoolteacher sat for a while, misery etched on his features.

There is one thing I can do, he thought. And I won't shy away from it.

FOURTEEN

It had taken some persuasion. Half-truths, nods, suggestions and intimations had been needed, but eventually the bursar of the University College of South Wales and Monmouthshire had agreed to Chard's attendance. It was a ticketed event which had been fully subscribed. A debate on the future of Ireland, with prominent guest speakers from America and Ireland, together with three members of parliament. It would be a function which, if he was indeed in Cardiff, Sean MacLiam would be compelled to attend. Not that he was a Fenian as far as Chard was aware, but he'd always had a keen interest in the land of his birth.

The bursar had initially refused Chard's request to attend, particularly as he had no jurisdiction in Cardiff, but eventually he was left with the distinct impression that the inspector was on a special assignment from the Home Office to keep an eye on the Irish speakers. There was a limit to the bursar's assistance however, and the invitation was limited to the after-debate refreshments.

So it was that Chard stood at the doors of the debating hall, waiting for the attendees to emerge and make their way to the function room. Dressed formally in top hat and frock coat, the inspector intended to merge in with the crowd, and hopefully spot his man.

Eventually he heard a round of applause and a hubbub of voices getting louder as everyone made for the exit, so he stood back, hopeful the evening would not have been wasted.

As the crowd of students, speakers and invited guests emerged, Chard scrutinised each one in the hope of identifying his former friend. One of the last to appear was a slim figure with fair hair and Chard couldn't restrain a satisfied smile.

So, it's true, and Farrington was correct, he thought.

Knowing there were rumours of anarchists in Cardiff and confirming Sean MacLiam was involved was one thing, thought Chard, but finding out if an assassin was being harboured in their midst would be a much more difficult task.

'Sean, old friend! Can it be you?' exclaimed the inspector, putting his hand on the slim man's shoulder.

'Eh? What?' came the startled response.

'You must remember me. It's Thomas. Thomas Chard, from your university days in Manchester.'

'Oh, goodness. Yes. Yes, of course. Good to see you, old man. What brings you here?'

Chard held out his hand, which the Irishman, still shocked, shook reluctantly.

'I was in Cardiff on business and thought I'd listen to the debate,' the inspector lied.

'I didn't see you in there.'

'I was right at the back. What did you think of it?'

Sean regained his composure and walked with Chard at his side into the function room.

'It was disappointing. It was a classic example of why the country is in such a damn mess.'

The two men took a glass of wine from a silver tray held aloft by one of the servants hired by the university for the evening.

'In what way?' asked Chard. He noticed that Sean was slightly flushed and had obviously been irritated by the debate.

'Our politicians tend to learn their craft in university debating societies. As you're aware, the participants are allocated an argument to defend, and they do their best to do so, regardless of their own beliefs. The object is to win the debate. That's all that matters. They carry that principle into the House of Commons. Whether an issue is right or wrong is of no concern. They follow the lead of their party and they argue the point, the object being to win at all costs. We saw it in the debate just now, did we not? We had guest speakers who were for or against a free Ireland, then half a dozen students had been allocated to each side to support their arguments in debate.'

'What's wrong with that?' asked Chard, seeing a fervent look in the Irishman's eyes. 'I would have thought you would have wanted to see a fiery argument on the issue.'

'No, you don't understand, do you? The students didn't really believe in half of what they were saying, but what is more important is that there was no attempt to reconcile each other's views. It was conflict for the sake of conflict, with no attempt at reconciliation.'

'Please take no offence at what I'm about to say, Sean,' began Chard, 'but from memory I would have put you down as someone entirely supportive of the Fenians' aims, irrespective of conflict.'

The Irishman sipped his wine and thought carefully before replying. 'I support a free Ireland, but believe it can only be achieved through the will of the people, and without mindless violence, which some idiots support. I also believe the will of the people needs to be heard here, in the rest of Britain.'

'In what way?'

'I've been lucky, Thomas. After leaving Manchester I inherited a fortune from an uncle in America. It allowed me to travel throughout Europe and learn from great men; scholars and philosophers from the continent. They showed me the truth of how the common man is manipulated and milked of his labour to provide profit for the people who really control us. Not just the common man, for that matter, but also those of the middling sort.'

'I don't think I follow…' answered Chard, wanting to draw out as much information as possible. 'Do others think like you?'

'I'm not alone in my views. No gods, no masters. That is our motto; but I've said enough. What about you? You say you are here on business.'

'Yes, I'm just in Cardiff for a couple of nights, on a commercial matter. Perhaps we could meet up tomorrow evening, and talk more?'

'That would be most agreeable. I have to leave now anyway, but we can indeed see each other at the—'

The invitation was interrupted by a red-faced man with white sideburns, who hailed Chard with no consideration for the ongoing conversation.

'Ah! Inspector Chard! I see you have a drink. I assume you've finished your inspection and didn't find any seditious villains, eh?'

Chard hastily approached the university bursar, grabbed him by the shoulder, and steered him away, before he could say any more. He said a few short, sharp words in the man's ear, then turned back to look around at Sean; but he had already vanished.

'Bugger and damnation!'

***

It was midnight, and nothing could be heard other than the soft moan of the wind passing through gaps around the stable door. Sir Henry Longville V.C. sat on a hay bale and by the light of an oil lamp stroked the muzzle of his chestnut mare.

'I know it's late, old girl, and that I'm keeping you awake, but you're always there to listen to me, aren't you?'

The horse snorted and twitched its ears.

'I told her just the other day. You've known all along of course; it's been our secret,' continued Sir Henry, giving the horse a gentle scratch. 'A few weeks, that's all I have, but seventy years is all we're promised so I've had a decent innings.' The stab of sudden pain in his stomach came out of the blue, as if to bear witness to his words. It took a moment for the agony to subside. 'I'll have to go soon, to take some more of Dr Matthew's concoction. It'll get me through the night at least. I'm afraid we won't do much more hunting together, but I'm sure you'll be well cared for after I've gone.'

The horse gave another snort and shook its head as if to deny what its master was saying.

'We have to face facts, old girl. I shall let you rest now and go for my nightly walk as far as the gate. I haven't much time left, so I don't want to waste it by sleeping any more than is necessary.'

Sir Henry kissed the horse's muzzle, and gave it a final pat. As if acknowledging its dismissal, the animal turned and moved across to the far side of the stable before lying down. Picking up the lamp, the old man walked towards the stable door and out into the night.

The house had deliberately been chosen for its remoteness, in the hills above Pontypridd. It was not impressive to look at, but was large and well-furnished. A long driveway kept it at a distance from the nearest road, and the gate sported no sign to encourage visitors. Lady Annabelle and the staff would be sound asleep, so there was no-one to impinge on the ageing knight's thoughts as he walked slowly, contemplating his future.

'Damn!' he cursed aloud, realising he'd left his cigarettes in his study. He glanced back at the dark outline of the house, only to immediately turn back again, thinking he'd heard someone whistling.

Holding the lamp forward he called out, though not too loudly, 'Who's there?'

No answer came and he immediately felt foolish. There were bushes on either side of the driveway a little further ahead and he cursed himself for feeling a little jumpy. 'Ridiculous old fool!' Sir Henry walked on beyond the bushes to within sight of the gate and relaxed, his thoughts focussing on how best to make use of the next few days.

Suddenly, he heard the sound of footsteps on gravel just behind him. His reactions, still fast despite his age and infirmity, allowed him to turn and face his attacker, swinging the oil lamp as he did so.

Avoiding the blow, the assailant punched his victim hard between the eyes with his right hand, causing Sir Henry to turn away. In an instant the garrotte was around the old man's throat and pulled tight. The oil lamp fell to the ground as he desperately clawed at the wire, but there could only be one fatal outcome.

FIFTEEN

Chard took another mouthful of his fried breakfast, contemplating the previous night's events. At least there had been progress. Sean MacLiam was definitely in Cardiff and so Swansea was now irrelevant. The question remained, was he harbouring an assassin? It was still unlikely. As Farrington said, the likely target for any assassin would be either the Prince of Wales, the Queen herself or a member of the Privy Council. By now, all of them would be in Balmoral, with the exception of the Prince of Wales, who according to the papers, was miles away in Norfolk. Also, even if it was possible to find his former friend again, how could he now gain his confidence? It would take some thinking about, with no distractions. At least he didn't have to worry about his report on introducing detectives into the Glamorganshire Constabulary. It was virtually complete. His recommendations, with supporting evidence, would be on Superintendent Jones's desk by the end of the week. Things were definitely looking up, he thought, as he mopped up some fried egg yolk with a piece of bread. Any day now, there might be a telegram from Farrington to say the assassin had been caught, and his services were no longer required.

The inspector's contemplation was interrupted by a knock on the front door, which was answered by Lucy.

'Sorry to disturb you, sir, but it's Constable Morgan,' she announced moments later.

Chard put down his cutlery and went to the door in his shirtsleeves. Barney, who had been lying splayed out like a rug, gave a yawn and padded behind his master.

'What's the matter, Morgan?'

'There's been a murder, sir. Sergeant Morris said to fetch you immediately.'

'Go back to the station and I'll be with you shortly,' replied Chard.

'No distractions, my arse!' he said to Barney, after the constable had left.

***

At the police station, Chard found Sergeant Morris waiting for him with a young man who looked shaken.

'Update me, Sergeant. What's happened?'

'Apparently a murder, Inspector. This lad is from the household of Sir Henry Longville. He found his master dead in the grounds early this morning.'

Chard turned his attention to the young man, who stood nervously wringing his cap in his hands. He had a face which had not been blessed by nature: pock-marked and lumpy with a slight turn in his eye.

'And your name is…?' enquired the inspector.

'Hughes, sir. Jack Hughes. I'm the handyman and I help look after Matilda, Sir Henry's horse.'

'I saw it tied outside. A beautiful animal. So you can ride?' asked Chard, trying to put the lad at ease.

'Just a little, sir. I'm not allowed on Matilda usually, but I had to get here quickly,' said Hughes, looking at his feet.

'Tell me exactly what has happened.'

'I was up early and heading towards the stables, when Mair, one of the maids, told me Lady Annabelle wanted me to find Sir Henry. I carried on to the stables, thinking he might have been with Matilda, but he wasn't there. I thought he might have taken a walk down to the end of the driveway, which he sometimes does in the evening; that's where I found him.'

The lad started to shake, and Chard placed a comforting hand on his shoulder. 'Take your time…'

'I'm alright sir,' Hughes replied with a sniff. 'He was just lying there, on his back. His face was all swollen, and his tongue was sticking out to one side. Then there were the marks around his neck. *Duw*, it was horrible.'

'What did you do?'

'I ran back to the house and told Mrs Reece, the housekeeper. Then I waited whilst Lady Annabelle was informed. Everybody was in a panic. First, I was told to fetch Sir Henry's body in, but how was I to do that in a right and proper manner? I'm the only man in the house—'

'Sir Henry had no valet or butler?' Chard interrupted.

'That's right, sir. If I was to fetch his body on my own, I would have had to put him over my shoulder like a sack of potatoes, or drag him, and that wouldn't have been proper. He was good to me—'

'Continue,' prompted the inspector.

'It was Mrs Reece who suggested I should take a sheet and cover his body. After that, I was instructed to take Sir Henry's horse and ride here as fast as I could.'

'How is the widow... Lady Annabelle?'

'Her ladyship was upset, saying such a thing shouldn't have happened. I've never seen her so upset.'

'Thank you, Hughes. That will do. If you take your horse and lead the way, I'll follow with one of my constables. We'd best take the van. As this appears to be a clear case of foul play, the body will need to be taken to our mortuary.'

Sergeant Morris gave a polite cough. 'If you don't mind me saying so, Inspector, from what the lad says, the property is off Llantrisant Road, on the way to Pen-y-coedcae. The van will be a bit slow, so you might be a bit quicker going ahead in one of the gigs. Constable Morgan is around here somewhere, so he'll be able to drive you.'

***

Even the light gig, pulled by one of the better horses in the station's stable, found it hard going. The route to Sir Henry's property took Chard and Constable Morgan out of the town via the steep Graig hill, continuing its upward ascent on Llantrisant Road into the countryside. With no identifying sign on the entrance to the property, the policemen would have driven past the simple wrought-iron gate, had it not been for Hughes leading the way on the chestnut mare.

They found the body halfway along the drive, covered by the sheet placed there by Hughes earlier on. Standing alongside was a young maidservant, trembling with fear, and a mature woman in a dark grey dress. She stood expressionless, with an iron poker held in her hand.

Hughes dismounted, and after a nod from Chard led his horse away to the stable.

Chard got down from the gig and approached the woman holding the poker.

'Lady Annabelle, I presume? I am Inspector Chard.'

'I am afraid you're wrong, Inspector. I am Mrs Reece, the housekeeper. Her Ladyship instructed me to guard Sir Henry until you came. We have foxes in the area, you understand. Mair here was supposed to do it, but was afraid the murderer might return.'

Chard glanced at the maidservant, who looked away in embarrassment.

'Where is her ladyship?'

'Indoors, in mourning. Lady Annabelle came out to see the body, then was overcome with emotion. She is not in a fit state to see anyone.'

'I will have to talk with her at some point, but perhaps it can wait until tomorrow. I'll take a look at the body first.' Chard bent down towards the corpse.

As he pulled back the sheet to reveal Sir Henry's distorted features, the maid gave an involuntary scream.

'Get back to the house, you foolish girl!' ordered Mrs Reece.

Chard pulled back the sheet further to reveal the full extent of the injuries to the neck, and grimaced. It wasn't a pleasant sight and he felt a little nauseous.

'Over here, Constable Morgan.'

Morgan got down from the driving seat of the gig and tied the reins to a nearby tree.

'Get your notebook out and do a rough sketch of the position of the body,' ordered the inspector, before addressing Mrs Reece once more. 'Hughes said the body hasn't been moved. Is that correct?'

The housekeeper nodded.

'Also note, Constable, that there appears to have been a blow to the front of the face, around the eyes. Mrs Reece, was Sir Henry known to carry money about his person at night?'

'I wouldn't know what a man keeps in his pockets, Inspector. It's none of my business.'

Chard grunted and pulled back the sheet fully. After inserting his hand into each jacket pocket, he eventually shook his head. 'If there was anything on him, it's gone now.'

The inspector started to pull the sheet back up, forcing himself to look at the staring eyes and protruding tongue of the victim one more time, when something caught his eye.

'Morgan, come here.'

'Yes, sir?' The constable bent forward to see what Chard was looking at.

'There looks to be a piece of paper just visible inside his mouth. Get your hand in and pull it out.'

Morgan gave an almost indiscernible glance of annoyance, put his fingers into the mouth of the corpse and removed a scrunched up, moistened piece of paper. Placing it on the ground, he flattened it out. 'There's just a drawing of a flag. Nothing written on it at all, just a black flag.'

Chard furrowed his brow and was just about to speak when the police van arrived, the horses' coats glistening with sweat from the arduous journey.

'Have the lads take Sir Henry's remains to the mortuary, whilst I have a few words with Mrs Reece.'

As Morgan walked off to speak to his fellow constables, Chard turned his attention to the housekeeper. Her expression indicated stoic acceptance of the horror in front of her, but Chard could perceive she felt shaken.

'I don't suppose you know of any significance there might be to the drawing of a black flag?' asked the inspector, taking out a pencil and notebook.

Mrs Reece shook her head.

'Did Sir Henry have any enemies?'

'I wouldn't know, Inspector.'

'Did you notice if he seemed out of sorts?'

'Sir Henry has not been quite himself recently. He went into town last week and ever since then he has been rather morose. I am not in a position to know why,' replied the housekeeper.

'Was he in the habit of being out in the grounds at night?'

'Not until recently.'

'Was everyone in the house when Sir Henry went for his walk?'

'As far as I know, yes.'

'Have you noticed any trespassers recently? Anyone acting suspiciously?'

Mrs Reece thought carefully, but then shook her head.

'Are you sure?'

The housekeeper turned her head away as Morgan helped Constables Jenkins and Scudamore take the corpse to the van.

'We do have occasional callers. I deal with them usually,' she replied, once the body had been removed.

'What sort of callers?'

'Deliveries, mainly. We all live at the house and everything is ordered in. We also hire casual labour around the garden when needed. Young Jack can't do it all.'

Chard scratched one of his sideburns with the top of his pencil. 'Yes, he told us he's the only male member of the household. Sir Henry had no valet.'

'The master said he didn't require one. He does not socialise and it is an informal household in many respects.'

'Have you worked for the family for very long? From your accent, it sounds as if you're from the local area.'

'Not quite. I'm from Llantrisant, and I took up my position here just over three years ago.'

'Was Sir Henry a local man?'

'No, Inspector. Sir Henry and Lady Annabelle are from Cumberland, or so I believe.'

'Do you know why they came to live here?'

'None of my business, Inspector, and I dare say none of yours,' replied the housekeeper, abruptly.

Chard was about to snap back a vicious retort when he recognised that the woman was trying to hold back tears over what must have been an alarming experience.

'I think perhaps I've asked enough questions for now. Constable Morgan will walk you back to the house. We'll return tomorrow to take formal statements from all the staff, and to talk with Lady Annabelle.'

Whilst the housekeeper was escorted away by Constable Morgan, Chard searched the ground close to where the body had lain. Unfortunately, there were no items of interest to be found. No torn threads, personal items, or discarded murder weapon. There were a number of partial footprints in the gravel, but nothing that could be put to practical use. When Morgan returned, he found his inspector frowning as he made a final entry in his notebook.

'Anything of interest, sir?'

'Unfortunately not. I would have liked to have found a discarded empty wallet, or a few coins – something to indicate a robbery. As things stand, we don't know if Sir Henry was killed by chance or deliberately murdered. He might have been killed by a thief living rough who came across him by accident, or some enemy who planned to murder him.'

'It's a bit remote here, so it could be someone on the run, like an escaped prisoner,' suggested Morgan.

'That's one possibility. I'll check with Cardiff prison to see if anyone has escaped, but I doubt they would flee in this direction. In the meantime, whilst I take the gig back to the station, you can have another word with Jack Hughes and get the names of the adjoining landowners. We need to check if anyone unusual has been seen in the area. I'll send more men to assist as soon as I can.'

'What if it was planned, sir? How would the culprit have got here?'

'The same way as we did, in which case he would own a horse and it might have been noticed late at night on the road. On the other hand, the murderer might have taken a hansom cab from town to Pen-y-coedcae, earlier in the day. It would be a relatively short walk to come back in this direction at night.'

'But then how would he return to town?'

'It's a fair walk, but all downhill. Just to be on the safe side, we'll also interview residents in Pen-y-coedcae,' replied Chard, walking to the gig. 'We'll know more tomorrow. There's more to this than meets the eye.'

SIXTEEN

Chard was glad to get back to the station. Although he could manage a gig, and could ride a horse at the trot, he had no great affinity with the beasts. Controlling the descent on the steepest part of the hill proved a challenge. Even at the bottom of the hill, entering the town, the left turn in front of the railway station was taken at a considerable speed. He reflected it was no wonder the junction was known as the Tumble, due to the number of accidents.

The journey had done little to improve Chard's mood, for he was already cursing himself for having let Sean MacLiam slip through his fingers. What the hell am I going to tell Farrington? he thought. I can tell him MacLiam is definitely in Cardiff, but how the hell do I trace him, because I doubt he's using his real name? On top of the questions which kept going around his head in respect of MacLiam, there was now this murder.

'Is the Superintendent in?' he demanded of Constable Temple as he entered the station.

'He's busy, sir. Inspector Hulme is in his office,' replied Temple, with a hint of insolence.

'Good, that's ideal!' Chard ignored the constable's attitude; it was clear that he was still being held responsible for Morgan's demotion.

Heading straight for his superior's office, Chard knocked and, at the barked command to enter, walked in.

'Sorry to interrupt you, gentlemen, but it is urgent,' he said.

'We were just discussing you, as a matter of fact,' said Superintendent Jones. 'As you've indicated your report will be completed by the end of the week, I was advising Inspector Hulme here that he can return to Aberdare station on Monday. You can then take over your correct post. In full uniform of course,' he added with emphasis.

'As you wish, sir,' agreed Chard, ruefully. 'However, for the moment there is something more pressing. I've just been at the scene of a rather brutal murder.'

'Sergeant Morris mentioned a murder, but I didn't ask the details. He said you were dealing with it,' said Hulme.

'I'm afraid the victim is a knight of the realm, by the name of Sir Henry Longville.'

'I don't recognise the name.' Superintendent Jones frowned.

'He seems to have been quite reclusive. I'll be interviewing the widow tomorrow. In the meantime, I'll need every available constable to search the area, including any who are on leave.'

'I'll arrange that for you, Chard,' responded Hulme helpfully. 'We can go to my office afterwards and draw up a plan as soon as the Superintendent gives us leave.'

'Of course,' agreed Jones. 'But first, Inspector Chard, do we have a motive for the murder? Any suspects?'

'Not yet. It appears to be a random killing for no particular purpose. What concerns me, however, is the method used. Sir Henry appears to have been strangled with a garrotte, and what with similar deaths at Merthyr and Barry Docks so recently…'

Superintendent Jones looked askance. 'You think they are connected in some way? Surely not!'

'I know it sounds unlikely, but if you don't mind I'd like to have a word with our colleagues at Merthyr.'

Jones nodded. 'I suppose it can't do any harm. But first of all, you had best go with Inspector Hulme to plan the search for the killer.'

It was half an hour later, after having studied local maps, updated Sergeant Morris, and sent for Sergeant Jackson to get back on duty, that Chard was free to call Inspector Greene on the telephone.

'I just wondered if you've caught the suspect in the garrotting case?'

'He's in our cells. We found him hiding in an attic yesterday morning. What's your interest?' asked Greene.

Chard hesitated. Clearly, if there was some kind of connection with the murder of Sir Henry, Inspector Greene probably had the wrong man.

'It's to do with the report I was carrying out. Such a quick arrest clearly shows you are very efficient. Apart from what you mentioned when we met, were there any other clues?'

'Such as? I told you everything we knew at the time,' answered

Greene, sounding rather irritated.

'For example, did the victim have anything unusual on his person? Was there anything stolen?'

'He still had his wallet, so the motive wasn't theft. I can't remember what else he had. Is it important?'

'For completeness I would just like to know those details,' replied Chard.

'I'm afraid I don't have the time to waste, Inspector Chard. If you insist, then I'll ask one of my sergeants to check and get back to you.'

'That would be very kind. I appreciate it.'

After putting the telephone down, Chard waited patiently for the call back. It was a long time coming, but when it did, Chard was pleased to find it was the same cheery sergeant who he'd met on his visit to Merthyr.

'I've got a full list here, Inspector. One wallet containing three pounds, two shillings and sixpence; a bunch of keys; the note arranging the meeting with the killer—'

'What did it say?' interrupted Chard.

'It read *I have the means to bring down Thorpe. If you want the information then bring this note with you to the Beehive in Castle Street at ten tonight. Come alone. A well-wisher,*' replied the sergeant.

'Who is Thorpe?'

'A political rival, Inspector. Apparently, the victim went to the rendezvous but was killed sometime later, on a different street.'

Chard's suspicion that Inspector Greene had the wrong man was reinforced by the sergeant's words. 'Thank you, Sergeant. That will be all.'

'Oh, I hadn't finished my list.'

'Sorry?'

'My list of the things in Mr Jeavons' possession. It's a bit odd, really.'

'What is?'

'He had a piece of paper on him. It was just a drawing. A black flag.'

***

Chard's mind was racing as he walked across the Tumble junction and up the Graig Hill. It couldn't be a coincidence. Unfortunately, the

Barry Docks station was not contactable by telephone, but he had sent an urgent telegram. If the murdered Constable Richards also had the drawing of a black flag in his possession, then it would raise all sorts of questions.

Fortunately, Chard's destination was not too far up the hill and soon he stood at the gate of the most feared and despised place in Pontypridd. The workhouse, although humanely run compared to earlier times, was the refuge of last resort for the hungry and destitute.

However, there was one aspect of the institution which was of universal benefit. The workhouse also contained the town's infirmary. The rich could afford doctors, whereas the poor could not. In addition, although the town's mortuary was located a couple of miles to the south, the infirmary had its own facilities. Originally it had just been a cold room for temporary storage of deceased inmates, but in recent times it had been improved to enable the examination of corpses by the police's medical examiner.

Once allowed through the workhouse gates by one of the orderlies, Chard went straight to the infirmary block to find Doctor Henderson.

'Good morning, Doctor. I hope I find you well.'

The corpulent physician with a large grey moustache looked up from the papers he had been inspecting, and placed them back on the clipboard attached to a patient's bed.

'Inspector Chard. I trust you are recovered from your ordeal? The business in Shrewsbury must have been rather a shock.'

Chard frowned. 'Yes, it was. On the subject of which, about Miss Roper…'

'I'm sorry, Inspector. She misled me. After all I'd previously done for her, I expected honesty. To her credit, she realised her failings and resigned her post. It's something we may both come to regret, because I have yet to find a suitable replacement. But unfortunately, it's the way it has to be.'

Chard nodded, though he felt guilty that May Roper's absence from her post, lying to the doctor in the process, had all been in the cause of helping him to clear his name.

'Have you had a chance to look at the body?'

'What body?' asked the doctor. 'Oh, you mean the one the constables took into the mortuary earlier. You haven't been told then?'

'Told what?' asked Chard, puzzled.

The doctor looked rather sheepish. 'If you remember, I was a little reluctant to take on the responsibility of being your medical examiner. Frankly, I am busy enough here as the infirmary doctor. And now Miss Roper has gone…' The doctor held out his hands and shrugged. 'I only agreed to taking it on because you had fallen out with Doctor Matthews and he didn't want to carry on dealing with you.'

Chard recalled the anger on the face of his former friend when it came to light he'd been having an affair with his housekeeper. A situation made worse when circumstances gave the appearance that he had only started the affair in order to investigate her.

Doctor Henderson noted the sadness in Chard's eyes as he continued his explanation. 'You will remember, I am sure, that on the night before your arrest, you brought the body of an infant to the infirmary.'

'Yes. The Pennels' child. A sad case.'

'It was late and I was at home, but the message from yourself was that it was an accidental death. The child had died in his sleep after having been given a calmative tonic. Constable Morgan subsequently gave me the broken bottle from which it came.'

'That's correct. The poor mother was distraught.'

'Despite your inference that I should effectively ignore other possibilities, I felt constrained to consider the possibility of negligence. If the child had been given too much of the tonic, then the mother could be culpable. It put me in a difficult situation,' explained the doctor.

'Surely you didn't have Mrs Pennel arrested? Nobody's mentioned it to me since I've returned,' said Chard anxiously.

'I did feel very uncomfortable about what I might have to do, but then chance intervened. I was in town when I ran into Doctor Matthews. Although he had spent nearly all summer in his home town of Swansea, he retained a few of his richer clients in Pontypridd. He still has his house here, even if he only uses it for overnight stays. We hadn't been on the best of terms ourselves at our last meeting, but we started to exchange pleasantries and soon we found ourselves having a coffee together. I explained my dilemma over the Pennel child and Doctor Matthews kindly offered to come and give his opinion.'

Chard listened to Doctor Henderson's tale, taking every detail in, but also wanting to ask about Doctor Matthews's housekeeper, Alice Murray.

'Anyway,' continued Doctor Henderson, 'we carried out a post mortem on the child. As it transpired, the child had a heart defect. He could have died at any time. Frankly, I wouldn't have spotted it. Doctor Matthews has to take the credit. I consider myself a very capable physician, but my experience was in the military. I can mend a bullet wound and repair broken bones, and my time at the infirmary has broadened my expertise in dealing with sickness and infirmity. However, Doctor Matthews is, I freely admit, more proficient in some areas of medicine than myself.'

'I am pleased for Mrs Pennel's sake that the death wasn't her fault, but where is this leading?'

Doctor Henderson held up a finger, indicating Chard should remain patient. 'I'm getting there. After we finished the post mortem, we agreed to meet up in the evening in the bar of the New Inn. Over a glass of port, we discussed how we'd been getting on. I freely admitted I'd regretted taking on the position of medical examiner. I was busy enough with my main role as infirmary doctor and frankly, I don't need the money from the retainer. I haven't an extravagant lifestyle and just want a relatively peaceful life. Doctor Matthews in turn confided that he did enjoy his former position. He only left it due to his anger at you. Also, he does have rather extravagant tastes and has two properties to look after. When he stopped living here on a permanent basis, he lost some of his best clients, just retaining one or two who didn't need regular attention. The reduction in income, and the loss of his retainer from the constabulary, had hit him hard. To cut a long story short, I talked some sense into him. He's now staying in Pontypridd more frequently, and has already agreed to take over as medical examiner.'

'What about having to deal with me?' asked Chard

Doctor Henderson grimaced. 'That's a difficult question. At the time he agreed, you were in Shrewsbury gaol. What his reaction will be now you're back, I can't honestly say. We'll find out when he comes to look at this fresh cadaver. He's been informed it's here, so he'll probably come in later this afternoon.'

'Very well. Ask him to meet me here tomorrow afternoon at three o'clock, by which time I may have at least one other body for him to look at.'

'Why? You're not planning to murder someone are you?' joked the doctor.

'No. But trust me, there are times when I feel like it...'

***

By the time Chard returned to the police station, the reply to his telegram was waiting on his desk. It took only a moment to read the short affirmation, before going straight to Superintendent Jones's office.

'I have seen that expression on your face before, Inspector. It usually means you have a fixed purpose and you want me to do something about it,' said the superintendent, raising an eyebrow as Chard entered the room.

'Sir Henry, Constable Richards and the Merthyr councillor – the deaths are all connected,' Chard replied confidently.

'Really? How? What could a knight of the realm, a local councillor and a simple police constable possibly have in common?'

'The killer left a clue. They all had in their possession a piece of paper with a black flag drawn on it. I don't know what it means – yet – but it's too much of a coincidence.'

The superintendent thought for a moment, then nodded. 'I see. What do you require in order to proceed?'

'Thank you, sir. I would like the bodies of PC Richards and the councillor taken to our mortuary as soon as possible. They can be examined tomorrow afternoon and returned immediately afterwards.'

'There will be some resistance from Merthyr station and perhaps the Chief Constable himself. They believe they've already caught their man,' warned Jones.

'The wrong man. Unless of course he has an accomplice. He couldn't have killed Sir Henry if he was already in custody. As for any resistance by the Chief Constable, we have three murders and the highest profile one is that of Sir Henry, which is our case. I'm sure he can be persuaded to see it that way. Don't you agree, sir?'

'Indeed, I do. It may, however, cause a little animosity with A Division, so don't blunder your investigation,' he warned.

***

'*Dydyn nhw ddim yn dod*,' was all of the conversation the Irishman could catch, before Ada Quill walked away from Willy into the night.

'What was that?' he asked as the little man closed the door.

'She said they're not coming,' replied Willy.

'I didn't know you spoke Welsh.'

'Never bloody asked,' came the mumbled retort.

'Damn and blast!' swore Wilson, following Willy as they rejoined Eddie Ward and James Eden.

'What's the matter?' asked the printer.

'Ada said she's fed up with us; and as for the others, they're not coming,' muttered Willy.

'I know Ted's been getting at Charlie for ages, trying to get him on his side. He must finally have succeeded,' suggested James.

Ward gave a snort. 'I blame Victor. He's a sly one behind that smile of his. I wouldn't trust him any further than I could throw him.'

'Four of them and four of us, with Ada, by the sound of it, wanting to have nothing to do with either of us. It's a pity,' reflected Wilson, running a hand through his hair. 'It's a shame the new recruit has disappeared, James.'

'Probably been coerced to join Victor and his cronies,' said Ward.

Eden shook his head. 'After he set fire to the mail, he ran off like a frightened rabbit. I kept up with him and tried to calm him down, but he went to pieces. He hasn't got the balls for it.'

'In which case he won't be joining Ted, Victor, Frank and Charlie,' surmised Wilson. 'They're going to do something rash which will bring the authorities down on our heads. At some point it would happen anyway, but my plan was to build a strong following before that eventuality.' He shook his head in despair. 'They'll undo everything we've done so far. I think it would be wise to suspend our activities for the time being. James, you had best return to Pontypridd and I'll contact you in due course. Eddie, just ensure all of our posters and leaflets are well hidden until we need them again. After tonight we were all due to meet again on Saturday. Willy and I can come here then, just in case Ada and Charlie have a change of heart. As for Victor, Ted and Frank, the next thing we'll hear about them is when they've either set fire to a building or blown something up.'

***

'Good evening, Mr Chard.'

'Hello Bert. I'll have a Jameson please.'

'On the shorts from the off is it, Thomas?' commented a familiar voice.

'Oh, good evening, Gwen. No, you've got the wrong idea. I won't be drinking too much tonight. I've got a lot on my mind.'

'You've been working too hard, that's the problem. We've hardly seen you since you've been back.' The landlady gave a broad consoling smile. 'Go and have a chat with your friends. It'll cheer you up.'

Chard glanced towards the far end of the room where Dic Jenkins and Will Horses were standing in their usual spot, deep in conversation.

'I say the daft-born bugger has gone missing,' Dic could be heard saying as Chard came within earshot.

'I've searched around the town and can't find him, but I'm sure he's fine, mun. It's probably his missus who's keeping him in,' replied Will.

'She wouldn't want him under her feet all day. I did hear he'd been seen in the Llanover last night. Terrible depressed he was, by all accounts. There'll be ructions if he's told his missus he's lost his job.'

'Perhaps he was building up the courage to tell her.'

'She probably knows already. Perhaps she's thrown him out and he's too ashamed to tell us. Oh, *shwmae*, Mr Chard. Didn't see you come in,' said Dic, finally noticing the inspector.

'I can see the pair of you are deep in conversation. Dai gone missing then?' asked Chard.

'We're getting a bit concerned. Losing his job and his change in fortunes seem to have unhinged him,' said Will.

'Have you called at his house?' suggested Bert, bringing over Chard's whiskey.

'Have you been listening to our conversation?' demanded Dic.

Bert smiled, which due to his missing front teeth looked alarming. 'Of course. That's a barman's job.'

Dic scratched his bulbous nose. 'We've not been to his house because Mrs Meredith is not someone I would like to face. She has a wicked temper by all accounts.'

'If she's that bad, why did he marry her?'

'Apparently they were happy once, but then lost three little ones on the trot, all before they were a year old,' replied Dic sadly.

'Look. If you're that worried about Dai, I'll try and call at his house tomorrow,' volunteered Chard. 'I can't promise because I've got police business to attend to, but I'll do my best.'

'That's very good of you,' said Will. 'You must be busy what with that business with the mail set on fire outside the post office.'

'*Duw, Duw*, it was a bad thing to do,' agreed Dic.

'Oi! Dic Jenkins. No blaspheming!' cautioned Gwen, who had appeared without warning, wagging her finger before crossing herself.

Chard tried to hide a smile. Very religious despite her occupation, Gwen would allow no 'Gods', whether sworn in English or Welsh. As he mused to himself, something seemed to stir in his memory.

'Excuse me all, but I need to think about something. I'll come back to chat later,' said the inspector, leaving his friends to take a table at the opposite end of the room.

Taking a sip of his drink, he recalled the defaced wall of the church and the daubed 'No God' slogan, which had been interrupted. Then his mind went to the words of Sean MacLiam. 'No Gods, No Masters.' Could there somehow be a connection? In addition, there was the arson attack. Was Sean really a leader of anarchists who were spreading their acts of vandalism further into South Wales? Was it a coincidence that these murders were also taking place at the same time? What was the meaning of the black flag symbol left with the bodies? Could that be connected? It was looking to be a three-pint problem, he concluded, going to the bar.

SEVENTEEN

It was rare for Chard to take the open offer of the use of Super-intendent Jones's horse, but this morning it was convenient. It had been a leisurely ride, taken at a slow pace suiting Chard's riding ability. Arriving at Lady Annabelle's house, he found Constable Morgan already there, standing next to the gig. Chard tied his horse alongside the vehicle, then the two policemen made their way to the front door, which was opened by a servant.

'Come this way, gentlemen.'

Chard and Constable Morgan followed the maid into a delightfully furnished room, and took the two comfortable chairs offered. Having sent off an urgent telegram to Farrington first thing that morning, he hoped for a quick reply. He had asked if the black flag had any signifi-cance. If the answer was yes, then it might mean there was an anarchist connection, but did that really make sense?

The inspector's thoughts were rudely interrupted by a loud bang as a small child barrelled through the door into the room, chasing a rubber ball. The infant suddenly stopped, surprised to see strangers, then stared at Constable Morgan's helmet, which was resting on his lap. He went to touch it, and Morgan pulled it out of his reach. Losing interest, the little boy turned towards Chard and pointed at his bowler hat.

'No, young man. You aren't having that,' said Chard with a smile.

Just then, the maid who had let them into the house appeared, red-faced with embarrassment. 'There you are, Master George. Come away from there now,' she ordered, picking him up.

'I am so sorry, but he's a handful, and of course he doesn't under-stand what's going on.'

'It's quite alright,' replied the inspector. 'How old is he?'

'Four years old this week. It's so sad. He doesn't understand that his father's gone,' the maid replied sadly. 'The mistress will be along very shortly,' she added before leaving the room.

Constable Morgan raised an eyebrow, clearly having shared the inspector's original assumption that the boy had been Sir Henry's grandchild.

It was just a few minutes later when Lady Annabelle entered. Chard guessed she was probably in her mid-thirties, though the sadness etched on her face made her appear older. As befitted the occasion, the widow wore a black high-necked dress, unadorned with anything other than some fine lace at the cuffs. Her blonde hair was fashioned neatly but not extravagantly. Both men stood as she entered.

'Please seat yourselves, gentlemen.'

'Thank you, Lady Annabelle. I am Inspector Chard and this is Constable Morgan, who will make the necessary notes of our conversation. Afterwards, we will need to speak to all of the staff and take formal statements. I appreciate this is a trying time for everyone, yourself in particular, but we will try and make this procedure as easy as possible.'

'I understand, Inspector.'

'We met your little boy just now,' said Chard, hoping to ease the atmosphere.

'The poor child won't be in a position to comprehend all this,' replied Lady Annabelle, waving a hand forlornly. 'Please just proceed with your questions.'

'I understand your husband was in the habit of taking a late-night walk in the grounds.'

'Yes, that's right.'

'Did he tend to carry money on his person, or anything else valuable?'

'Not to my knowledge.'

'Have you been aware of anyone acting suspiciously in the area?' asked Chard.

Lady Annabelle shook her head.

'He hadn't planned to meet anyone last night?'

'Pardon?'

'I was wondering if there was any significance to his walk last night in particular. I ask because the motive for the attack is not clear.'

'Why would he want to meet anyone late at night?'

Chard fingered one of his sideburns in thought. 'I don't know. You see, the possibilities are limited. Either the killer encountered your husband by chance, or it was a deliberately planned act. If it was by chance, then we have to wonder who would be wandering around somewhere this remote. If it was a vagrant, then they would be on foot and unlikely to have gone too far. We have constables checking every premises in the area as we speak. Even if it was a vagrant, what was his motive? Surely, he would be after food or somewhere to sleep and if challenged would most likely run away.'

'And if it wasn't by chance?' asked Lady Annabelle, her face very pale.

'It means the villain went to a lot of trouble, and there would have to be a strong motive. Did your husband have any enemies?'

'No. He did not.'

'Are you sure?'

'Yes, of course I am sure,' said Lady Annabelle, her voice strained with emotion.

'In which case, looking for other motives, do you know if your husband had made a will?'

'Yes. Everything is left to myself. His children from his first marriage are both deceased. There are no other provisions.'

'You are sure?'

'The matter was discussed very recently,' replied Lady Annabelle, her lips trembling.

Chard raised an eyebrow but decided not to pursue the statement.

'Did your husband have any business interests?'

'None. He has investments of course, but they are handled by our solicitors in London.'

'No political interests then? For example, did he know a gentleman called Jeavons, a councillor in Merthyr Tydfil?'

The widow shook her head. 'He hated politics, and politicians for that matter.'

'Did he ever mention the term "anarchists" to you?' asked Chard.

The inspector's hopes rose as Lady Annabelle nodded.

'I don't know what this has to do with anything, but yes. He used to express his anger about social disobedience and used the term alongside communists, trade unions and such like.'

'Did he have a particular dislike of them? Something from his past perhaps?'

'When he was serving in the army, before he won his Victoria Cross, his regiment had to put down a number of riots in northern towns. He also helped to quell the disorder in Trafalgar Square some years ago. That was before I met him, when his first wife was still alive. She died of cholera, you understand.'

'You only came to live here in recent years, I believe.'

'Henry wanted to leave his past life behind. Everything reminded him of his previous marriage and he wanted a fresh start. I wish we hadn't left, I truly do.' A tear rolled down Lady Annabelle's cheek.

'Don't fret, your ladyship. I will find who has done this, and they will pay the penalty. You have my word on it.'

The widow gulped and then, unable to contain herself, she gave a great wail. 'It's so pointless! So pointless!'

'Murders often are,' agreed Chard, softly.

'No! You don't understand!' blubbed Lady Annabelle, her attractive features distorted with anguish. 'He was dying anyway! He only had weeks to live!'

Chard and Morgan exchanged a glance of puzzlement, as the housekeeper, Mrs Reece, rushed into the room, alerted by her mistress's distressed voice.

'There, there, Lady Annabelle,' consoled the housekeeper. 'Shall I ask these gentlemen to leave?'

'No, it's alright,' sobbed the widow, dabbing her eyes with a handkerchief.

Mrs Reece gave the policemen a withering look before leaving the room.

'I think I should explain,' continued Lady Annabelle. 'Although there were some years between us, Henry had always been a very active man despite his age. On Monday, he told me some terrible news. His doctor had told him he had a tumour and there was no cure. I was as prepared as anyone could be for his passing – but not like this. As I said, it was so pointless.'

'In which case, the murderer couldn't have known about your husband's condition,' said Chard.

'Obviously not. As far as I am aware the only people who knew were myself and Dr Matthews.'

'Would that be Dr Ezekiel Matthews, by chance?'

'Yes. Do you know him?'

'We are acquainted.' Chard glanced towards Morgan and indicated that the constable could close his notebook. 'Thank you, Lady Annabelle. You have been most helpful. I will leave Constable Morgan to take formal statements from all the staff, whilst I return to the station to direct the investigation.'

Lady Annabelle pulled a bell cord and Mrs Reece escorted Constable Morgan to speak to the staff whilst Chard took his leave.

The inspector rode back to Pontypridd and went directly to the stables behind the White Hart, a pub on the Tumble junction. The superintendent preferred to keep his horse there, paying for a good stabling to ensure the animal was given the best attention possible. After handing over the reins to the stable lad, Chard crossed the junction onto the forecourt of the railway station, where several cabs waited for business. He looked for a familiar figure in a long coat and battered top hat, and spotted him almost immediately.

'Good morning, Will. How are you and Merlin today?'

'Fine, thank you, Mr Chard,' replied Will Horses. His horse, Merlin, swung his head around and seemed to nod in agreement.

'I don't suppose you've had any fares from the town up towards Pen-y-coedcae recently, have you?'

'I can't say I have. It's not a popular route. Too bloody steep. I take it you're asking because of the murder.'

'News has got around then,' grunted the inspector.

'We had a couple of constables asking us cab drivers about recent fares earlier on. I don't think anything useful came out of it,' said Will with a shrug. 'Have you been round to Dai's house yet, Mr Chard?'

'He still hasn't been seen?'

'No. Not seen him in any of his usual haunts,' answered Will, clearly very concerned.

'I'll try and call round to his house this evening. I'm sure there's nothing to worry about. I would go sooner, but…'

'I know you're busy…' Will's sentence was interrupted as a group of people appeared on the forecourt, having alighted from the Cardiff train. 'Sorry, but business calls,' said the cab driver, giving an apologetic shake of the head before walking towards his potential fares.

***

'Well, Farrington? What have you to report?' demanded the Home Secretary.

'The latest reports from my men in Scotland and the North East give no indication of any unusual activity among the known anarchist groups,' answered the black-clad figure.

Sir Matthew grimaced. 'The Privy Council has finished its meeting without incident. As good as that news might be, it means that if this assassin is indeed in the country, then he has yet to strike. From what you've said previously his target must be the Prince of Wales.'

'We've spoken to his private secretary to get details of His Royal Highness's itinerary, Sir Matthew. Unfortunately, he tends to change it at the last minute without telling anyone. Nevertheless, I am redeploying most of my men to the eastern counties, whilst keeping those who have infiltrated anarchist groups in place.'

'And you say there is absolutely no sign of this assassin?'

'Not as yet, Sir Matthew.'

'Then perhaps he isn't here and you've caused a lot of concern for no good reason,' snapped the Home Secretary.

'If he is here, then I'll catch him. Dead or alive.'

'Believe me, you better had!'

Farrington strode into his office, and in an unusual display of frustration, slammed the door behind him before throwing his black leather gloves on his desk.

A few minutes later, there was a knock and a nervous clerk entered. 'Telegram for you, sir.'

Farrington snatched the message and on reading it paused in hope before shaking his head. No. It was possible, but just too unlikely that it was directly relevant. On the other hand, he told himself, you never know. Taking a pen, he drafted a quick reply.

***

Chard walked through the workhouse gates and headed for the infirmary. There had been no reply to his telegram at the police station. Inspector Hulme was complaining at being unable to search for the arsonists who had set fire to the mail on Monday night, because all his men were now being used to search for Sir Henry's killer. There was also a complaint from the Merthyr police to Superintendent Jones about Chard interfering with their case in respect of the murder of Councillor Jeavons. As a means of avoidance, the inspector had taken his midday meal in the town, not returning until it was time to set off for his meeting at the mortuary.

As Chard entered the infirmary, he caught the eye of Doctor Henderson who, knowing that the meeting with Dr Ezekiel Matthews would prove difficult, gave him a sympathetic pat on the back before he went into the mortuary room.

'Good morning Ezekiel, it's been a long time,' greeted Chard on entering.

There was only one slab in the centre of the white-tiled room. A sheet lay over the cadaver that rested there; two others, also covered, waited their turn on trestle tables.

Standing next to the slab was a stocky man with brown wavy hair brushed backwards and a small waxed moustache. He wore a long white apron and his shirtsleeves were rolled up.

The doctor scowled. 'Not long enough, and it's Dr Matthews.'

The inspector took in a breath, then nodded his acceptance of the new relationship. 'As you wish, Dr Matthews. Have you had time to examine all three of the bodies?'

'I have, and in my opinion, they were strangled by a material of approximately the same diameter.'

'The same murder weapon then, a garrotte?'

'Did I say so?' answered the doctor scornfully. 'It may be, perhaps it was not. What is the connection between these three poor souls?'

'Nothing. That's the problem. It just seemed too coincidental for three people to be garrotted in a short space of time. The only link is that a piece of paper was found on each of them with a black flag drawn on it.'

Doctor Matthews's nose twitched, which it often did when he was intrigued or excited. The unconscious habit made his short, waxed moustache move at the same time, and the overall effect always made Chard think of a rodent examining a piece of cheese.

'That, I admit, is interesting,' said Matthews, lifting the sheet off the body on the slab.

'Is there anything else you can tell me from your examination of the bodies?'

'If you want me to say the injuries are identical in every way, then you're going to be disappointed, Inspector.'

Chard felt a twinge of disappointment at the failure of his old friend to address him by his Christian name. It would take some time for the wounds to heal, but he couldn't regret the brief affair he'd had with the doctor's housekeeper. Nor could he help but hope for reconciliation with Alice one day. 'In what way do they differ?'

The doctor turned and pulled back the sheets on the other two cadavers, exposing their throats. 'In two of the cases the mark left by the garrotte is horizontal, but in the case of Constable Richards the mark shows an upward pull, which might indicate the killer was significantly taller.'

'Not necessarily. Richards was quite tall himself. It could be he was attacked from above by someone shorter whilst he was sitting,' suggested Chard.

'Quite so.'

'Anything else?'

Doctor Matthews pointed to the figure on the slab. 'Sir Henry received a heavy blow to the face, whereas the other two are unmarked except for the actual strangulation.'

'He was a military man, so may have been more difficult to subdue,' suggested Chard.

'Possibly,' agreed the doctor.

'I understand from my discussion with the widow that Sir Henry was one of your patients.'

Matthews nodded. 'A very valuable one.'

'She also said he did not have long to live.'

'It is one of those twists of fate that had he not been murdered, he would otherwise have suffered an unpleasant demise in the next few weeks due to a tumour.'

'Which just adds to the lack of a motive,' sighed Chard. 'My only lead at the moment is the black flag drawing. Hopefully something will come of that. I'll arrange for the bodies of Richards and Jeavons to be removed once I get back to the station. Thank you, Doctor.'

Matthews simply gave a nod of acknowledgement and turned away.

'I understand you kept the rental of your house in Pontypridd,' said Chard, pausing at the door.

'It was convenient to have somewhere to stay overnight when visiting my wealthier patients. I've spent most of the last few months at my home in Swansea.'

'Wouldn't it be more convenient to stay here permanently, now you're continuing as our medical examiner?'

Matthews shook his head, clearly irritated by the question. 'I can easily be contacted by telegram. Two days a week is sufficient unless you have a sudden spate of deaths, or my patients have a compelling need for my services. I do have others under my care in Swansea, you know.'

Chard gave an understanding smile, aware from their previous friendship that the doctor's patients in Pontypridd were far wealthier. 'And how is Mrs Murray…?'

There was a pregnant pause, and Chard cursed himself for mentioning his former lover so soon. The doctor reddened slightly as if he was going to make an angry outburst, visibly taking a deep breath as he composed himself.

'I have not told her the full details of your arrest and subsequent adventures in Shrewsbury. The knowledge that you were still married whilst paying her attention would only make the situation worse. If you and I are to maintain a professional relationship then the subject is not to be mentioned again. Do I make myself clear, Inspector?'

'Perfectly, Doctor,' replied Chard.

He left the mortuary consoling himself with the thought that the house rented by the doctor was too large purely for overnight stays, and the hire of occasional servants must be proving more costly than regular staff. Surely he must resume using it as his main residence, and perhaps Alice would return.

EIGHTEEN

By the time Chard returned to his office, Constable Morgan was waiting for him.

'Come in, Constable, and give me your report.'

The inspector pushed the door open and placed his bowler hat on his desk before taking his seat. Morgan stood facing him and consulted his notebook.

'Frankly, sir, nothing of any great significance came from my interviews with the staff. They saw nothing suspicious. All were in their beds at the time of the incident. None of them had any knowledge of any social contacts Sir Henry might have had; he appears to have kept himself to himself. He stayed around the house, except when exercising his horse.'

'How long have the staff been in Sir Henry's service?'

'Ever since he came to the area.'

'No former servants? Ones who might have been dismissed?' asked Chard.

Morgan shook his head. 'I asked that, sir.'

'They used occasional casual labour though, didn't they?'

'A handful from the local area when extra hands were needed. Mrs Reece usually did the hiring, but occasionally Sir Henry or Lady Annabelle might do so if the housekeeper was indisposed. I have a list of their names and can check if they can account for themselves.'

'Good. Please do that. Any itinerant labour recently?'

'Sometimes they have strangers offering to sharpen knives and so on. There were a couple of occasions last month, but nothing recently. There was no knowledge of any dispute with hired help.' Morgan shrugged. 'The staff seemed mystified and the maids were terrified by such a thing having happened.'

'I see.'

'Oh, by the way sir, I believe you know a Mr Meredith. A teacher at the school on Tyfica Road.'

'Yes, I do. What's that got to do with the murder?'

'Nothing sir; it's just that as I was passing the front desk, I saw Constable Scudamore being harangued in Welsh by a fearsome lady. After she'd gone, I asked him about it and he said she was a Mrs Meredith, wife of the gentleman you know. Apparently, her husband has been missing for the last couple of nights. I just thought you should know, sir.'

'Thank you for telling me. I'm sure Scudamore will have taken a description. I know we've got our hands full at the moment, but…'

Before Chard could finish his sentence, there was a knock on the door, and Constable Temple appeared.

'Telegram for you sir.'

Chard took the telegram, opened it, then dismissed both Temple and Morgan as he started to read the contents. Leaning back in his chair, his brow furrowed, the inspector read the message again. It was the reply from Farrington. The black flag was, as he half-hoped and half-feared, an anarchist symbol. That was the connection between the murders, and somehow Sean MacLiam had to be involved.

***

Ted Schwartz stubbed out his cigarette on a cracked saucer and shook his head.

'All of this wasted time! We should have done this ages ago,' he said to the other three men sat around the table in his rented room. 'I lost my brother in the Trafalgar Square riots and wanted to hurt the authorities ever since, but I haven't done enough!'

'It was Wilson who got us all together,' said Charlie. 'And he provided money, as well as getting the people behind us.'

'People who wanted to do sod all. Happy to let us take the risks, whilst they threw us a few coppers to make themselves feel as if they were doing something,' grunted Frank Edwards. 'When I go to North Wales soon, then you'll see some action. It'll be all over the papers.'

Victor Blandford gave his usual enthusiastic smile and patted the large man on his shoulder. 'Though, as we've already discussed, there are things we can do here first. And I don't mean the petty things Wilson had us doing. Damn shame there are only four of us.'

'It would have been three if I hadn't talked Charlie round,' said Schwartz, his unusual accent cutting through the conversation.

'I just thought about it again and came to the conclusion Wilson is just playing games,' said the docker.

Blandford grinned. 'We're glad you did.'

'It's a pity James couldn't be persuaded,' added Janssen.

Frank Edwards gave a snort. 'No bloody loss. He's wet behind the ears, with the face of a spoiled brat despite his size. Glad to be shot of him!'

Ted Schwartz lit another cigarette. 'A shame about Ada, though. She's as tough as any man.'

Blandford nodded. 'There I agree with you.'

'Leave her out of it,' muttered Edwards. 'She wouldn't listen to me, so there's no point taking the matter further.'

'I'm going to try and talk her round,' said Janssen. 'I think it's worth a try.'

'Really?' teased Schwartz. 'You think you're so good with the women that you can even charm Ada when Frank can't?'

The handsome docker looked embarrassed. 'I was being serious. If I talk sense to her, she'll join us. I expect Ada will turn up for their Saturday meeting and I'll catch her then.'

'Don't you go switching sides!' warned Edwards.

'You have my word I won't.'

'I believe you,' interjected Victor Blandford before Edwards could respond. 'But now, gentlemen, we need to decide our first target and I have just the place...'

***

A dishevelled figure sat on a patch of grass close to the river. It was a chilly evening; the light had faded and it had started to rain. For the seventh or eighth time in the last hour Dai took the folded sheet of newspaper out of his pocket, even though his tired eyes could no longer read the print. It didn't matter, for he knew the content. The article in question told the sad tale of an orphanage forced to close. They had defaulted on their mortgage, having failed to make payment by a specific deadline. It had come as a shock to the charity running the orphanage, because they had managed to scrape together the necessary money and had sent it in good time. Tragically, it transpired that the payment had been posted in Pontypridd on Monday evening, just before Dai himself had set the postbox ablaze. The landowner, wanting the orphanage for industrial development, had decided to show no mercy.

'It's all my fault,' wept Dai, putting his head in his hands. 'I've lost my job, I've got no money, my wife hates me, I'm a criminal – and now I'm responsible for what's happened to the orphanage.'

Slowly, the distraught former teacher started to rock back and forth in despair, all reason gone.

'I will do it! I will do it!' he swore to himself. Then he let out a wail of anguish that no one heard.

***

Eddie Ward walked to the back of his print shop and unlocked the door of the small storeroom that his apprentice was forbidden to enter. Before entering he glanced behind, thinking he'd heard a noise. The printer shook his head. Nothing after all. Young Albert, his apprentice, had long since left for home, knowing a Thursday night was when his master preferred to work on alone.

'There'll be no more of that,' Eddie muttered to himself.

He would no longer spend Thursday evenings printing pamphlets asking for money; and posters demanding an end to authority. It was something he should never have got into; but once he'd started, how could he stop? Ted or Charlie would probably have set fire to his premises and caused him to lose his livelihood. Eddie shrugged, convincing himself that there was nothing to be concerned about. Wilson paid well and if his group was caught then what would the authorities do to a printer who was just fulfilling a contract, eh? Absolutely nothing, he reasoned. At least there would be a temporary break, at Wilson's insistence. And with Ted in particular having gone his own way, he wouldn't feel afraid to say no if Wilson asked to restart in the future.

Inside the storeroom he grabbed the last remaining batch of anarchist leaflets and put them under his arm. Having an open fire in a printshop was never a good idea, so he'd lit a brazier out in the yard, and that was where the leaflets were destined. A sad waste of paper and ink, but Wilson had already paid for them. As he left the storeroom, he thought he heard a noise again, over by the printing press. Cautiously he approached, but then gave a sigh of relief as a skinny tabby cat appeared. It casually approached and rubbed itself against the printer's legs.

'Oh, it's you! Mousing I suppose,' said Eddie with a smile.

Cursing himself for his nervousness, the printer went outside to the yard, where the brazier was glowing in the darkness. Dropping the leaflets into it, and seeing the paper smoulder, then burn, Eddie rubbed his hands in contentment. He was just about to turn around when he heard footsteps. Reacting too late, he felt something encircle his neck.

'What...?' Eddie's words were silenced as the wire tightened. Panicking, he kicked out behind him, catching his assailant on the shin, but to no great effect. Placing both hands to his own neck, the printer desperately tried to get his fingers beneath the garrotte to prise it away. Fingernails tearing and bleeding in the attempt, the constriction continued unabated and he could feel the bile rise in his throat. Gradually the reality reached him. This is the end, nothing to be done. Arms dropping to the side, Eddie slumped to the ground.

The killer looked around. No-one in the yard and all was quiet except for a dog barking somewhere in the distance. Quietly whistling a tune, he dragged Eddie's lifeless body into the centre of the yard, where the printer's apprentice would clearly find it next morning. From his pocket he took a piece of paper which he unfolded and placed on the chest of the corpse. On it was drawn a large black flag. Taking a large stone from the ground he placed it on top of the paper to ensure it couldn't blow away.

'There. That should do perfectly,' he said, rubbing his hands in satisfaction.

NINETEEN

Arriving at the police station very early to ensure there was little risk of being overheard, Chard used the telephone in the superintendent's office to telephone Farrington.

'We've had three murders down here, all connected to anarchist activity.'

'Anybody of note killed?'

'If you mean anyone of high social rank, one knight of the realm, Sir Henry Longville. Other than that, a local councillor and a police constable. There's no obvious connection between the victims. All were left with a drawing of a black flag in their possession.'

There was a pause on the line before Farrington replied, 'I'll look into Sir Henry and see what I can find. How were they killed?'

'Garrotting.'

'A method preferred on the continent.'

'But not entirely unknown over here,' said Chard

'Do you believe MacLiam is involved?'

Chard hesitated. 'I fear so. Though I can't confirm the man you're after, this assassin, is with him.'

'Where is MacLiam?'

'Somewhere in Cardiff. I'm afraid I haven't been able to locate his exact whereabouts. I need to inform my superior and the Cardiff Borough police of the full facts.'

'No! Under no circumstances must you let it be known there's serious anarchist activity in the area. If, God help us, he succeeds, then we may need to cover the incident up. As things stand, there is no evidence that your killer is the assassin. He may not even be there.'

'I can't ignore three murders!'

'I'm not asking you to. By all means investigate them, but don't start a hue and cry to capture every anarchist there. In the unlikely event our target is in Cardiff, then such action will make him disappear. You need to locate MacLiam, find out if he is harbouring the assassin, and determine who he intends to kill. That's something you should already have done.'

'It's a damnably hard task when I can't reveal my mission. Can't you provide some of your own men to assist?'

'My instinct tells me Lucheni is somewhere in the eastern counties and the person in danger is the Prince of Wales. All my resources must be directed there. No, Chard. You're on your own. Don't fail me.'

'Sod him!' Chard exclaimed, putting down the receiver. Farrington or no, people are dying, he thought, and it's not a time for secrets.

Superintendent Jones was not coming in to the station until the afternoon, but on his return, he would have to tell him.

Several hours later, he was still of the same mind. Finding MacLiam on his own would be impossible. He had spent the previous evening walking the streets of Cardiff, hoping for a sight of his former friend. Several discreet chats in less than salubrious pubs had produced potential leads, but none proved useful. With one exception. He'd heard a whisper of a name. Someone called Wilson might be worth speaking to, if he could be found. It hadn't taken long to realise Wilson was the English equivalent of MacLiam. Following that logic, Sean Padraig MacLiam may be calling himself John Patrick Wilson. It would be a starting point and he would mention it to the superintendent that afternoon.

Picking up the folder on his desk, Chard gave a sigh. He had completed the report recommending funding for the recruitment of detectives, but it was pointless. The whole exercise had been manufactured by Farrington as an excuse for his mission, and the money would never be approved. Hopefully, his efforts might impress Superintendent Jones and put him back in his good books, but the vengeance from Farrington if he revealed the full extent of the anarchist problem was a matter of concern.

'To hell with it, I need a drink!' he exclaimed aloud, and headed for the door.

***

Mrs Dodds looked at her basket and felt pleased. There'd been some really good bargains at the market today. Her Jonny would be delighted with the evening meal, that's for sure, she told herself. The pleased housewife pulled her shawl more tightly across her shoulders to keep out the chill wind, then set off for a final walk along Taff Street before returning home. The pavement was, as expected for a Friday, full of shoppers, with people having to step into the street in order to pass. It was something to be done with care as carriages and omnibuses clattered past in both directions.

Passing the side alley to the Captain's Brewery, she saw someone she thought she recognised. It was a man standing on the edge of the pavement, looking very like Mr Meredith from a few doors up her street. Except Mr Meredith was always very presentable. This other person wore dishevelled clothes and had wild unruly hair. His spectacles seemed to be hanging from one ear on a broken frame and he had a wild look about him.

Perhaps it is him and he's unwell, she thought, before deciding to attract his attention. 'Mr Meredith!'

The man glanced in her direction, looked away in the direction of an oncoming omnibus, and then back to her once more. He gave a smile, and a wave, then stepped out into the road.

***

Chard looked at his pocket watch as Barney tugged on the lead. Having needed a drink, and yet knowing there would be a meeting with the superintendent to come, the inspector had decided instead to return home for a cup of tea and something to eat, prepared by Lucy.

'Five minutes more, then I'll have to return to the station,' he informed the dog, who as usual ignored him.

Lucy had planned to take Barney for his midday walk, but Chard needed someone to listen to his concerns, and the Staffordshire bull terrier fitted the bill. It had just been a short walk to the end of Gelli-wastad Road and back, the dog visiting each tree and lamp post on the way, but Chard's head now felt a little clearer and more at ease. He had just reached his front door and handed the lead over to Lucy when Constable Davies rode up on his bicycle.

'You appear to have got the hang of it,' said Chard with a smile.

'I'm afraid there's been an incident, sir. I think you need to come and see,' the grim-faced constable responded. 'I'll leave the bike here and go with you.'

Concerned by the constable's demeanour, Chard let Davies lead the way down through the town centre until they reached Taff Street. They were greeted by complete pandemonium, with the narrow street blocked by a halted omnibus and a vast crowd of pedestrians.

Constable Temple was trying to do his best to keep people back, but to no avail. Some onlookers were pushing forward for a view, only to turn away looking pale, one vomiting against a wall. Further up the street a number of distraught ladies were weeping.

'Get back! All of you get back, I say!' Chard bellowed, his voice heavy with authority. Most of the crowd turned in response, and when the massive frame of Sergeant Morris arrived to add to the presence of Constable Davies, they parted. As Chard walked through the throng, the driver of the omnibus, a short man with a shock of white hair beneath his cap, came forward with hands clasped in front of him.

'I couldn't do anything about it,' he said. 'He just ran out in front of me.'

Chard moved him to one side and walked to the front of the vehicle. It was an unpleasant sight. A pedestrian had gone underneath the horses and a wheel had crushed the poor man's skull like an eggshell.

The inspector instinctively turned his head away from the sight. 'Do we know who he is?'

'We think it's the missing person we'd been told to look out for. A lady in the crowd came forward and said he waved to her before stepping into the road. It seemed to be a deliberate act to get himself killed.'

The shock hit Chard and he forced himself to stare once more at the mutilated form that lay beneath the 'bus.

Seeing the inspector's discomfiture, Sergeant Morris stepped forward and took control of the situation. 'Temple, get a couple of sheets from the linen shop down the road to cover the body. Davies and I will try and clear the street. At least if we can clear one side, we can get the traffic passing in turn. When you return, I'll remain on traffic control whilst you and Davies remove the body. Now get going!'

Chard walked away from the bus, lost in his own thoughts, oblivious of the chaos around him. What made Dai do it? He'd been upset about losing both his jobs, and was unhappy at home, but this? What had tipped him over the edge? Why hadn't he himself tried harder to find Dai Books? Surely finding a missing friend should have been more important than searching aimlessly for MacLiam last night? Will and Dic had at least been making more of an effort to find him.

'Inspector!'

Chard shook his head clear at Sergeant Morris's call, and stepped out of the way as a wagon squeezed its way around the omnibus, which would be unable to move on until the corpse was removed.

With the sergeant and constables fully occupied, Chard took out a notebook and jotted down details from the 'bus driver and several witnesses. It would be a long afternoon.

TWENTY

James Eden hesitated as he approached the police station. This is it, a time to steady my nerves and go ahead with it, he told himself. Easier said than done. Taking a deep breath, he walked through the entrance and approached a constable standing behind the front desk.

'I'd like to see a senior officer.'

'That would be me, then,' replied Constable Scudamore. 'Everyone is out on duty and there's just been an incident in the town centre. Unless you want to see the superintendent of course,' he added with a hint of sarcasm. 'Now what seems to be the trouble?'

Eden drew himself upright, standing stiffly as if on parade. 'I've come to hand myself in.'

'Really? And what for, exactly?'

'I have been a member of a group of anarchists, acting against the government of this country.'

Scudamore looked at the young man with curiosity. 'Acting against the government? In what way?'

'Our group has displayed posters advocating change, defaced walls and set fire to postboxes. I want to confess all.'

'In which case, young man, I'll take you for a sit down in one of our cells until my sergeant gets back.'

Eden held out his hands, expecting to be handcuffed, but on seeing the evident edginess, Scudamore adopted a friendly tone. 'No need for that. You've come here willingly, so just follow me. I'll even bring you a mug of tea.'

***

It was an hour later when Chard walked through the door, in the company of Sergeant Morris.

'Is the Superintendent in?' asked the inspector.

'He's in his office, sir,' answered Scudamore.

Chard nodded. Even though still shaken by the afternoon's events, he realised his discussion with the superintendent could not be avoided. The whole truth about the mission confided by Farrington must come out. As he was about to go upstairs to pick up his report, Scudamore spoke to Sergeant Morris.

'You'll never guess what, Sergeant. There's some young bloke waiting in the cells who wants to confess to being an anarchist.'

'What did you say?' interrupted Chard, turning back.

'I was just telling the sergeant here that someone walked in, saying he's an anarchist.'

'He came in of his own volition?'

Scudamore nodded.

'Then bring him up to my office. You had best handcuff him for security though.'

Five minutes later, Chard was at his desk with James Eden standing before him.

'You may leave us, Constable. Return to your other duties,' instructed the inspector.

Once Scudamore had disappeared from view, Chard indicated for the prisoner to sit. He looked at him carefully. A well-built young man, clearly wanting to look calm, but the edginess was discernible.

'I am Inspector Chard. I understand you want to confess. Let's begin with your name,' said the inspector, taking out a notebook.

'James Eden.'

'Where do you live?'

'I rent a room in Wood Street, Treforest.'

'I think I may have seen you around the town, perhaps at your place of work, or out on the town?' Chard probed.

'I doubt it, Inspector. I work in Cardiff and rarely come into Pontypridd at night.'

'Where do you work? I note there's an ink mark on your cuff.'

Eden glanced at his right wrist. 'I am employed at the Coal Exchange, but today I've taken leave of absence. My employers have no idea I'm here. I had been uncertain whether or not to confess, but this morning it became clear to me that there is no option.'

'It's to your credit that you have come to us voluntarily. I understand you want to confess to being an anarchist.'

'That is correct.'

'And what crimes have you committed?'

'None, directly that is.'

Chard studied the innocent-looking face before him, and leaned back in his chair with a puzzled expression.

'None? That doesn't seem like much of a confession.'

'I joined a group of anarchists because I thought all of them had the intention of changing society for the better. A leader had been elected and he seemed a decent man, who might have unlawful methods, but not ones that would actually harm people. It was just a matter of giving out leaflets persuading people not to trust their councillors, setting fire to the odd property and such like.'

'You set fire to things?'

'No. But I knew about such things and watched whilst others performed the act. The postbox set on fire in Pontypridd this week, for example.'

Chard rubbed his chin in thought. 'I see. We'll discuss that in a moment. But let's start with this leader of yours. What's his name?'

'Wilson, John Wilson. We meet in Cardiff. I'll give you all the names and descriptions of the members of the group.'

The inspector blessed his good luck, and tried hard to keep the excitement from his face.

'Such information would indeed prove helpful and may lessen your sentence for aiding and abetting. But what intrigues me is why you decided to come and give yourself up. You could have just walked away from the group and not told us.'

Eden trembled slightly as he spoke. 'The group has split into two factions. Those who follow Wilson and those who want to cause violence. There are three men in the latter, Victor Blandford, Frank Edwards and Ted Schwartz. They may also have recruited a docker called Charlie Janssen.'

'That still doesn't explain why you've confessed.'

'This morning the body was found of a man called Eddie Ward. It made the first edition of the morning paper. Like myself, he'd remained loyal to Wilson.'

'What happened to him?' asked Chard.

'He'd been strangled. I fear not only do the breakaway group want to cause the establishment harm, but they also want to wipe us out as rivals.'

'Where did this killing take place?'

'Cardiff. The borough police are investigating it, but as you are the nearest police station to where I live, I thought I'd get a fairer hearing here.'

Chard stared at Eden carefully, looking for any change in expression.

'Are you aware of any other murders of this type recently, with a black flag placed on the body?' The latter detail had not been reported in the newspapers.

'No. I read about a policeman being strangled in Barry Docks, though.'

'Do you know who the killer of this man, Eddie Ward, might have been?'

The prisoner shook his head. 'Victor is clever and devious and I wouldn't put it past him. Frank is a bully and Ted has a nasty streak in him. It could be any of them.'

'Where can I find them? It will weigh heavily in your favour if they can be caught,' promised Chard.

'I have a proposal, which you may not accept. But it's the only way you'll arrest them, or at least most of them.'

'I'm listening.'

'Let me go and leave me to find out where they are going to hold their next meeting. I believe I know where to find Wilson, but he isn't the problem. It's the other group you need to catch, and soon. Frank has to travel down from Merthyr and unless they've already planned something untoward, he'll probably want to get back up the valley sooner rather than later. That suggests they'll be meeting somewhere in Cardiff early tomorrow evening. I should be able to find out the location by then.'

Chard looked dubious as the young man continued.

'I've made an excuse for my absence from work today, but I have to be at the Exchange tomorrow. There's a special ceremony taking place at five o'clock and I've been asked to help with the arrangements. If I'm fortunate enough to be freed by the magistrate, then I've a chance of keeping my job. With that in mind, would you be prepared to trust me and meet me at the Exchange around five o'clock tomorrow? I would then lead you to the men you want.'

Thoughts raced through the inspector's head. He wanted Wilson, and perhaps this was the chance to get him. Yet that was no good if he didn't get the assassin, if indeed he was in the county. This other group sounded as if they could contain a professional killer; either the assassin who Farrington was after, or someone else who had murdered four victims by strangling them with a garrotte. If he did agree to the proposal, then he could delay telling Superintendent Jones absolutely everything, at least for a little while longer.

'I'll give it some thought, but before I do, tell me more about the fire in Pontypridd. You said you watched without actually carrying out the deed. Who was the arsonist?'

'A local man called Dai Meredith. I believe he had been a teacher.'

Chard was struck speechless as James Eden continued.

'Victor Blandford recruited him. I felt rather sorry for the man. He clearly wasn't sure what he was doing or why he was doing it. His wits were addled if you ask me. As soon as it happened, he ran off.'

All Chard could say was 'I see…' before remaining silent for almost a minute.

Finally, he spoke. 'Let me have a full description of everyone involved. Then I'll have you released. But I warn you, if you betray this arrangement, you'll feel my wrath!'

***

Feeling perhaps fortune was on his side, Chard felt hopeful as he walked into Superintendent Jones's office.

'Ah! I was expecting you, Inspector. I take it you have finished your report?'

'As promised sir,' replied Chard, taking the completed bound report from under his arm and placing it on the polished oak desk.

The superintendent picked it up and gave the initial pages a cursory glance, before going to the summary at the end of the report. 'I'm sure your case will be clearly presented and I will read through the detail later. What I am eager to see are your recommendations.'

The inspector watched impassively as Jones read the concluding pages, his expression changing from concern to doubt, then from contemplation to acceptance. Finally, he closed the report and shook his head.

'I will wait until I've read the report fully to see if the points you've made are backed up by the supporting detail. However, your proposals for a detective inspector at four of our stations with a supporting officer under their command will never get approved. It would be too costly.'

'Our efficiency would be improved, sir. Quicker results and less cost in the long run.'

The superintendent stroked his moustache absent-mindedly. 'A good point if it was being argued from a position of strength. However, whilst Inspector Hulme has been here, carrying out your regular duties, I have allowed you time and space both to compile your report and also to carry out the functions of a detective. Exactly in the manner described in your recommendations. Is that not so?'

Chard nodded.

'In that time you have, to your credit, established a link between the murders of three disparate victims. Yet the killer remains at large. I think your case would be much stronger if you had made an arrest. Do you see my point?'

'I do sir. With regard to which, I have something to report.'

'Really? Then enlighten me,'

'News has reached me of another murder. This time in Cardiff. I have a possible lead from an informant and I would like to pursue the matter tomorrow evening.'

'Not our jurisdiction, as you well know.'

'I wondered if you might be able to arrange something with the Cardiff Borough Police? Perhaps just say we are following a lead on one of our cases and we would appreciate if they could help us by providing a sergeant and a couple of constables to arrest a suspect. You needn't tell them it also has a connection to their case.'

'They do tend to like it if we ask for their help,' agreed the superintendent. 'It inflates their egos. And if we are only asking for assistance from the lower ranks...'

'I'd like to take Sergeant Morris with me.'

Superintendent Jones shook his head. 'No, I think sending both you and a sergeant might prove inflammatory. Take one of the constables.'

Chard felt concerned. He didn't want to explain that potentially he was going to be rounding up two groups of anarchists. The redoubtable Sergeant Morris would have been a great asset, but perhaps he could manage without him.

'Where do you want the Cardiff officers to meet you?'

'Outside the Coal Exchange, just before five o'clock.'

'Then leave it to me. Thank you for your report. I can see you've put a lot of effort into it. Well done. But don't forget that Inspector Hulme finishes here tomorrow and will be returning to Aberdare station. I want you back in uniform first thing on Monday morning to resume regular duties, so catch this damn killer!'

***

Despite his brief spell of optimism that afternoon, the sombre reality of the tragedy surrounding Dai Books' death hit Chard hard. The walk to the Ivor Arms in the cold, dark evening had been a slow, thoughtful one. Barney, despite his imploring looks, had been left behind, for on a Friday night the Ivor Arms would be crowded.

'And stay out!'

Chard's arrival at the pub coincided with an inebriated customer being pushed forcibly out of the door by Gwen, who immediately crossed herself for her unseemly behaviour.

The drunk staggered, turned to gesture rudely at the landlady, then hurriedly ran as best he could up the street for fear of being chased.

'Oh! Thomas, come on in. Sorry you had to see that. As you know, I don't allow riff-raff here and he won't be allowed back in again.'

'Not to worry, Gwen. Are Dic and Will here?'

'Yes. We've all heard the news. A terrible business.'

Gwen turned and led the way into the pub, forcing a way through the crowd of customers. Those nearest the door were Friday night drinkers of the casual sort and in high spirits. In contrast, the far side of the room was packed with the regulars, men and some women, who knew Dai Books of old and were sad at his passing. It made for an awkward atmosphere.

'I'll have to help Bert behind the bar,' Gwen apologised. 'Can I get you a drink?'

'No, Gwen, I'm not thirsty tonight. I just want to talk to Will and Dic.'

The landlady put an arm around Chard and gave him a sympathetic hug, before returning to her work.

'*Shwmae*, Mr Chard,' said Will Horses, raising his glass in a morose greeting.

Chard noticed it was only a half-pint glass and barely a sip had been taken out of it. Dic had no drink in front of him at all.

'Like me then, not very thirsty,' said the inspector. 'Do you think we could take a walk somewhere quieter?'

'Aye, I'm with you,' responded Dic.

Will nodded, put his drink down on the bar and headed for the door.

Once the three were outside, Chard suggested they walk up towards the canal basin.

'Is it true he killed himself deliberately?' asked Will.

'It looks that way,' said Chard.

'They'll have it down in the papers as suicide then?'

'I'll do all I can to argue that he didn't know what he was doing, and it was an accident.'

'Do you think that was the case?'

'I've had information he'd been drawn into something so far from his normal behaviour that it indicates he wasn't in his right mind.'

Dic, who had been walking in silence, suddenly interrupted the discussion.

'It's our fault. We let him down.'

The three men halted and stood together, taking in the enormity of the words.

'I'm afraid you're right,' agreed Chard.

'Aye, we didn't realise how bad a state he was getting into,' agreed Will.

Dic pulled on the edge of his drooping black moustache. 'When he told us he'd lost his first job, we pulled his leg about having to become a teacher. Teased him mercilessly, we did.'

'And we used to take the mickey about that dragon of a wife of his, thinking it was funny how much grief he was getting at home,' said Will.

'I'm no better, because I joined in as well,' confessed Chard.

'It's made all the worse because when we last saw him, he clearly wasn't in his proper mind. He'd lost the teaching job and needed calming down. We should have stopped him from having so much to drink,' said Dic.

Chard indicated they should walk on, which they did in silence, going past the canal basin and on towards the Newbridge Chainworks where the Bunch of Grapes stood close by. A good pub, which being away from the town itself was less busy.

Once inside, the inspector bought a round of drinks and the three friends sat to resume their discussion.

'We didn't know what state he was in, but we should have done. It's easy to make fun of someone's misfortunes, but much harder to try and understand their point of view and help them. That takes effort,' said Chard.

'You're right. It's a bad group of friends we are,' admitted Dic.

'You mentioned earlier that Dai had been drawn into something. What did you mean by that?' asked Will.

Chard took a swig of his beer, then wiped his mouth with the back of his hand before answering. 'I'll do my best to keep it out of the papers, but I understand he got into bad company. In your search for him did you hear anything of the sort?'

'He was seen drinking in the Llanover the other night. There was some kind of altercation with a man who had just called in,' answered Will.

'A young man, wearing spectacles?'

'I didn't get a description. Why?'

'Because according to my information he'd been befriended by a young man called Victor Blandford. Medium height, dark hair, spectacles and "a pleasant manner", according to my notebook.'

'Never heard of him,' muttered Dic.

'In fairness, if he was a wrong 'un then Dic would know him. No offence, Dic *bach*.'

'None taken.'

Chard gave a wry smile. 'He's involved with a group from Cardiff rather than around here, together with another young man called James Eden.'

Will and Dic both shook their heads and shrugged.

'Were they the reason Dai did what he did?' asked Will.

'They might have been the cause of the thing that drove him over the edge. If that's the case then they'll pay for it. Hopefully, I'll have all the bastards locked up by this time tomorrow.'

'I'll drink to that,' said Will, raising his glass.

His companions joined the toast, and after finishing their drinks, the three men made their way home, each lost in their own thoughts.

***

It was a tricky job, putting it together by the light of a small lamp. Harder, in fact, than it had been to obtain the necessary sticks of dynamite. The fence at the quarry had gaps in the wire and the lock on the explosives store had been easy to open. Just a tap with a hammer at the right point and the padlock just sprang open. Four sticks should be enough and judging by the lax security they wouldn't be missed. The difficult bit was here, now, attaching the wires and setting the clock.

'Get in, you bugger,' he muttered, forcing the final wire into place. 'Tomorrow's the big day!'

TWENTY-ONE

Chard spent the following morning at the police station, sat in his old office on the ground floor with Inspector Hulme. Mundane as it was to wade through the following months' rotas, check the receipts for the station's necessary expenses, and get up to date with the recent arrests and prosecutions, it did at least distract from other matters. By midday, everything had been done and after thanking Inspector Hulme for having covered his post so dutifully, Chard was left with nothing much to contain his impatience. Eventually, after instructing Constable Morgan to join him at three o'clock outside the railway station, the inspector went home and decided to take Barney for a walk around Ynysangharad Fields.

'I'll let you off the lead if you'll behave yourself,' he promised the dog as they crossed the New Bridge. Once off the road and in the fields, which were privately owned but kindly accessible to the townspeople, he let Barney loose.

Chard stood and watched the river flow by, whilst his dog foraged amongst the bushes. It was a cold day, which had deterred others from taking a stroll, so there was no-one in earshot. 'I might be getting somewhere, Barney.'

The dog heard his name and emerged from amongst a pile of leaves, looking guilty, which was his customary expression.

'I mean, the Superintendent seems to be happy with my report. The constables are less hostile, though I'm still not entirely forgiven. I've got a plan to help Morgan, which should help him. As for May? She's in Bristol and there's bugger all I can do about that.'

Barney plodded over and sat on Chard's foot, recognising his master wanted company.

'Get off, you daft animal.' Chard reached down and scratched the dog's ear.

'As for this bloody anarchist business and these murders…' Chard picked up a stone and threw it towards the river in frustration. 'Four dead in total and none of them really connected. Three of them represent some kind of social authority apart from this latest one, the printer in Cardiff; and only one of them is strictly speaking my direct concern.'

Used to his master talking to himself when they were alone, Barney gave a yawn and lay down.

'They must be connected, but none of it makes sense. I still don't think Sean MacLiam, or John Wilson as he now calls himself, could possibly be behind all this. He's not the killing type. Hopefully, this young Mr Eden has told us the truth and the assassin is part of the breakaway group. His turning up has been a miracle, because it must end today. If I catch Farrington's man for him, then all well and good. If he isn't one of them, then it doesn't matter. My involvement will be over and I can go back to living as normal.'

A spattering of rain made Chard grimace. 'The weather's turning, Barney. You'd best get back on the lead. Time to go.'

The Staffie watched with doleful eyes as the lead was re-attached, then dog and master turned back the way they'd come.

'Daft you might be, but you're a good listener. If everything works out, I'll buy you the biggest bone in the butcher's shop,' promised Chard.

***

Chard and Constable Morgan had hoped to arrive very early for the rendezvous at the Coal Exchange, but a thick fog had descended on Cardiff which delayed their cab. By the time they arrived at the front steps, three police officers were already there waiting for them.

'Good afternoon, Sergeant. I'm Inspector Chard and this is Constable Morgan.'

'Sergeant Wisdom, Inspector. I understand you wanted our assistance in arresting a suspect. Is he inside?'

'No, but I have an informant in the Exchange and I'm due to meet him in a few minutes.'

'If you don't mind me saying so, Inspector, your plain clothes won't cause comment but one police uniform should be sufficient. We don't want the business of the Exchange to be interrupted, or the gentlemen inside to be distracted. I'll accompany you, but the constables should perhaps wait outside.'

Chard thought he would rather just take Morgan, but there was a certain diplomacy to consider, so he nodded his agreement.

For such a grand, impressive building, the doorway was not particularly imposing, and the elderly doorman seemed almost uninterested in the people coming in and out.

'Ever been here before, Inspector?' asked the sergeant as they walked through the ornate vestibule.

'Never, but I'm quite interested in…' Chard's words faltered as they entered the Great Hall and he took in the magnificence of the architecture. High galleries, the woodwork embellished with exquisite marquetry, reached up to a magnificently ornate ceiling which covered a vast, well-lit room capable of holding up to a thousand dealers, brokers and agents. Fortunately, as the day's business had all but closed, there were fewer than a hundred people present.

'There you are, Inspector. I'm pleased to say that I have the information.'

Chard turned to see James Eden approaching, an earnest look on his face.

'There's a long service presentation taking place in an anteroom at five o'clock, but I've helped set things up and I'm free to come with you now.'

'Where are we going?' asked Chard.

'They're meeting at Ted Schwartz's lodgings at half past five and it's almost five o'clock now.'

'What about Wilson?' demanded Chard.

'I've told you, he's not the one you want. I can lead you to him easily enough afterwards. Ada Quill and Willy Rabinovitz might be with him, but they won't be a threat even if they're there. It's the others you want. One of them is a killer and my money is on Ted.'

'I didn't realise we were after a killer,' commented Sergeant Wisdom. 'I should have been—'

'Help! Help! You there… Sergeant… help!'

The outburst came from a thin, bald-headed man in a frock coat. He was red-faced and his eyes bulged alarmingly.

'Calm down, sir. What's the trouble?' asked the sergeant calmly.

'A bomb! I've found a bomb! I was doing my daily rounds when I came across it in the room next to our records office. If it goes off it will destroy priceless historical documents.'

'We've been having renovation works this last fortnight; workers are in there every day,' explained Eden.

The commotion had not gone unobserved and the word was spreading, leading to a mass unruly exodus.

'I'll take a look. Lead the way!' Chard pushed the terrified man back in the direction from which he came. The sergeant and Eden followed behind as they were taken through a side door, into a corridor, then down a flight of steps.

'I'll come no further!' insisted their guide, pointing to a closed door. 'It's on the floor in the middle of the room.'

'Out of the way! I'll look,' said Eden, pushing past to enter the room. It was dimly lit, the only daylight coming through a small window set high into the wall. 'I see it!' he exclaimed to the others in the doorway.

'Let me take a look,' said Chard.

'Shit! There's a clock on it and it's about to hit the hour! I think it's going to go off!'

'Back!' yelled the inspector, but as he did so, Eden threw himself at the device, ripping out the wires.

Chard felt his whole body tense up, mid-breath. It was seconds before his mind accepted that there was no explosion and he allowed himself to exhale.

TWENTY-TWO

'We owe you a debt of thanks, Mr Eden,' exclaimed the wide-eyed sergeant. 'I've never seen such bravery.'

'Yes, I agree,' said Chard.

The clerk gave an embarrassed smile.

'Who on earth would have done such a thing?' asked the sergeant.

Chard grimaced. 'We have a pretty good idea, and with your help they'll be in custody by the end of the evening. My intention was to search for a killer who has strangled his victims. However, having seen the lengths to which the villain and his associates are prepared to go, I think you should apprise your inspector and issue firearms. Constable Morgan and I will meet you outside in, say, half an hour?'

The sergeant gave a brief nod and then hurried away.

'When he gets back, I'll lead you to Ted Schwartz's place,' said Eden.

Chard nodded. 'Good, but what about the man Wilson? Where can we find him?'

'Just a few streets away, but he can wait until later.'

'I'll be the judge of that,' snapped the inspector. 'If he's that close, we can get him now. If your account's correct, we won't find much resistance.' Inwardly, Chard knew the priority had to be the arrest of those responsible for the bomb, but if Wilson got away, Farrington would not be pleased. Any resulting delay was a risk that had to be taken.

'But what if the others get away?' asked the clerk.

'It will take time for the sergeant to explain the situation to his inspector and then get back here through the fog. Now come on and lead us to Wilson!'

***

Wilson gave a sigh of regret as he watched Ada disappear into the fog, then walked back into the workshop. At least he'd had apologies from two of his former followers. He returned to the task of checking for anything that might lead the police to their identities or whereabouts. It was probably unnecessary, but if there was one of the hotheads who couldn't be trusted, it was young Victor Blandford. The devious little bastard would be quite likely to tip off the police out of spite.

'Such a shame, after the months of effort,' he declared to the empty room. The truth was that his life had been empty before leading his small band of followers. He had money, plenty of it – but no real purpose in life. His wife had been a firebrand and wanted to change the world, before consumption finally took her away. On her deathbed she'd made him promise to follow in her footsteps, but that was easier said than done. He did want to carry out her wishes but hadn't known how to go about it. Fighting for an independent Ireland would have been the obvious cause, but the violence carried out by the 'Brotherhood' appalled him. Instead, he'd written to academics and social reformers on the continent, to understand the principles of socialism, anarchism and nihilism. Through the contacts made, he realised social change was best done gradually. But he couldn't do it on his own and, leading a solitary life, he'd lapsed into despair and a meaningless existence. That was until, by chance, in the back room of a pub, he'd fallen into the company of this small, squabbling group of disparate people. Becoming their leader had given him hope and purpose, but now he would need to begin afresh.

'Who's there?' he called as a loud creak interrupted his thoughts. He cursed himself, realising he hadn't locked the door. There was little light coming through the single window, and the solitary lamp he'd lit failed to illuminate the doorway.

'It's me,' replied Willy, shuffling into the room. He was wearing a flat cap and a long shabby coat which looked as if it had suffered decades of mistreatment.

Wilson looked relieved, and smiled benevolently. 'Ah, our faithful friend. Don't worry, you won't starve. I'll still see you all right for money, so you'll have a roof over your head. Ada's not long left, and there's little to do here. Just a few bits and pieces on the floor. I'll put them in the bag over there, but that'll be it. Once I've finished, I'll walk with you into the town.'

The Irishman went towards the bag, halting on hearing a click behind him. Turning back, he was astonished to see that Willy had produced a revolver, and it was aimed at his head.

'Willy? What on earth are you doing?'

It wasn't just the pistol which held Wilson's attention. It was also Willy's manner. Instead of his usual subservient slouched posture, he stood straight-backed with a confident expression on his face. Despite his lack of inches, he seemed to dominate the space around him.

'The name's Nestor Lucheni, to be perfectly accurate, though I have used many others.' The voice was different. Each word precisely spoken but with the hint of an accent that Wilson couldn't place.

'But what's the meaning of all this? I don't understand...'

'Of course you don't, but I will explain. Sit down in that chair!'

Wilson, utterly confused, did as he was ordered.

'I would have explained to you my true identity and purpose when I first arrived, but fortunately I was sceptical about my instructions.'

'What instructions?'

'I was told there was an active anarchist cell here and you were named as its leader. I could have gone to any one of several groups, but the ones in major cities probably have government informants. I also had a special reason for coming here, apart from my mission.'

'Mission? What mission?'

'Don't interrupt! As I started to say, I would have explained things on meeting you, but I decided to wait and see what sort of man you were.' Willy's expression turned to one of utter contempt. 'You turned out to be a child, playing little games. I was disgusted to be part of your infantile attempts to inflate your ego. I have seen young men barely out of school die for a cause. Yet all you've done is set fire to a few things or give out leaflets and stick up a few posters. You are quite pathetic.'

The Irishman, confused and hurt by the stinging words, looked away.

Willy scoffed at his captive and with his free hand took an object from his coat pocket, which he held behind his back.

'You mentioned you had a special reason for coming here?' asked Wilson, looking up at his captor.

'South Wales specifically, you mean. Yes. I'd never been here before and was curious to see what it was like.'

'But I heard you speaking Welsh to Ada,' argued Wilson.

'I was born in the Ukraine but my mother was Welsh. Her father had gone to work for the Hughes mining company. After he died, my mother married an Italian who also worked in the mines. Then he was killed in an accident leaving us destitute. It was my first experience of capitalism and if we were treated badly by the company, it was as nothing compared to how some of the other working-class widows and orphans suffered.'

'I am sorry to hear that,' replied Wilson, still trying to gauge exactly what situation he was now in. Did Willy intend to kill him? Surely if that was the case, he would have fired his pistol by now?

'What do you intend to do with me?' he asked.

'I had originally intended to just disappear, tempted as I was to put a bullet in you. However, as it happens, you can help me with my mission.'

'Oh yes, you haven't told me about that. I'm sure I'd be able to help,' replied Wilson, trying to buy some time.

Willy gave a friendly smile, but there was something in his eyes which made Wilson's blood run cold. 'I promise to tell you in a moment.'

The assassin stepped closer and placed the muzzle of his revolver against the Irishman's forehead. Unseen by his captive, Willy brought his other hand from behind his back and pricked Wilson's wrist with a needle.

He flinched at the sudden sharp stab, but daren't move further, with the gun pressed firmly into his skin.

'I have to make sure this works in case it has lost its potency since I first arrived here. In a few seconds I'll know. You just seemed to be the obvious candidate to try it.'

Wilson felt a cold feeling travel up his arm and through his body. At the same time, he felt his heart pounding and he started to weaken.

Willy removed the pistol from Wilson's forehead. The Irishman instinctively tried to get up, but failed.

'Perfect! You'll last for another ten or fifteen minutes, but that's your lot. They'll say it was a heart attack. I think I'll leave you now. There's a train I need to catch.'

Willy started to walk away, but then stopped and came back. 'I made a promise to you, didn't I? I said I'd tell you my mission, and

I do keep my promises.' The assassin bent closer to whisper into the helpless Wilson's ear. The Irishman's eyes opened wide with shock as he heard the words. After trying once more to get out of his seat, he slumped back, immobile.

Willy laughed and walked out, humming a tune to himself.

***

'Are you sure this is the place? I can barely see ten feet ahead in this fog.'

'Yes, Inspector. I've been here many times before. If my information is correct, you'll find Wilson inside, but he's not the man you need. I keep telling you it's Ted Schwartz. Wilson would never plant a bomb. I don't think Charlie Janssen knew anything about it either, or he would have warned me to keep away from the Exchange.'

'Constable Morgan, lead the way. If the door's locked we'll have to break it down,' ordered Chard.

Stepping forward, Morgan tested the door. 'It's open sir.'

'Is there a back way out?' Chard asked Eden, who shook his head in response.

Morgan drew his truncheon and Chard, wishing he'd drawn a firearm from the station's armoury, gripped his heavy-handled walking cane tightly. Given a nod from the inspector, Morgan opened the door and strode inside. A lamp, oil running low, flickered dimly on a window ledge.

'Bloody hell!' swore Chard, recognising the figure slumped in a chair. 'Morgan, check there's no-one else in here!'

The inspector ran towards the stricken Wilson, followed by Eden, and checked if the Irishman was still breathing.

'He's still alive.'

'Looks like he's had some kind of seizure,' suggested Eden.

'Sean! Sean! We'll help you. Stay with us!' encouraged the inspector. 'Too… late. He's… killed… me…'

'Definitely no one here, sir,' reported Morgan, putting his truncheon away.

Chard ignored the constable. 'Who did this, Sean?'

'Willy… a… killer…' The breathing was becoming shallower and

Wilson's eyes were fully closed.

'Good God!' exclaimed Eden, looking shocked.

'Tell me! I need to know what he intends to do,' insisted Chard, placing his ear to Wilson's mouth, which moved almost silently.

Morgan and Eden watched as a puzzled expression formed on the inspector's face. Then a long quiet sigh seemed to escape from Wilson's lips. Chard checked his pulse, then frowned.

'He's gone.'

There was an uncomfortable silence before Chard turned to Eden. 'What do you know about this Willy, other than what you already told me yesterday?'

'Nothing. He seemed to be just a pathetic little vagrant.'

'Constable, take a look around and see if there's anything here of interest.'

'We need to hurry back,' insisted Eden, 'or the others will get away.'

'I suppose so,' agreed Chard. 'There's a bag over there that might prove useful, so we'll take that.'

'And what about this, sir?' asked Morgan, bending down to pick something up from under the one large table in the room.

'What is it?'

'It looks to me like a homemade garrotte!'

***

Back at the Coal Exchange, the Cardiff Borough sergeant, together with his inspector, waited impatiently. A dozen constables, each armed with a Lee-Metford rifle, stood before them. As soon as Chard's party approached through the fog, the sergeant could be seen talking to his superior, who strode forward angrily.

'Inspector Chard, I presume! I'm Inspector Kimble. What is going on? We were told you'd come here to make a routine arrest. Why didn't you advise us that there was a maniac trying to blow up the Coal Exchange?'

'Because we didn't know. The person I was after is no longer here, but this young man…' Chard pointed at Eden, '…not only prevented an explosion, but also thinks he knows where the culprit might be found.'

'If we're not too late already,' muttered the clerk.

Chard ignored the comment. 'I appreciate this is not my jurisdiction and so I will not interfere. Mr Eden here is providing valuable information on my case but I am happy for him to go with you. My constable will accompany you as well, but only to escort our informant back to Pontypridd after you've finished with him.'

'What about yourself?' demanded Kimble with a look of suspicion. 'If we catch the bomber then the arrest will be ours, you know.'

'By all means take the credit. I'm not bothered,' said Chard, 'I have other things to do.'

Constable Morgan's expression betrayed his confusion at Chard's attitude, but a gesture from his inspector made it clear he was to obey.

'Then we'll make a start. Come on, men!' Kimble ordered.

Chard watched as the armed policemen disappeared into the fog, then made for the entrance of the Coal Exchange. Since the bomb alert, most of the occupants had either gone home or remained outside for fear of a second device. Only a few had gone back inside to retrieve their things. Chard tapped one of them on the shoulder with his cane.

'I am Inspector Chard. I need a telephone. Where can I find one?'

'There's one in that office to the left, Inspector.'

Chard took the card with Farrington's phone number from his inside pocket and rushed towards the office, praying he would be able to get hold of him straight away. He was in luck.

'I hope you're calling to tell me you've found MacLiam. Not that I really suspect him of involvement with an assassin, but it would be useful to cross him off our list.'

'I've found him alright. He'd used the English equivalent of his name, John Wilson. But he's dead.'

'Go on.' Farrington's tone was serious, as he sensed the gravity in Chard's voice.

'Unknown to him, the assassin had been laying low among his followers, presumably using them as a source of money until he needed to move on.'

'Do you have the man?'

'No. It was he who killed MacLiam. I'm sorry to say he's already set off on his mission.'

'Damnation!' swore Farrington. 'How the hell are we going to catch him now?'

'I spoke to MacLiam before he died and he whispered something to me with his last breath, but it didn't make sense,' said Chard.

'It might be a code. Tell me! We might not have much time!'

'He was speaking in gasps. It sounded like "mission… going to kill… Harden."'

'I know of no one of importance with that name. Could it relate to a place?'

'There's a chance he meant Hawarden, a town in Flintshire. I've been there once, long ago. But I don't see the relevance.'

'Wait on the line! However long it takes, just stay there!' snapped Farrington.

Over the telephone, Chard could hear footsteps walking away, a door opening, and Farrington shouting loudly at some subordinate. Fully ten minutes had passed before Farrington returned to the other end of the line. His voice was different, almost panic-stricken.

'You were right. It is Hawarden. Do you know what Lucheni, the assassin, looks like?'

Chard tapped his jacket pocket which contained a summary of the descriptions provided by Eden. 'I do.'

'Then get on a train to Hawarden immediately. No! Wait until I've checked my Bradshaw's.'

There was a delay as Farrington consulted his railway guide, before speaking in a more controlled manner. 'There's no way you'll catch him tonight. Take the milk train north in the morning. I'll meet you at Shrewsbury station, and we can travel to Hawarden via Wrexham. We might not get there soon enough, so in the meantime I'll send a telegram to ensure his target stays well away.'

'Who is his target?' asked Chard.

The reply came as a shock. 'Oh, good Lord no!' he exclaimed.

TWENTY-THREE

William Ewart Gladstone walked slowly down the staircase, grasping the banister tightly and measuring each step. At eighty-six years of age and in ill health, having guests to stay at Hawarden Castle was rather a strain for the former Prime Minister.

'How was His Grace this morning?' he demanded of the butler waiting at the foot of the stairs. 'Sufficiently rested, I hope.'

'Indeed, he was, sir,' the butler replied. 'Mr Henry has gone with him to Holy Communion and they should be back shortly to take breakfast.'

Gladstone gave a snort. It was a good job that his son, Henry Gladstone, was present to escort the archbishop for an 8 a.m. service. Too damn early! And after such a stormy night! The wind had howled, keeping him awake for what seemed like an eternity.

'Mrs Gladstone is already in the breakfast room, sir,' informed the butler.

'Not that we can start eating until the archbishop gets back.' Gladstone sighed to himself.

'Before you go sir, there is the matter of your telegrams. They've been coming in regularly since the archbishop arrived yesterday.' The butler held out a silver salver on which at least two dozen telegrams sat, unopened. 'One of them is marked urgent.'

Gladstone scoffed. 'I opened three "urgent" telegrams yesterday morning, and they were nothing of the sort. All congratulating me on the visit of the Archbishop of Canterbury and asking if he will drop in for tea, and such like. Fawning sycophants, the lot of them. Leave the telegrams where they are and I'll look at them this afternoon.'

***

Chard sat uncomfortably alongside Farrington as the train rattled its way up the line beyond Shrewsbury, heading towards Wrexham. He wasn't intimidated as such, but the black-clad figure carried an air of arrogance and threat which deterred any attempt at civil conversation.

Finally, after travelling in silence for nearly half an hour, it was Farrington who spoke.

'I've noticed some trees have been uprooted by last night's storms. There's a chance that the telegraph lines are down. I know the one I sent yesterday evening must have got through, but I also left instructions for others to be sent after I left for the railway station. They may have failed. It's a damn shame Hawarden Castle doesn't have a telephone installed.'

The words were spoken hurriedly, and for the first time Chard realised Farrington was worried. 'In which case we'd better hope the train keeps to time,' the inspector said.

'Are you armed?' asked Farrington.

'No,' answered Chard, more abruptly than he'd intended. 'I take it that you are, as is your man Drake.'

Farrington glanced across the carriage to the thick-set individual wearing an overcoat and bowler hat. 'Of course. I just hope you can recognise Lucheni from the description.'

'So do I,' agreed the inspector.

***

The Most Reverend Edward White Benson, Archbishop of Canterbury, had enjoyed an excellent breakfast. It had been a busy weekend, with a journey from Stranraer to Carlisle, then to Hawarden for a full formal dinner with the Gladstones and their guests the previous evening. The night's storm had disturbed his sleep and the early morning communion had been a little inconvenient. Especially so when now, only three hours later, he had to return to the church for the eleven o'clock service. Yet, he felt obliged to demonstrate that he was full of vigour. Despite his sixty-seven years, the archbishop had the reputation of being fitter than many younger men and was determined to prove the point.

'Let us not take a carriage. We can walk to church… if you can keep up,' the clergyman boasted.

Mrs Drew, the former prime minister's daughter, glanced in the direction of her brother Henry and, ensuring the clergyman couldn't see, rolled her eyes in annoyance. Age and infirmity allowed her father to remain in the castle and her mother to travel by carriage, but the archbishop could not be expected to walk alone. Their guest's attendance at morning service was no secret, having been planned for weeks, and the locals would no doubt be out on the street to catch a glimpse of the great man.

'My wife and my niece will accompany mother in her carriage, but my sister and I will be only too happy to walk with you, Your Grace,' said Henry.

'Good. That's settled then. I'm looking forward to your husband's sermon, Mrs Drew. Let's depart, then, shall we?'

Smiling politely, Mrs Drew followed the direction of the archbishop's outstretched arm and led the way into the hall, where servants were summoned to bring their coats, ready to face the cool morning air.

***

'Where first? Hawarden Castle or the church?' asked Chard as the three men hurried from the station.

'The porter said the castle is at the far end of the village, so St Deiniol's will be nearer,' replied Farrington. 'Listen! The bells are ringing the call to service. We'd better run, in case the telegram didn't get through.'

Farrington, Chard and Drake ran onto The Highway, the road leading into the centre of the village, eventually catching sight of the tail end of a crowd heading up Church Lane. A police constable stood, hands behind his back, watching them disappear from sight.

'Constable! Is the archbishop at the church?' demanded Farrington once they got within earshot.

The policeman turned around, looking annoyed at being hailed so abruptly. A glance at Farrington's grim visage moderated his response.

'You've just missed him, and I doubt there'll be room in the pews for any outsiders. Those who can get a seat are already inside,' he answered, before turning away.

Without saying another word, Farrington ran towards Church Lane with his companions in pursuit. The lane was narrow with a high stone wall on one side and buildings on the other. Drake overtook his employer and pushed aside the stragglers in the crowd making their way towards the church. A short distance ahead, the lane widened into an open space in front of the gate leading to the church grounds.

Farrington, taller than Chard, pointed ahead. 'The archbishop has stopped to talk to the crowd at the gate. They're crowding around him. Is our man there?' he demanded, not trying to hide the urgency in his voice. By now they were only about thirty yards behind.

Chard peered, trying to make out anyone meeting the assassin's description, but there were a number of short men visible, let alone anyone concealed within the crowd. Desperate to try something, he bellowed "Lucheni!"

No-one paid any notice, eager as they were to hear the archbishop's address – with one exception. A man wearing a flat cap, looking pathetically dishevelled, turned his head for a moment, and in that split-second Chard recognised the expression of someone with evil intent.

'There he is!' yelled the inspector.

'Where?'

'He's gone into the centre of the crowd. Run!' ordered Chard.

Once again, it was Drake who took the lead in clearing a path through the bystanders as the archbishop finished his address and passed through the gate, carrying on down the church path with his escort.

'The archbishop seems safe,' said Chard.

'I hope so,' replied Farrington. 'Where's the man you spotted?'

'I don't know,' answered the inspector, looking around him. With the archbishop gone, and knowing that the church was already full, the crowd started to break up. But there was no sign of Lucheni.

'We have to find him! He won't have gone back up the lane; he'd be too easily spotted. Drake, you head right towards the rectory; I'll go ahead and search around the church. Chard, take that path to the left.'

Chard watched as the two others sped off. In truth he was winded, and forced to acknowledge he perhaps wasn't as fit as he'd believed. After taking a few moments to compose himself, he set off in the direction suggested by Farrington, towards St Deiniol's library.

***

Inside the church, the service started as soon as the archbishop sat down alongside Mrs Gladstone in the seat usually taken by her infirm husband. As everyone knelt for the Absolution, Mrs Gladstone noticed the archbishop's arm, which was twitching in a most peculiar manner. There followed a gurgling noise in his throat which caused the old lady to jerk upright in alarm. A moment later, the clergyman fell forward in helpless collapse.

***

'No sign of the bugger!' Chard muttered to himself, after a quick circuit of the library grounds. In his mind, the obvious route of escape would be to head beyond the library and circle back to the railway station. Though if the fugitive was unsure as to how close his pursuers were, he might not want to risk crossing the clear ground between the library and the tree-lined hedge beyond. Hopefully Lucheni would be caught elsewhere by Farrington or Drake. At least they were armed.

I haven't even got my cane with me, Chard thought with regret. The sturdy implement with its weighted handle had proved useful on more than one occasion, though Lucheni looked small enough to over-power without it, unless he had a gun.

Satisfied there was no sign of Lucheni outside the building, Chard went to the main door and turned the handle. It was unlocked, raising the question of whether or not to enter and search the library room by room.

'Chard! Any sign?'

The inspector turned to see Farrington approach, followed closely by Drake.

'He wouldn't have had enough time to run to the tree-line without me seeing him, and I've done a quick circuit of the building. If he came this way, he must be inside the library. I was about to search.'

'No,' objected Farrington. 'I'll go in with Drake.' He produced a revolver. 'You go around the back and observe if he comes out that way.'

Chard nodded his agreement and, after the two men went inside, he hurried to the back of the building and waited close to one of two rear exits.

*****

Henry Gladstone and the churchwarden carried the archbishop to the rectory and laid him on a couch.

'Carefully, now,' said Dr Burlingham, a local doctor who had been in the congregation. 'Remove his collar and loosen his clothing. I've sent for my nurse and Dr Roberts, but in the meantime you'll have to assist.'

'I think he's still breathing,' offered Mrs Drew, who had followed her brother.

'Very faintly, though. If you'd like to help, perhaps you could remove his shoes and massage his feet whilst I feel his pulse.'

Henry Gladstone looked bereft as the doctor felt the unconscious clergyman's wrist, repositioning his fingers several times before shaking his head.

'It's very weak, if there at all. I'll have to try the Sylvester method.'

The doctor took the clergyman's arms and pressed them over the chest, then pulled them backwards over the patient's head to draw in air. He performed the action several times, checked the pulse and repeated the process.

'Dr Roberts has arrived,' someone called from the hallway, and moments later the village's other doctor appeared, carrying his medical bag.

'Good,' said Dr Burlingham, his manner understandably abrupt. 'This isn't working. We'll have to try an injection of ether. Do you agree?'

Roberts nodded. 'I'll see to it straight away.'

Whilst the syringe was being prepared, Burlingham continued to work on the patient, without success. Eventually the medication was ready and the injection was made in the archbishop's left side. Everyone prayed.

*****

Chard had been waiting for around ten minutes when he heard a faint creak.

Instantly alert, he moved closer to the exit door and held his breath. In that moment, every small sound seemed amplified, and he felt as if he could smell the presence of his quarry.

Slowly, quietly, Lucheni emerged.

'Got you, you little bastard!' uttered Chard triumphantly as he grabbed the assassin's left arm and twisted it.

Lucheni was forced into a crouched position, unable to stand upright, but then… a sudden click as the hammer of the pistol in his free right hand was cocked. Despite Chard's hold, Lucheni was able to twist his body just enough to allow him to point the gun.

'Let go, or I'll blow your balls off!'

'You won't fire because it'll give your position away to my colleagues, who are both armed,' replied Chard, trying to sound confident.

'If you don't release me I'll be caught anyway, so what have I got to lose? Now let me go and I won't fire. It wouldn't be in my interest.'

'But I could still call out, which means you'd still be in trouble and would have to shoot me. Whatever you do, my two associates are going to know where you are.'

'We already do.' The interruption came from the doorway through which Lucheni had come.

Chard breathed a sigh of relief as Farrington and Drake stepped through, pistols drawn.

'There's no way out for you. Drop the gun!' ordered Farrington.

Lucheni grimaced and threw his pistol on the grass. Chard relaxed and released his grip.

The assassin looked dejected; a defeated pitiable figure… who unexpectedly moved like lightning, producing a syringe from his pocket and placing it against Chard's neck. He moved behind the inspector, his head appearing around Chard's shoulder to taunt the two men with guns.

'I think I'll be making my way out of here now, don't you? I wouldn't do anything hasty if I were you, or this man will die.'

Lucheni whispered into his captive's ear. 'Step back. One pace at a time, but don't dawdle. Do as I say and I'll release you when I get to the trees.'

Chard knew it was a lie. Once at the trees Lucheni would plunge the needle in, if only to delay his pursuers. But there was no option other than to play along. He noticed Farrington murmur something to Drake, but neither man moved.

The distance between them was somewhere around twenty yards, and Lucheni was glancing backwards towards the treeline, when Farrington tapped Drake gently on the shoulder.

Some deep instinct for survival made Chard throw himself to the ground, risking the prick from Lucheni's needle. Heart juddering with shock when the sound came, he waited a second before raising his eyes to see Drake standing with firing arm outstretched.

Feeling nauseous, Chard slowly got to his feet and turned to see Lucheni's body splayed grotesquely on the grass, blood oozing from the hole in his chest.

Farrington walked forward, a grim smile on his lips, with Drake a yard or so behind.

'What the hell was that?' demanded Chard, his voice a mixture of shock and anger. 'If I hadn't have dived forward you would have killed me.'

'The bullet would have gone through you and hit him as well. Sorry, old chap, but it was the only way of getting our man for certain. Drake! Throw the body in the trees and stand guard. I'll make the necessary arrangements to remove it discreetly. The locals may have heard the gunshot but I'm inclined to think they'll believe it's some farmer shooting at a rabbit.'

'I assume you're finished with me,' Chard asked, still fuming at Farrington's sang-froid.

'Perhaps. Let us check on the archbishop first,' Farrington answered with a contented smile.

It was an expression that was not to last. The two men arrived back at the church to find that the service had finished and a crowd was gathered at the church gate. The policeman they had seen earlier was trying to maintain order amidst the hubbub. Chard tapped an old man on the shoulder and asked what the commotion was about.

'It's the archbishop. Dead as a doornail. Heart attack, they say,' replied the old gent.

Overhearing the conversation, the colour drained from Farrington's face. He pulled Chard away from the crowd and spoke sternly.

'Listen carefully. This is a matter of the highest political importance. Lucheni was never here, understand? He had no connection to the man called Willy in South Wales and there's to be no investigation along those lines. He just disappeared. I repeat, do you understand?'

'What about the archbishop's inquest?'

'There will be no inquest, not a genuine one at least. It can't get out that he was assassinated. The fall-out would bring down the government, and God alone knows how many other assassination attempts on prominent persons will follow. Your duty is clear.'

'In which case I will co-operate. But it comes at a price…'

TWENTY-FOUR

'Good morning, Inspector.'

Chard grunted an acknowledgment.

Only Sergeant Jackson could make such a pleasantry sound sarcastic without crossing the border into insubordination.

The sergeant knew Chard preferred to be out of uniform, but this morning, in accordance with Superintendent Jones's expectations, he was immaculately turned out in full formal dress. The inspector headed for his former office on the ground floor, sighting Constable Morgan on the way and gesturing for him to follow.

'What happened on Saturday?' Chard asked as he closed the door behind them.

'It was a disaster, sir. Inspector Kimble started shouting orders as soon as we got near. Someone in the fog, probably some youngster acting as a lookout, whistled a warning. By the time we got to Schwartz's place, the occupants had all run for it. Where did you go, sir?'

'Never you mind. Do we still have Eden?'

'He came back voluntarily and I put him in a cell.'

'Good. I'll question him after I've given the superintendent my report about Saturday's events. Was anything of interest found at Schwartz's house?'

'I'm afraid not,' replied Morgan.

'A damn shame. The whole gang should have been caught.'

'What about the man called Willy? I've put the garrotte in my desk drawer. Do you think it might be him who whistled the warning?'

'Take the garrotte to Dr Matthews. He can compare it with the marks on Sir Henry's body and hopefully confirm it is the murder weapon. Forget Willy Rabinovitz. He's no longer of interest.'

***

'I've read the morning paper, so I've been expecting your own account. Take a seat,' instructed Superintendent Jones.

It was rare for Chard to be offered a seat in the superintendent's presence, but the pleasure at seeing his subordinate back in full uniform had clearly warmed Jones's mood.

'The discovery of a bomb was coincidental and not intended to play any part in my investigation. I went to the Coal Exchange to meet my informant and then we were to round up a small gang of trouble-makers, one of whom is our killer. Unfortunately, the bomb incident delayed my plan.'

'This informant. Is he reliable?'

'He threw himself at the bomb and stopped it from going off. We have him here, but I'll release him after a further interrogation,' replied Chard.

'Who planted the bomb?'

'Probably one of the gang I was trying to catch; possibly our killer. I don't know at this stage.'

Jones shook his head, clearly dissatisfied with the answer. 'The paper indicated no arrests were made.'

'That's correct. The bomb incident changed everything. It became a matter for the Cardiff Borough Constabulary and their approach alerted the suspects. However, their names and descriptions are known, so I'm hopeful there'll be quick arrests.'

'Most unsatisfactory, Chard. Our killer could strike again.'

'I'm confident that won't happen. There'll be no more garrotting.'

'How can you possibly say that?'

'It's just a feeling sir. With them all on the run, I'm sure whoever the killer is will want to keep a low profile. I just want them all locked up so I can work out who should hang. They are all suspects and most are no doubt guilty of some crime or other. However, one or two, like my informant, might have been drawn into the group in innocence, persuaded down the wrong path when in a vulnerable state of mind.' Chard thought of Dai Books, whose involvement he had resolved to leave out of his account.

'Nevertheless,' said Jones, 'forgetting the bomb, which is not our responsibility, we still have no result. That does not bode well for the acceptance of your report. Incidentally, having read the excellent presentation and content, I have fully supported its recommendations.'

'On the contrary, I am pleased to say we do have a result, though not an arrest.' Chard suppressed a smile at the superintendent's quizzical expression before continuing. 'I discovered the identity of the man responsible for planning the arson attacks at our post office and at a number of locations in Cardiff. He was the man holding the gang together, though he was not our killer, nor did he plant the bomb. Unfortunately, he died of a heart attack before I could arrest him. His name was Wilson.'

'That's something, I suppose, but what about the killer?' demanded Jones. 'Three murders on our books and no one arrested yet, and Merthyr playing merry hell because I told them to let their suspect go. Are you sure it's the same person responsible?'

'There's every indication that is the case. As for where we go from here, it really does depend on catching the gang, and if the Cardiff police beat us to it, I'll have to request permission to interrogate them myself. Obviously, now I've returned to my old duties, I can't spend every minute on the case and with that in mind, I'd like to raise something from my report.'

'Such as?' asked the superintendent suspiciously.

'The recommendations mention a detective inspector at each of our four largest stations, ideally supported by a detective sergeant.'

Jones gave a grunt. 'Don't mention sergeants to me; I've enough of a problem there as it is. As you know, due to our lack of resources I had to bypass the normal procedures and promote Jackson on the grounds of seniority. Scudamore was unlucky to miss out, but he'll get the next post, if I receive the funding.'

'I wasn't thinking of Scudamore, sir. He's a good man and will make an excellent sergeant, but he's not cut out to be a detective. Even out of uniform, his manner and general bearing mark him as either a military man or a police officer. If he were to make discreet investigations someone would recognise him as a policeman from a mile away. I had another idea, one which might meet with your approval.'

'Such as?'

'We support the detective inspectors with a detective constable who would have twelve months to demonstrate their aptitude. If found to be suitable, they would then be eligible for promotion to detective sergeant,' proposed Chard.

Superintendent Jones looked thoughtful. 'This is all hypothetical, of course, because we won't get the funding, but I'll play along. How does this thinking apply itself to our current problem?'

'Hypothetical, I agree, but just supposing it does happen, I would have to nominate such a constable. I do have someone in mind, but I would rather have some hard evidence of his suitability in advance, so we'd both be in agreement over the selection.'

'Given your previous plea against Constable Morgan's demotion, I am assuming he's the officer you would recommend?'

Chard nodded. 'It isn't just that I feel responsible for the demotion. When in Shrewsbury he showed admirable qualities which would make him particularly suited to the role.'

Jones gave a benevolent smile. 'I bear him no ill will, you know that. But there had to be a punishment. Discipline is all-important. So, what is your suggestion?'

'When required, I would like to use him to work on this case, under my direct instruction. He may need to operate in plain clothes and travel outside our area, until the killer is brought to justice. You have my word that someone will swing for these murders.'

***

'I just saw Eden leaving the station,' said Morgan as he stood in front of Chard's desk.

'I've let him go,' said Chard. 'He's confessed to watching someone commit arson, thereby aiding and abetting, but on the other hand, his employers, despite this morning's absence, will treat him as a hero. Taking into account the information voluntarily provided in aiding our investigations, a magistrate would let him walk free.'

'Did he tell us anything else, sir?'

'He recounted his discussion with Inspector Kimble on Saturday and confirmed that he gave the same descriptions already provided to ourselves. As far as Kimble is aware, Eden had reported an offence to me and believed the culprit to be one Ted Schwartz, a man known to associate with a small group of anarchists. He refused to tell Kimble what the offence was, so at the moment the inspector is unaware it relates to the death of the printer. Neither did he reveal his involvement in the arson attacks, nor did he mention what happened when we found Wilson, for fear of it leading to awkward questions and being detained.'

'Perhaps it would be better to keep him here, for his own safety. I expect he's worried about Wilson's murderer still being on the loose,' suggested Morgan.

Chard shook his head. 'He thinks that he'll be forgiven this morning's absence from work due to the weekend's events, so he'll keep his job. Having him kept in jail would put that in jeopardy. I've assured him he'll be safe, and if he wants a constable posted on his street, then we can arrange it.'

'What do we do next, sir? Sergeant Jackson said you wanted to talk to me about something important, but he didn't say what it was about.'

'That's because I didn't tell him,' replied Chard with a satisfied smile. 'Let us consider the position we're in. We have a murderer who has killed four unconnected victims.'

'Willy Rabinovitz, sir,' said Morgan.

'No. Forget him for the moment. Someone must hang for those crimes and it's going to be another of Wilson's gang.'

Morgan looked puzzled and waited for Chard to say more, but there was just an uncomfortable silence.

'Dr Matthews has confirmed the garrotte I found is the likely murder weapon,' the constable added.

'That's as may be, but I want a confession from someone. There's also the matter of the bomb, and instinct tells me it's the same culprit. As for the cases of arson, we know Wilson planned them. Eden can give first-hand evidence against Victor Blandford, but otherwise was not present at any other incident.' (Except for the one involving Dai Books, thought Chard.) 'We need to catch all those involved and interrogate them thoroughly, whilst not stepping on the toes of Inspector Kimble.'

'All we can do is wait then, sir.'

Chard shook his head. 'Not entirely. As you are aware, I consider myself responsible for your demotion. I want to give you the chance to redeem yourself in the superintendent's eyes. To that end, I have work for you which is not to be disclosed outside these four walls. You will answer to me, and only to me. Do you understand? There is a chance your efforts will be wasted and a pointless exercise, but I've just got this feeling that won't go away...'

Morgan frowned. 'Might I ask what my duties might entail, sir?'

'Initially as much research as can be done from your desk, then afterwards—'

The explanation was interrupted by a knock on the door.

'Enter! What is it?' snapped Chard as Constable Jenkins walked in.

'Message from the superintendent, sir. It's Cardiff Borough Constabulary on the telephone. They've arrested someone called Schwartz and they say you can interview him tomorrow morning.'

TWENTY-FIVE

'I understand you've got Ted Schwartz in your cells, Inspector.' Kimble gave a dissatisfied grunt. 'He tried to sneak back to his lodgings yesterday morning, but I'd placed a man in the house opposite, just in case. Not that I can hold him for much longer. We questioned him hard through yesterday afternoon, and last night. He denies knowing anything about the bomb. Unless you've got some evidence I don't know about, we'll have to let him go. Talking of which, I'd be obliged if you told me everything you do know. You told us you were going to make a routine arrest, without giving details of the offence. Then there's a bomb found in the Exchange and immediately you are able to point the finger at a group of suspects. What's going on, Inspector Chard?'

'I'll explain. We've had three murders in the county and there's evidence that the perpetrator belonged to a group of troublemakers. I understand a printer was found murdered in Cardiff recently, and he might be another victim. Our informant advised there were four likely suspects and they were planning something big. The assumption is that it was the bomb. The four were due to be meeting at Schwartz's on Saturday.'

Kimble nodded, satisfied with Chard's explanation. 'I see. As you can appreciate, with the bomb incident being very much on our doorstep, we wanted the opportunity to break him first. However, as we've been unsuccessful, you're welcome to question him yourself. Follow me.'

Chard was taken to a small room, with only a glimmer of light coming from a small window set high in the wall. It was bare of furniture except for a table and two chairs.

'If you'd like to make yourself comfortable, I'll get my men to bring Schwartz.'

Following a short wait, the prisoner was brought in and handcuffed to a chair by two burly constables. He looked in a sorry state.

'You can leave. I'm safe enough,' Chard said to the officers, who made to object until they saw the determined expression on the inspector's face.

Once they'd departed, Chard took a good look at Schwartz. One side of his face was badly bruised, his lips were crusted with dried blood and his right eye was blackened and completely closed.

'If it helps, which I'm sure it doesn't, I don't approve of their methods of interrogation,' said Chard.

'Piss off!' The words were spat out, causing a dribble of saliva to run down Schwartz's chin.

Chard smiled. 'That isn't going to get you anywhere. You need to listen carefully to what I have to say.'

The inspector waited silently, staring at the prisoner for half a minute, before continuing. 'Inspector Kimble is interested in the planting of a bomb, which thankfully injured no one at all.'

'Bloody bomb! I know nothing about it. There was a loud whistle in the street, I looked out and saw a copper, so I ran for it. It's only natural ain't it?' Schwartz's strange accent combined with swollen, bloodied lips made his words difficult to understand.

'You weren't on your own though, were you? Don't deny it,' cautioned Chard.

The prisoner said nothing.

'As I was saying. Inspector Kimble is interested in the planting of the bomb. I, on the other hand, have three murders, possibly four, which I need to solve. Someone has to hang for it and it might as well be you.'

'Me?' There was alarm in Schwartz's voice.

'I have an informer who is prepared to give a statement that you not only planted the bomb, but also strangled three or four other men with a garrotte,' lied Chard.

'What? Who? Is it Wilson? I bet it is. Just because we broke away from his leadership.'

'It isn't him. He's dead.'

The prisoner looked shocked. 'Was he one of the ones strangled?'

'That's not important right now.'

'If it isn't Wilson then who can it be? I know! It's bloody Charlie. The lily-livered bastard! It's why he didn't turn up!'

'Calm down, there's a good fellow. Perhaps I can help, if you are willing to co-operate. On the other hand, if you're not…'

Schwartz bent his head forwards, staring at the floor as he considered Chard's words. After a few moments he looked up and spoke resignedly. 'Go on. Ask what you want from me.'

'That's better,' responded Chard, with a reassuring smile. 'You see, between the two of us, I don't think you are the murderer,' he said quietly. 'It might be Frank Edwards or Victor Blandford, for example. I don't really care which one, but someone has to hang. At the moment you're all I've got.'

'If Charlie's helping you, then I'll make a statement that I saw him commit arson in Cardiff.'

'You were there at the time?'

'Yes, I'll swear to it. I don't mind being charged with aiding and abetting, but I didn't actually do it.'

'Good! But that still doesn't let you off the hook. I understand you were planning to do something big. I suppose that must have been the bomb, so who did the deed? If you tell me the truth then we'll have you charged with the minor offence. Charlie Janssen will be arrested for arson, and as the bomb didn't go off, I'll arrange for any charges connected with it to be dropped. However, if any other major act is carried out, you will be considered an accomplice.'

Schwartz shifted uncomfortably in his seat as Chard continued.

'Needless to say, I'll ensure you also get landed with the blame for the murders. I won't need proof, just the word of one of the others eager to save themselves at the expense of your neck. Remember, one of your gang did plant the device without your knowledge, and it's likely that person is also the strangler. I'll give you a few moments to think about it.'

There was a tense silence as the prisoner considered his options.

'It can't have been Charlie who planted the bomb, not if he's your informer,' said Schwartz eventually. 'I know Frank worked with explosives in North Wales. Victor is clever enough to make one, but it depends how complicated it was. The intended plan, devised by Victor, was to derail a mail train just outside Cardiff. In order to lift the rails, keep lookout and arrange an escape, it would have taken four of us to do it. There's no chance of it happening now. Truthfully, I don't know where Victor or Frank are. Victor lives in Pontypridd and Frank is in Merthyr but intends going to North Wales very soon.'

'That still doesn't help you. I need at least one of them,' pressed Chard.

'We talked about the need for money and Frank wanted to rob the payroll of the Cyfarthfa Ironworks. It's possible he might still go ahead with the idea.'

'Surely it'll be protected.'

'There are two payrolls. Both are collected from the bank in Cardiff and come up by train. The major part is collected on Friday and has two men guarding it. However, the lesser payroll for the office staff arrives on a Wednesday. It's carried in a locked leather case by one of the managers on the ten o'clock train. That's the one Frank would be after.'

Chard smiled. 'Thank you. I will keep my side of the bargain, providing I catch Frank Edwards.'

After going to the door and calling the constables to take Schwartz back to his cell, Chard went to find Inspector Kimble.

'I have no evidence that Schwartz is the killer I'm after, nor that he planted the bomb. He will, however, make a statement confessing to aiding and abetting an act of arson. That should keep him in custody until he goes in front of a magistrate. He's been co-operative, so don't treat him too roughly, eh? Let me know if you catch any other suspects and I will reciprocate.'

***

Idris Morgan was in the process of opening a telegram when Chard walked into the police station. Reading the contents, the constable sighed, rolled it into a ball and threw it into a wastepaper basket.

'I've only called in to see how you've been progressing. I take it you aren't having much luck,' commented the inspector.

'Some, but not much, sir. There's a limit to what you can do by telegram. I've managed to get hold of the society columnist for the East Cumberland News, and the reply I just received says he might be able to help.'

Chard gave an appreciative nod. 'Well done. That sounds hopeful.'

'I haven't finished, sir. He wants to discuss the matter in person.'

'In which case, you know what you need to do. I thought it would come to this. The reporter probably wants to barter – a promise of a future scoop in exchange for what he knows. I just hope I'm not sending you on a wild goose chase. Send a reply agreeing to his terms and try and catch a late afternoon train. With luck you'll make it by midnight.'

Chard watched Morgan clear his desk, and wondered if he was doing the right thing. There might be nothing to it, but there was something which just didn't sit right…

'Constable Temple! Send a telegram to the general manager of the Cyfarthfa Ironworks. Tell him to expect me this afternoon on a most urgent matter.' Chard considered telling the superintendent to inform Merthyr Division of his visit, but decided it would only cause complications. 'If anyone needs me, that's where I'll be,' he added, before walking out.

***

'Inspector Chard to see you, Mr Baileys,' informed the clerk, as Chard was seen through to the impressively large office of the ironwork's general manager, a rotund man with a bald head framed by tufts of grey hair.

As much as Chard disliked wearing his uniform, there were times like this when its natural authority paid dividends in impressing people of high social standing.

'Inspector, I understand this is an urgent matter?' asked Baileys, with a concerned expression on his face.

'I am afraid there's a possibility that an attempt will be made to steal tomorrow's payroll. We have become aware that someone has been considering making such an attempt, and we're trying to find him. Rather than take the risk, I propose laying a trap.'

The manager looked shocked. 'I can't believe such a thing could happen. Who is this individual?'

'Frank Edwards, who may possibly have been a recent employee of yours. Perhaps you can check your records to see if you have an address, though instinct tells me he may have moved on since the weekend.'

'I'll have it done immediately,' replied Baileys, calling one of his staff into the office.

Chard waited until the clerk returned with an address written on a piece of paper, which he gave to the inspector.

'I'll pass this on to my colleagues in case he's still there,' said Chard, putting it in his pocket. 'However, I was thinking of replacing your usual courier with one of my own men of a similar build. I assume Edwards knows the procedures for the payroll collection, so you'll have to run through them with myself in order that we don't raise any suspicion.'

'I'll call for our payroll manager, Mr Shunter. He collects the payroll himself and can give you all the detail you need.'

Whilst he waited for Shunter to arrive, Chard wondered who he might use to replace the usual courier. When the payroll manager entered the room, he knew there was only one possible choice.

TWENTY-SIX

Chard knew it was a wild shot in the dark. Superintendent Jones had thought so too, and was dubious of his inspector's choice of constable. Yet, as soon as Chard had seen Mr Shunter's generous proportions, he realised it would have to be Constable Davies who took his place. Consequently, it was Davies who left the bank in St Mary Street, Cardiff carrying the large leather case which usually contained the payroll. On this occasion the money had been replaced with bundles of blank paper.

Chard grimaced as it started to rain just when he needed to leave the cover of a shop doorway in order to follow Davies at a discreet distance. The roads and pavements seemed particularly busy, but Davies's size meant that he could be picked out from the crowd and easily kept under observation. Chard's eyes scanned the passers-by. Frank Edwards was known to be a large, powerfully-built man over six feet tall. He might be difficult to overpower, but the inspector was confident that his heavily-weighted walking cane and Constable Davies's bulk would prove sufficient. Not that he anticipated an attempt in the town centre. It was more likely Edwards would board the train somewhere outside Cardiff, if indeed his instinct was right.

Davies went directly to the station, looking straight ahead as instructed. The last thing Chard wanted was for the constable to look nervously around, anticipating an attack. Thankfully he was doing an excellent job. There was a queue at the booking office and Chard stopped to buy a newspaper, waiting as inconspicuously as possible until Davies moved towards the platforms. Then the inspector had to rush to buy his own ticket, losing sight of Davies in the process. Fumbling for change, Chard paid his fare, then rushed up the stairs to the relevant platform.

'Where the hell...?' he uttered, before noticing a carriage door closing at the front of the waiting train.

Sprinting forward, he threw himself into the second carriage just before the guard slammed the door and waved the train away.

Chard slumped in his seat for a moment to catch his breath. 'This had better not be a waste of time,' he muttered.

There were two elderly ladies and a vicar in the carriage but no one else. Chard hoped Edwards was not already in the forward carriage, waiting for his quarry. He shook his head to clear the thought. Davies knows what Edwards looks like and would have called out when he got on board, he reasoned.

At the first stop, Chard went to the window and looked to see if anyone answering Edwards's description was waiting to look for the courier and enter his carriage. If such an event was to occur, Davies knew to stall whilst Chard leapt out and tackled the man from behind. The inspector frowned on seeing a young woman waiting on the platform, but nobody else.

Anticipation grew with each scheduled stop, but every station proved anticlimactic. By the time the train pulled in at Merthyr Tydfil, Chard came to the conclusion that his wild gamble had failed to pay off.

The inspector allowed the two elderly ladies to descend from the train onto the platform before following suit. Davies could be seen showing his ticket to a guard on the way out of the station. Taking his own ticket from his waistcoat pocket, Chard hurried to catch up. Once outside, Davies would take a cab for the short journey to the ironworks, whilst his superior followed in another. Chard then anticipated an embarrassing discussion with Mr Baileys before both policemen returned to Pontypridd.

At least it's not raining up here, Chard thought as he walked onto the station's forecourt. But by God it's not pleasant. He liked the smell of the coal which fired the railway's steam engines, but when merged with the smoke from the town's industries and the moist atmosphere, the air felt thick and cloying.

The thought made him lose concentration, and it was almost too late that he noticed the tall figure of Edwards step out from behind a two-horse brougham carriage and approach Constable Davies. There was a glint of steel as a knife was produced and pressed against the policeman's kidneys. Edwards whispered something into Davies's ear, evidently instructing him to go towards the Brougham's open door. The driver of the vehicle wore an old overcoat with a cap pulled down to disguise his features, but clearly was an accomplice.

As Davies struggled to squeeze himself into the carriage, Edwards's knife arm momentarily moved away from the constable, and that was when Chard struck.

'Police! Give yourself up!' he yelled, swinging his ebony cane with both hands. The round brass head of the cane made an audible crack as it connected with Edwards's elbow, causing him to cry out in pain. Somehow retaining his grasp of the knife, he passed it into his other hand, waving it before him to keep the inspector at bay. Relieved at the inspector's intervention, Constable Davies stepped backwards from the carriage's doorway as the driver picked up the reins.

'Keep back,' warned Edwards, slashing the air wildly with his knife.

'I've got him,' yelled Davies, grabbing his man around the waist.

'Back, I say!' shouted Edwards, who despite the disabled arm was powerful enough to break the constable's hold and slowly back up towards the rear of the vehicle.

Bystanders were starting to be attracted by the spectacle, and when a railway official began shouting for help, it was enough to make the carriage's driver crack his whip.

'No...' implored Edwards, and while he was temporarily distracted, Constable Davies hit him with his full eighteen stone of body weight.

Big as he was, Edwards crumpled to the ground with the policeman on top of him, the knife skidding from his hand to land at Chard's feet. Ignoring the weapon, the inspector ran towards the carriage, but he was too late, able only to thrash the rear wheel impotently with his cane as it sped away.

Taking a pair of handcuffs from his pocket, Chard threw them to Davies. 'Slap these on him and we'll take him into the local station.'

***

'When are you going to get me a doctor? You've broken my bloody arm!' complained Edwards an hour later.

'They'll get you one soon enough,' answered Chard.

Inspector Greene had sent for a doctor from the infirmary, but was far from happy about it. Already smarting from Chard's interference in his investigation of the murder of Councillor Jeavons, he was indignant to find Pontypridd policemen executing an arrest in his own town. Fortunately for Chard, Superintendent Hughes and the Chief Constable were delighted at the good relations it would foster with the owners of the Cyfarthfa Ironworks. As an exercise in diplomacy, Chard suggested that Inspector Greene could process the arrest through Merthyr Division's records, providing he could interview the prisoner first.

The two men sat in a white-tiled room in Merthyr police station, facing each other across a table. Edwards, securely – and given his injury, painfully – handcuffed, looked defiant and angry.

'How did you know?'

'Schwartz told me you were thinking of robbing the payroll before returning to North Wales.'

'Bastard! I'll kill him!'

'You no doubt stole the carriage, but who was driving it?' demanded Chard.

Edwards spat on the floor.

'Suit yourself. I'm only trying to help. There's a chance it'll help save you from the noose.'

'What do you mean? Attempting a robbery isn't a hanging offence,' snapped the prisoner.

'You're correct, but murder is.'

'What are you talking about?'

Chard could see the concern and uncertainty on Edwards's face. 'There have been four murders, the most recent being that of a man called Ward, a printer in Cardiff. I need to find someone to hang for it, and it might as well be you.'

'I didn't do it. You can't have any proof.'

'My word against that of a dangerous man, captured in the process of robbing a payroll in broad daylight outside the railway station? I think I know who they'd believe; unless you've got an alibi of course.'

Edwards went silent. He was aware of the murder of Jeavons in Merthyr and word had got to him about Eddie Ward.

'Was it the same murderer?'

Chard considered his response, then nodded.

'I was with someone, the night that Eddie Ward was killed,' said Edwards eventually.

'Who? Tell me and it might save you from the hangman.'

'I was in Cardiff on the night Eddie died, but I was staying with a Mrs Quill. She'll vouch for me.'

'Where does she live?'

Chard took out his notebook and wrote down Edwards's reply, before giving a reassuring smile. 'I was wondering where to find Ada Quill.'

'How do you know her name?' asked the prisoner.

'She's one of Wilson's little band of followers, like you.'

'Wilson's an arsehole.'

'He's dead.'

Edwards looked shocked, then blurted out, 'I didn't do it!'

'Calm yourself. Apparently, it was a heart attack. When did you last see him?'

'It was when we all had a bit of a bust up a few days back.'

'I don't suppose you've been planting bombs recently?' asked Chard raising an eyebrow. 'You seem a very angry man, just the sort to want to kill a lot of people in one fell swoop.'

Edwards reddened with anger. 'Don't try blaming me for that! I wouldn't have a clue how to put a bomb together. If I did, I'd have blown up Lord Penrhyn and all his family in North Wales. I've lost my wife and two children due to sickness caused by us not having enough to live on. You'll find out I'm wanted up there for assault. It's why I came here out of the way for a while. My only remaining child is with my brother and his wife. I just wanted to do something whilst I was down here to fight back against the evil bastards who control our lives.'

'I am aware of the relationship between Penrhyn and his workers,' commented Chard, an element of sympathy in his voice. 'The only members of Wilson's group that I can't find are Blandford and Janssen. I'm guessing one of them was your accomplice, the carriage driver.'

'I don't know where Victor has gone and as Charlie's a docker, I'm guessing he got on a ship. That's all I can tell you,' replied Edwards, grimacing with pain as he tried to move his arm.

'That will be all for now,' said Chard, getting up from his chair. 'Once you're back in a cell, they'll take the cuffs off, which will lessen the discomfort in your arm; and the doctor will be here soon. The information you've provided may have saved you from the noose.'

'Mrs Quill next,' he muttered to himself as he walked out of the door.

TWENTY-SEVEN

Idris Morgan felt unsettled. He had hardly ever travelled outside of South Wales and yet in the last few weeks things had changed. Firstly, he'd travelled to Shropshire and the Black Country to help clear Inspector Chard's name and now here he was in the far North of England. At least the journey hadn't been entirely wasted. Arriving in Carlisle late on Tuesday evening, he'd found the newspaper office easily enough the following morning. As expected, the reporter, Fittson by name, wanted something for his column – a detailed description of how the body was discovered, and a promised exclusive when the murderer was caught. In return, he'd take Morgan to see some of Sir Henry's former employees that very day.

Morgan sighed as he recalled the subsequent journey, which had taken them some miles to the west of Carlisle. Fittson had already made some enquiries and located two former servants who had little to tell them, other than Sir Henry's political leanings and his hatred of socialists. They did however, mention that Sir Henry's valet had been given a handsome sum on his dismissal, sufficient to set him up in business as a publican near the coast. Unfortunately, arriving at the Plume of Feathers in the evening, the former valet had been dismissive to the point of rudeness, refusing to discuss his former employer. Despondent, Morgan had returned to his hotel room intending to return to Wales the next day, but on that morning, just as he was about to leave, Mr Fittson turned up with one more lead.

'Stroke of luck, old chap. I was talking with some colleagues in the Sportsman's bar late last night. One of them had written a review of a new tearoom here in Carlisle. The proprietor mentioned she'd been lady's maid to Lady Annabelle Longville. Here's the address.'

Now Morgan sat, waiting in a parlour for Mrs Lincoln to make herself available. It was a well-furnished room which smelled strongly of polish. The table in the centre of the room was covered by an intricately embroidered tablecloth and there was a piano close to the window.

How did she afford to set up her own place? Morgan wondered. It did seem curious, as did the valet's sudden apparent good fortune. Inspector Chard's insistence that he follow up on Sir Henry's background had seemed strange, especially when the killer was undoubtedly that Willy Rabinovitz fellow, who he seemed reluctant to consider. Yet, Morgan conceded, there might be method in the inspector's madness.

The constable's thoughts were interrupted by the entrance of a lady who was perhaps in her late thirties. She wore a plain high-collared white blouse, a black skirt, and an expression of concern.

'Mr Morgan, I understand. How can I be of service? My maid tells me it is something to do with my former position in the household of Sir Henry Longville.'

Morgan stood out of politeness and waited until Mrs Lincoln took a seat and indicated that he should resume his position.

'It's Constable Morgan actually. I'm a member of the Glamorganshire Constabulary,' he said, producing his warrant card. 'May I say what a lovely place you have here.'

Mrs Lincoln looked at the warrant, glanced almost imperceptibly at Morgan's damaged ear, frowned, then finally nodded. 'It's only a small tea shop, but it is well-regarded by my customers.'

'It must have been difficult to get started, with the costs I mean,' continued Morgan with a genial smile.

'My former employer was very generous.'

'Yes, to his valet too, I understand. But not to the rest of his staff. I spoke with two of them yesterday and they were paid a pittance when Sir Henry left the county.'

'I was held in great regard by Lady Annabelle. It was a pleasure to serve her.'

'Yet she did not ask you to go with her when they left for South Wales.'

'I didn't know that was where they went. Sir Henry made the decision not to take me... but he was very generous.'

It was a snapped reply and Morgan noticed the worry etched on the woman's face as she started to lose her composure.

'So you've already said, Mrs Lincoln. Any reason in particular?'

'That is a private matter. I believe I have no more to say. I signed papers... I would lose everything.'

'Were you aware that Sir Henry is dead... murdered?'

Mrs Lincoln looked shocked. 'How? Lady Annabelle and young George... how are they...?'

'They are fine. No one else was hurt,' comforted Morgan. 'I assumed the news might have made the local press. I've been to the local newspaper office and although they hadn't many details, the death had been reported.'

'I truly hadn't heard about it. My little business occupies much of my day and I have no time for gossip.'

'We are trying to find out the identity of the killer and knowing a bit more about Sir Henry's past might help. Now, can you please explain why Sir Henry was so generous to yourself and his valet in particular? I promise not to reveal the source of anything you tell me, other than to my inspector, and he is very discreet.' Seeing the woman's hesitancy, but having noted her initial reaction to the news, he added, 'It might ensure Lady Annabelle's safety from whoever did this.'

Mrs Lincoln remained silent for a few moments with head lowered. Finally, she looked up with an expression of resignation. 'If it's for Lady Annabelle's safety, I will tell you something of the matter. I knew little George wasn't Sir Henry's child. That is enough for you to know.'

'As far as the staff were concerned, was that something only you and the valet were aware of?'

'There was a little bit of gossip, but I was the only one that knew for certain,' she answered, shaking her head.

'Then why did he reward his valet?'

Mrs Lincoln got up abruptly and went to the door, checking that there was no-one outside, before returning to her seat. Speaking in hushed tones, she leant towards Morgan. 'I was by the door outside Sir Henry's study one morning and this is what I heard...'

***

'A complete balls-up!'

That had been the Home Secretary's view of things. He rarely used such coarse expressions, but Farrington agreed that the assessment was justified. The only way for either of them to keep their official positions would be to cover up the truth.

Farrington drummed his fingers on the top of his desk as he mused. There had been so much to arrange, not least the urgent appointment of a medical examiner and a coroner from his own department. They were both reliable men who had proved useful on several occasions when problematic people had succumbed to 'accidents'. Agents who had infiltrated the Irish Brotherhood reported no indication that the assassin had confirmed the kill. He simply hadn't had the time. Fortunately, there had been a gas explosion at a factory over sixty miles away in Birmingham on the same morning Lucheni was killed. Farrington's men had been able to arrange for the assassin's body to be 'discovered' amongst the rubble the following day. Without any evidence to the contrary, the coroner's report could not be questioned by the assassin's employers.

Things seemed to be under control, albeit that his own reputation in the eyes of the Home Secretary would be forever scarred. Farrington knew his own men could be trusted, but what about Chard? It had been a question repeated several times by the Home Secretary at each of the three meetings he'd attended since his return. If it wasn't for the murders committed in South Wales, he could just have the inspector 'removed'. The problem being that, unless the unsolved murders were closed down, enquiries might lead to Lucheni having been spotted in Hawarden. The fact that the attempted bombing of the Coal Exchange had made national headlines didn't help either. At least Chard seemed easily corruptible, though his asking price would cause the Home Secretary a headache.

'I think it's time Inspector Chard and I had another chat,' murmured Farrington as he started to compose a telegram.

***

'We picked her up last night, without any trouble,' said Kimble smugly.

It hadn't taken long for the Cardiff Borough inspector to act on the information supplied from Chard's interrogation of Frank Edwards.

'Good. It's one more of the gang and although I doubt she's the killer, I may be able to get something out of her which will lead me to the two remaining suspects,' replied Chard.

'Never mind your killer,' Kimble objected. 'What about the man who planted the bomb? He might try again!'

'I can say with a degree of confidence that he won't.'

'How can you possibly be so sure?'

'Just a hunch,' replied Chard enigmatically. 'Now, may I speak to the prisoner?'

Kimble gave a dissatisfied grunt. 'Same room as last time. You know the way,' he said curtly, turning his back.

Ada Quill was already waiting, handcuffed as Ted Schwartz had been on Chard's last visit.

'Mrs Ada Quill, I believe,' said Chard sternly.

'Why are you holding me? I've done nothing wrong!'

The inspector stared at the prisoner, taking in the hard look in her eyes. Clearly a woman who was not easily intimidated. The worry lines on her brow, rough complexion and premature grey streaks in her hair indicated a hard life.

'Frank Edwards told us where to find you.'

Chard noticed the shock register in the prisoner's face.

'Frank…? No! Where is he…?'

'Behind bars in Merthyr, Mrs Quill. He's been arrested for attempted robbery.'

Ada made to speak, but then closed her lips, sadness etched into her features.

'We are also aware he was a member of a group of anarchists led by a man called Wilson. You were also a member of the group,' stated Chard.

'Did Frank tell you that?'

'No. We already knew. At the moment we have no evidence against you of any crimes committed, but if I look hard enough…'

'What do you want of me? I'll not say a word against Frank, though.'

Chard nodded his understanding. 'Were you aware a man called Eddie Ward was murdered recently?'

'Yes. Word gets around quickly.'

'Where were you the night it happened?'

'At home. Frank was with me; he sometimes stays the night,' she said unapologetically.

'You see, I have a problem,' said Chard. 'Someone needs to be found guilty for a number of unsolved murders and for planting a bomb at the Coal Exchange. Top of my list are the people who broke away from Wilson's group, which include Frank Edwards and yourself.'

Ada looked frightened. 'It wasn't me or Frank! We were together.'

'Or you were both killing Eddie Ward,' reasoned Chard. 'What about the evening of the bomb? I understand there was a meeting held at Ted Schwartz's lodgings. It broke up before Inspector Kimble got there. So, tell me,' he demanded sternly, 'who was there? Schwartz, Edwards, Janssen, Blandford......perhaps yourself?'

'No! Ted isn't right in the head! I wouldn't trust him, and Victor Blandford makes my flesh creep. I didn't want any part of it. Neither would I stay with Wilson though. He was just a fool playing games. That evening I went and told him so. I heard he had a heart attack the same evening and as much as I was fed up with him, he was harmless and I hope I didn't cause it.'

'You saw Wilson that evening?'

'Yes, and Charlie probably wasn't at Ted's meeting either, because he was just leaving the workshop as I arrived.'

'Do you know where Charlie Janssen is?'

'No idea, and I wouldn't tell you if I did,' replied Ada, sticking her chin out defiantly.

'What about Victor Blandford?'

'Oh, I'd tell you about him if I knew. Which I don't.'

Chard thought for a moment, then abruptly walked to the door and called for the constable waiting outside.

Just as the constable came in, Chard paused, pushed the constable back into the corridor, and returned to stand opposite the prisoner.

'Just one more thing...'

When Chard came out of the room five minutes later, he had an enigmatic smile on his lips.

'You may release Mrs Quill. There is no case to answer and she has been most helpful,' he said to Kimble as he walked out of the station.

***

As much as Chard wanted to get back to his office to think through his next move, there was something more pressing which needed his attention. The coroner's inquest into the death of David Meredith was due to take place in Courthouse Street that afternoon.

Chard knew there was no benefit to be gained by a verdict of suicide, so he stood before the coroner in full uniform and gave his assured opinion that his friend had not been of sound mind when the incident occurred. It was enough to sway the decision and a verdict of death by misadventure was written into the records. After a quick word with Will and Dic, who had been in attendance, and a word of condolence to the widow, Chard rushed back to his office to find an unopened telegram on his desk. He opened it and groaned.

TWENTY-EIGHT

'I'll be out for the rest of the evening, Lucy,' Chard announced as he reached for Barney's lead.

The dog gave a yawn and raised himself from his prone position in front of the fire, to pad quickly towards the door.

'What if there's something urgent, Mr Chard? Will you be at the Ivor?' asked the maid.

'Yes, Lucy, but I have to call in at the station first.'

Farrington's telegram had instructed the inspector to telephone him that evening, probably oblivious to the fact that he didn't own one. At least there was a telephone at the station, and with neither sergeant on duty that evening, just a constable manning the front desk, there would be no raised eyebrows at him using the superintendent's office.

'If you hear a dog growling and making a general nuisance of himself outside, ignore it. I've just tied my animal to a post and he doesn't like it,' said Chard as he entered. 'I'll only be a few minutes.'

'Right you are, sir,' responded Constable Scudamore, thinking nothing of it.

Chard entered the Superintendent's office and made his call via the operator. The phone was answered promptly, as if Farrington had been waiting desperately for the call.

'Have you tidied up all of the loose ends?'

'If you mean, have I decided who I'm going to hang for the murders, then yes, but it might take a while,' replied Chard sharply.

'What do you mean? Do not play games with me Inspector.'

'I'm not playing games. What about your end of the bargain?'

'It might be possible to arrange what you want in a fairly short period of time,' replied Farrington begrudgingly.

'Good. However, there is likely to be one small problem beyond my control.'

'Such as…?'

'My constable overheard Wilson saying Willy Rabinovitz killed him.

He's a good man and won't let it go. There's also the question of the bomb planted at the Coal Exchange. That's something I can make go away, but not Wilson's death.'

'Would your constable be open to an inducement?' asked Farrington cautiously.

'If you mean, can he be bribed, the answer is no.'

'Where is Wilson's body?'

'As far as I am aware it's liable to be still in Cardiff's mortuary, possibly awaiting an inquest.'

The line went quiet as Farrington considered his options. Finally, he came to a decision. 'Let your constable make any enquiries he likes. However, be sure to remind him he will of course need medical evidence to show a murder did take place.'

'Understood,' confirmed Chard. 'I think that should settle matters and hopefully there will be no further need for me to call you. Just remember your end of the bargain.'

Farrington put down the receiver without replying.

Chard smiled at first, and then laughed out loud.

***

Half an hour later, the inspector was at the far end of the bar in the Ivor Arms, talking to Dic Jenkins and Will Horses. Barney had made himself comfortable by sitting on Dic's foot.

'It was good of you, speaking up for Dai like that this afternoon,' said Will.

'The least I could do,' responded Chard. 'We let him down and I hope he's looking down on us with a forgiving heart.'

'Amen to that,' agreed Dic.

Chard sniffed the air. 'Can you smell anything? It's been annoying me since I arrived.'

Bert Humphreys chimed in from behind the bar. 'It's Gwen's fault. Someone lent her a posh cookbook and she decided to make a fancy soup for the guests in the upstairs room. Unfortunately, instead of using three cloves of garlic, she used three bulbs. Stank the place out, it did. Have some more beer, it helps to forget about it.'

All three drained their pints in one gulp and ordered another round, the drinks arriving at the same time as a flustered Gwen appeared from the kitchen. Will made the mistake of glancing in her direction and immediately sniggering. Dic cringed as he saw the expression on Gwen's face as she bustled towards them, nearly bowling over several customers.

'What are you sniggering at, William Owens?' she demanded.

'Nothing.'

'Don't you lie to me. If you three, and yes I'm including you, Thomas, have been having fun at my expense, I'll bar the lot of you!'

Fighting the impulse to laugh, faced with the landlady's enormous quivering bosom and furious expression, Chard was pleased to see an excuse to escape the situation as the pub door opened and Idris Morgan walked in.

'Sorry, Gwen! Police business!' said the inspector, snatching his overcoat from the coat stand, pulling Barney off Dic's foot, and heading quickly in Morgan's direction.

'Sorry, sir, I know you don't like being interrupted in here,' said the constable.

'That's not a problem. I can see from the case you're carrying that you've probably come straight from the train. Let's go outside and find somewhere we can talk privately.'

***

The two men walked back towards the town, then up onto the apex of the Old Bridge. It was a clear night sky, for despite the hundreds of coal fires lit in the town to keep out the evening chill, the stars still shone brightly, reflected in the black waters of the Taff flowing below.

'This is quiet enough,' said Chard. 'Tell me what you've found out. I hope it's going to be helpful, because at the moment I feel I have the pieces of a jigsaw puzzle which won't quite fit.'

Morgan looked uncertain, as if he wanted to say something but didn't know how.

'You seem to have something on your mind. Spit it out,' prompted Chard.

'Before I tell you how I got on, there is something which in truth is bothering me.'

'Then by all means tell me before I die of old age,' replied the inspector good-humouredly.

'The man Wilson named Willy Rabinovitz as his killer and he's our likely murderer, but you've made no attempt to find him. Why?'

Chard, expecting to face the question at some point, chose his words carefully before replying. Willy had met his fate, but the enquiry had to be closed down. 'To be honest, Morgan, I should have reported the matter of Wilson's statement. However, Wilson was not necessarily a man of sound mind. There was no obvious indication of foul play at the time and my understanding of the initial medical report, kindly supplied by Inspector Kimble, was that of a heart attack.' It was a statement which came easily, for it was true, not that the Cardiff Borough's medical examiner was known for his competence or sobriety. 'If it bothers you, then by all means make enquiries with Cardiff to have the body exhumed and re-examined.'

'Thank you, sir. I will,' replied Morgan, still looking concerned. 'But surely Rabinovitz must still be our prime suspect for the other murders?'

'Of course not. I've never suspected him at any point,' replied Chard, smiling inwardly at having hidden the fact from Farrington.

'But I don't understand...'

'The description of Willy Rabinovitz is that of a man barely five feet in height. The strangulation marks on the throats of Councillor Jeavons and Sir Henry, both tall men, were horizontal. Those on Constable Richards showed an upward pull, which meant either the assailant was very tall or his victim had been sitting when attacked. It is possible Richards was sitting; but in the case of Sir Henry, for example, there was nowhere to sit at the murder scene. I also confirmed there were no marks on the knees of his trousers to indicate that he had been felled before the killer started strangling him. Willy was just too short to have done it. That's why I have always been certain of his innocence. As for the bomb at the Coal Exchange, I believe he was also innocent of that. Satisfied?'

'I suppose so, sir,' answered Morgan, still taking in Chard's explanation.

'Good. I believe I know who our killer is, but I'm not at all certain how everything fits together. Tell me how you got on. Was there anything in Sir Henry's past that I need to know about?'

'To get straight to the point, sir, a few interesting things came to light. I spoke to two servants initially, who said he was generally a decent sort. He did seem to have an undue hatred of socialists, communists and such like though, and had seen some service putting down outbreaks of disorder. The decision to sell up and move here was done with little notice, and nearly all of his staff were given a pittance for their past service. There were, however, two exceptions. The valet and the lady's maid were treated with extraordinary generosity, despite having been left behind. Each of them was given enough to set themselves up in business.'

'That is rather odd,' commented Chard thoughtfully.

'Wait until you hear why, sir,' replied Morgan with a broad smile. 'I spoke to Mrs Lincoln, the lady's maid, who revealed that her settlement was conditional on her silence. You see the child we saw wasn't Sir Henry's. That's all she would say.'

Chard furrowed his brow. 'And the valet?'

'He wouldn't talk to me, but Mrs Lincoln believes he knew Sir Henry was guilty of a murder, because she overheard a conversation…'

Chard listened intently as Morgan continued his tale, then when the realisation struck, smiled contentedly. 'The pieces are starting to fit the puzzle. I haven't quite got all the answers, but I know how to get them.'

A sudden chill breeze sprang up, causing Chard to shiver, and Barney started to tug on his lead.

'Well done, Constable. You deserve a good night's rest. I'll see the Superintendent first thing in the morning.'

***

The news that Superintendent Jones was out attending a meeting with the Chief Constable made for a frustrating start to the day. At least Chard knew exactly how he wanted to proceed, but it would need the superintendent's full agreement. In the meantime, there were a few enquiries to be made by telephone and telegram to confirm his suspicions. Fully absorbed in the resulting replies, Chard was interrupted late in the morning by Constable Morgan.

'You won't believe this, sir,' he complained.

'Take a seat, Constable. What is it?'

'It's Wilson. Nobody had claimed the body, so it was still in the mortuary yesterday and we could have had it re-examined.'

'Could have? You mean there's a problem?' asked Chard, keeping a straight face.

'Some relative turned up first thing this morning and carted it away for cremation! Can you believe it, sir?'

Chard marvelled inwardly at Farrington's efficiency. The deceit to Morgan did not sit easy, and the temptation to confide that Wilson's killer had met his own demise was almost overwhelming.

'Never mind, Morgan, we've got other fish to fry and you're going to play an essential part. When Superintendent Jones returns, we'll see him together.'

***

'I can scarcely believe my ears!' declared Superintendent Jones, his expression one of disbelief combined with outrage. 'And you're absolutely sure of this?'

Chard, standing before the superintendent's desk with Morgan at his side, nodded gravely.

'Positive, sir. The only problem is that the evidence is circumstantial, and I don't believe it will be enough for a conviction. They'll go free and the case will forever be "unsolved" in our records.'

'But I don't see how Lady Annabelle could possibly have benefitted from Sir Henry's death. After all, he was dying and I understand he had no intention of changing his will. Is that not so?'

The inspector grimaced. 'It's true. I've had a discreet word with his solicitor and he confirmed it. Lady Annabelle had nothing to gain and seemed genuinely upset by the murder. I admit it's the one thing which still puzzles me. Yet I am convinced she was complicit.'

'Would it not be better to leave her out of it for the time being and simply arrest the murderer?' asked Jones, stroking his moustache.

'Unfortunately, he seems to have vanished. Instructions have been given to locate him, but not to make an arrest. As I've explained, I fear he would be acquitted. Lady Annabelle is the key.'

'Then how do you propose to proceed?'

'I anticipate that within two or three months Lady Annabelle will pack up and leave at short notice. She'll meet up with our suspect and when we have them both together, I'll make the arrest.'

'Three months? I can't allow a murderer to go walking around at liberty for that length of time,' objected Jones. 'I'll allow you until Christmas at the very latest.'

'Thank you, sir. It might not be enough, but I appreciate your dilemma.'

'How will you be alerted if Lady Annabelle does move at short notice?' asked the superintendent.

'At this point I think it worth mentioning the commendable work done by Constable Morgan on my behalf in investigating Sir Henry's past,' remarked Chard, causing the constable to proudly straighten his posture.

'Duly noted. Continue,' Jones prompted.

'We have details of the staff at Lady Annabelle's house from the statements made at the time of Sir Henry's murder. Although they live in, they were all hired locally and we have their family addresses. Constable Morgan will, over the next few weeks, seek to become friendly with some of their relatives whilst out of uniform. Lady Annabelle will have to lay off the staff before leaving, and I would imagine Sir Henry's fine horse will fetch a pretty penny at the auctions. Even at short notice, word will get out quickly to the relatives, and hopefully to Morgan. Then Lady Annabelle can be followed, and the trap sprung.'

Superintendent Jones sat back in his chair, fingers entwined as he considered Chard's proposal. Finally, he leant forward and addressed Constable Morgan.

'It appears we are very reliant on you, Constable. Make sure you are worthy of our trust.'

TWENTY-NINE

It was cold, bone-numbingly so, and Chard hadn't even bothered to remove his overcoat despite having been at his desk for over an hour. A fire had been lit in the station, but its heat failed to reach the inspector's office. When he'd woken that morning, there'd been ice on the inside of the bedroom window and it was only the smell of bacon frying in the pan that had finally prompted him to rise.

'What's this?' he grumbled, picking up a letter that had arrived in the morning post. It was from Inspector Kimble. Chard read it, screwed it into a ball and threw it into his wastepaper basket.

I can't say I blame him, he thought. I'd indicated that I might help find his bomber but here we are in December and I'm no further forward. Morgan has been sniffing about for the last five weeks but no sign of Lady Annabelle making a move. Where Charlie Janssen and Victor Blandford are, God only knows. Ada Quill has been released. Ted Schwartz has served one month's hard labour, and now vanished, but at least Frank Edwards is serving five years for the attempted robbery.

Chard's sombre thoughts were rudely interrupted as the door of his office suddenly burst open.

Looking up in annoyance at the cause of the intrusion, he saw Morgan enter, dressed in plain clothes and with an excited smile on his face.

'She's on the move! I heard a rumour late last night and Ted confirmed it,' the constable garbled.

'Who's Ted? Not Ted Schwartz, I assume.'

Morgan shook his head. 'No, sir, the uncle of one of the maids. I've just been to see him. The staff have all been given a week's notice. Agents will be handling the sale of the property.'

'Any rumour of where Lady Annabelle is going?' asked Chard.

'Not yet, but I'll keep my one good ear to the ground,' replied Morgan with a smile.

'I'll get Sergeant Morris to appoint two men to work in shifts keeping watch on the house. I knew we were right,' said Chard, rubbing his hands with glee. 'I'll go and tell the superintendent our trap is about to be sprung.'

***

It had been a tense, frustrating week, waiting for the rushed departure of Lady Annabelle with her young child. Fortunately, the hired cart taking items of personal luggage to the railway station for onward transportation had been spotted by Constable Temple. Leaving his post close to the house, he had followed the cart to the railway station and made enquiries about the eventual destination of the luggage.

Lady Annabelle had set off in a hired cab early the following morning. She was travelling light, encumbered only by a single case and her child. Unknown to her, Constable Morgan was waiting at Pontypridd railway station, ready to follow in an adjoining carriage, and Inspector Chard had gone ahead to Liverpool's Lime Street Station.

If the winter chill had felt uncomfortable in Pontypridd, the wind's icy blast from the Irish Sea which tormented the city of Liverpool was infinitely worse. Somewhere a church clock struck midnight as Chard, accompanied by Morgan and two constables provided by the Liverpool Constabulary, approached the Midland Adelphi Hotel. There they found a detective sergeant waiting for them just inside the door. Chard's face, numbed by the stinging wind, felt some feeling start to return on entering the relative warmth of the hotel's hallway.

'The man arrived about two hours ago and I've placed the hotel register on the reception counter for you to examine. They're both in their room, Inspector Chard. I've advised the hotel manager that there's a police matter to be dealt with, but nothing else.'

'Thank you, Sergeant. We'll need a maid to take care of the child. Other than that, it's simply a case of arresting them. But I have to stress that they must be separated immediately and not allowed to communicate. The woman is best taken out first; unfortunately her companion is liable to make a fight of it.'

'With five of us, that shouldn't be too much of a problem and Constable Murphy there is a former wrestler. Your man will be in cuffs in seconds,' replied the detective confidently.

'You there! What is going on?' asked a small, fussy-looking man in spectacles who came rushing forward from an adjoining room.

'Let me introduce Mr Towle, the manager,' explained the detective sergeant.

'You are helping the police, for which we are extremely grateful,' said Chard in an attempt to placate him. 'I was just explaining to the sergeant here that we would appreciate the assistance of a maid. Could you oblige us?'

'Yes, of course, but I want to know what's going on.'

Chard gave his most reassuring smile. 'If you can kindly provide a maid and the pass keys to the third-floor rooms, then by all means you may follow us.' Chard put a finger to his lips for emphasis. 'Quietly, mind you.'

The policemen waited for the manager to return with the maid and the pass keys, then ascended the stairs to the third floor.

'Right, it's the fourth door on the left,' whispered Chard. 'Mr Towle, please give me the relevant key.'

The manager obliged, with a degree of hesitancy. 'But they seem very respectable people,' he murmured. 'You might catch them in a state of undress. We don't want a scandal!'

Chard ignored the comment and passed the key to Morgan. 'We get in quick. You take Lady Annabelle, and don't worry about using force. It's imperative we get her out of the way immediately and out of earshot.' The inspector noted Morgan's reluctant expression at having to manhandle a lady. 'Just pretend she's one of the whores who we clear off the street on the Tumble. That's an order.'

'Lady Annabelle? That's not the name she registered under. You mean she's a member of the nobility and you've just ordered your man to treat her like a whore? Oh my...!' exclaimed the hotel manager, starting to raise his voice in panic.

Chard raised his eyebrows in exasperation. 'No more delay! Detective, you secure the child and pass him to the maid. Constables, we take our man. Remember he's a killer!'

Morgan stepped forward quietly, put the key in the lock, and glanced back at his inspector.

'Go!' ordered Chard.

It took seconds to change the hotel's quiet gentility into pandemonium. Lady Annabelle screaming, being dragged unceremoniously from her bed clad only in her chemise; her companion clawing and spitting at the two constables as they handcuffed his naked body; the maid taking the crying child from the detective's arms and running out to the corridor; the hotel manager looking fit to burst with worry as doors of nearby rooms were heard to open, guests raising voices in complaint.

'Help me!' echoed Lady Annabelle's plaintiff cry from somewhere outside as she struggled to free herself from Morgan's firm hold.

'Be so kind as to help by finding a spare room for Lady Annabelle, and lock her in until we arrange transport to the nearest police station,' Chard said to the manager, having to raise his voice to be heard.

'I can't do that! She isn't even properly dressed,' protested Mr Towle. 'What has she done to deserve this treatment?'

'Aiding a murderer, and, oh, incest. Is that enough for you?' asked Chard sarcastically.

The inspector grunted with satisfaction as the manager left to do his bidding, then walked slowly across to the constables, who were standing either side of their subdued prisoner. The man's usual expression of naivety was for once missing, replaced with a mask of pure hatred. Chard stared him in the eye as he spoke. 'James Eden, or as I should correctly say, James Longville. You are under arrest for the murder of Sir Henry Longville… your father.'

THIRTY

'Well, Lady Annabelle, you are in a predicament,' began Chard. It had taken some time to bring both prisoners to Pontypridd. They had been kept apart from the beginning. James Longville had been covered with a coat on his journey to the police station in Liverpool, where he was kept overnight, clothed and put under guard on the early morning train. Lady Annabelle had been allowed to spend the remainder of the night locked in a hotel room, then escorted in silence by Chard and Morgan onto a midday train. Now she sat opposite the inspector in Pontypridd Police Station. Morgan, having been excused due to his night-time vigil, was absent from the room, but Constable Temple stood in his place, notebook at the ready.

'Where is my child?' she demanded.

'In a Liverpool orphanage. When you next see him, he'll be a grown man and won't recognise you,' replied Chard. The words were cruel, deliberately so, delivered without a note of compassion.

A tear began to form in Lady Annabelle's already red-rimmed eyes. Her dishevelled hair flowed untidily over the shoulders of her navy-blue dress, one of the few items of clothing she had been allowed to bring. 'My George is a delicate boy. I need to see him.'

'I dare say he could perhaps be moved to St Michael's in Treforest, but that will take time. You will no doubt be engaging a solicitor, and he can try to arrange it.'

Lady Annabelle nodded and straightened her posture as if in an attempt to regain her composure. 'On what charge am I being held?'

'Accessory to murder. We know James killed his father and we have all the proof we need,' lied the inspector. 'In the circumstances, given the abnormal relationship with your stepson, I expect they'll lock you up and throw away the key.'

The prisoner swallowed hard. 'I see… But I knew nothing of the murder.'

'Don't lie!' shouted Chard. The aggressive tone to a distressed woman did not come easy, but it was essential to break her, and her face betrayed a desire for self-preservation. 'When I interviewed you after your husband's murder, you told me both Sir Henry's children from his previous marriage were dead. It's true that his daughter had died, but his son had disappeared. No body had ever been found, and in fact you knew that James was still alive.'

'I panicked... It was the distress... I didn't know what I was saying...'

'No! You knew exactly what you were saying. It was an attempt to divert my attention away from the true killer, and might now see you rot in jail for the rest of your life.'

Lady Annabelle started to weep as Constable Temple fidgeted uncomfortably in the background.

'Your only hope is to tell me the truth. It may save you... And reunite you with your son.'

The words were the final blow that cracked Lady Annabelle's resolve. 'I tried to stop him. I swear I did,' she pleaded, the words sounding genuine, as if torn from her soul.

Chard softened his tone. 'Then tell me everything, from the beginning.'

Lady Annabelle lapsed into silence, and when she eventually spoke, it was in a restrained, quiet voice.

'I met Henry in London. He was, as you know, much older than me, but he moved in such grand social circles that I was dazzled. He had not long been bereaved, though you wouldn't have thought so, and we had a whirlwind engagement. The marriage took place in London with few guests. He had no family other than James, who didn't attend. After a honeymoon in Paris, we travelled to Henry's home in Cumberland. It soon became apparent that my husband's only real interests were horses and visiting former army colleagues away from home. Cumberland was boring and I felt lonely.'

'And James...?' prompted Chard.

'He was sixteen when he came into my room one night when Henry was away.' Lady Annabelle paused, before crying out loud, 'Oh God! It should never have happened! I should never have allowed it to happen!'

'Constable, go and fetch her ladyship a cup of tea,' Chard ordered

Temple, as the prisoner slumped forward, weeping uncontrollably.

Ten minutes later, tears still trickling down her cheeks, a calmer Lady Annabelle continued her story. 'When I became pregnant, there was gossip below stairs and Henry must have overheard one of the servants. From that moment on, he became distant and when George was born, although there was some similarity with my husband's features, he looked more like James. My husband never said anything to me. There were no accusations, but he knew. James was sent to study over the border in Scotland, but never arrived. He just disappeared. It was said that he'd died in a drowning accident and his body was never recovered. Soon after, all the staff were dismissed, my husband cut himself off from his social circle and we came here.'

'When did you next see your stepson?'

'Earlier this year. He appeared without warning, having ensured Henry was out, pretending to be a travelling cabinet maker and demanding to speak to the mistress of the house. It transpired that on arriving in Scotland, he'd been waylaid by men hired by his father's valet. After beating him to within an inch of his life they threw him into a river to drown. Somehow, he survived, was found and cared for by a crofter and after many months regained his health. After that, he resolved to take his revenge and followed us here.'

'What did he tell you about his plans?'

'He told me that if my husband was out of the way, I would inherit his wealth and we could start a new life together in America with George. I know there's an age difference of fifteen years between us, but if a man takes a younger wife, then no one blinks an eye, so why should it be different for a woman?'

Chard resisted the temptation to comment that the age difference was immaterial. Hers was an incestuous relationship with her stepson. Did he say he was going to kill him?'

'Yes... but I didn't think he meant it,' she added hurriedly.

The inspector wasn't deceived by the lie, but chose not to challenge it. 'But Sir Henry didn't have long to live. You would have inherited the money and been together anyway.'

'I didn't know that at the time. As soon as I found out, I wrote to James and gave the letter to our occasional gardener to post in town the day before Henry died. It was the only way to avoid the risk of my husband seeing it. For some reason the letter never arrived. I swear that I tried to stop James and he would never have hurt his father if he'd have known.'

'Obviously not,' replied Chard sarcastically. 'It does explain why you were genuinely distressed at your husband's murder.'

'I really was. It was all so pointless. Afterwards, James wrote to me and we made arrangements to meet in Liverpool before sailing to America. Tell me, Inspector, how did you know I was involved with James?'

'I didn't at first. I'd been struck by the particular viciousness of your husband's murder. The way the black flag drawing had been stuffed down his throat. It seemed...unnecessary. As if there was something personal in the attack. It unsettled me, and made me want to look more into his background, especially as the secluded lifestyle seemed so strange. There was clearly something unusual about your move from Cumberland, but at that point I was unaware of the motive. Our further investigations revealed that George was not Sir Henry's child. Subsequently I made enquiries which confirmed that James's death had not been registered. We had also discovered that Sir Henry had been overheard talking to his valet after the alleged drowning accident, in a manner best described as conspiratorial. Then came the recollection of my reaction when James first appeared before me to provide information against his fellow anarchists. I remember saying that his face looked familiar. Of course, I'd first seen that same naïve expression when I met your child, his son.'

Lady Annabelle sobbed at the mention of her child.

'In the meantime,' continued Chard, 'I had separately deduced that the man I knew as James Eden was a killer. The pieces of the puzzle finally came together and his true identity became obvious. Instinct told me that revenge would not be enough for him. Brutal killers tend to have a leaning towards avarice, and as the inheritance lay with you, his former lover, I reasoned that you were likely to be involved. His intention would have been either to marry you, or to kill you and George, reappearing sometime in the future to claim everything as the only living heir.'

'He would never have harmed me.'

'What do you know of the other murders?'

Lady Annabelle looked perplexed. 'What other murders?'

'Three other victims were murdered in the same manner. Were they part of your plan too?'

'I don't understand. What are you talking about? Why are you doing this to me?' demanded Lady Annabelle, collapsing into tear-filled hysteria.

'Never mind. Funnily enough, I believe you. Constable Temple, put your notebook away and look after the prisoner. I've had enough for now. Our other prisoner can stew overnight; it's been a long day.

***

'Feeling refreshed?' asked Chard the following morning as Constable Morgan, back in uniform, entered his office.

'Yes, thank you, sir. I fell asleep as soon as my head hit the pillow yesterday afternoon. Didn't wake until five o'clock this morning. How did the interviews go yesterday?'

'The one with Lady Annabelle was most productive, but I've saved James Longville. I think you deserve to be present for this one,' replied Chard with a smile. 'Tell Sergeant Morris I'd like the prisoner brought from his cell, then join me in the interview room.'

Ten minutes later, Longville was brought before Chard, accompanied by two constables who pushed their handcuffed prisoner into the chair facing the inspector. Morgan sat to one side, notebook at the ready.

Chard waited for the constables to leave, taking their positions outside the door, before starting his interrogation. 'We know your real identity. I assume you won't try to deny it?'

James's face, so full of aggression and malice the previous evening, had returned to the more familiar expression of youthful naivety. 'No,' he replied 'You know who I am and if it helps, I confess to having an incestuous relationship with my stepmother. Though when there are so many other terrible crimes in the world, I'm surprised at the lengths to which you have gone.'

'You know very well that incest is the least of your crimes. Let's talk about the murder of your father,' replied Chard drily.

'I don't know what you mean.' The denial came with a look of innocence.

'We've got the murder weapon, the garrotte.'

'Oh, you mean the one dropped by Willy after he murdered Wilson.'

'Wilson wasn't murdered. The coroner ruled that he had a heart attack,' snapped Chard.

'But Wilson said...'

'He was unhinged by coronary pain. It isn't relevant, particularly as we know for a fact that Rabinovitz didn't murder your father. He was too damn short! Our medical examiner will swear to it under oath. He is also able to confirm that the wire of the garrotte found is of the right diameter and length to have caused the marks on not just your father's throat, but also on three other victims.'

'It looked like standard piano wire to me. Anyway, if it wasn't Willy's, then someone else must have dropped it. Perhaps Wilson himself,' suggested James.

Chard stared at the prisoner, looking for some sign of nervousness: a tic of the eyelid, a sweaty brow, a trembling finger – but there was nothing. It was as if ice ran through Longville's veins.

'Wilson had two other visitors before we arrived,' resumed the inspector. 'Ada Quill told me Charlie Janssen had been there, and I did consider there was an outside chance he was the guilty party. However, on questioning her further, she was able to confirm that before leaving Wilson, she had helped to clean up the room. At that time – and she will swear this under oath – there was no garrotte on the floor where you say you found it. You changed your original plan because you thought you'd had a moment of inspiration, when in fact it was a disastrous mistake.'

'Plan? What are you talking about, inspector?'

There it was, Chard smiled to himself: a slight nerve tremor of the left eyebrow. 'Your intention was to plant the garrotte at Ted Schwartz's place. By insisting on going to find Wilson first, I threw things awry. His claim that Willy Rabinovitz had killed him quickly made you think of planting the garrotte there instead. If Willy really was going to be pursued for a murder, then surely we'd believe he was our strangler? An open and shut case. Because you thought it through in a split second, the realisation of his height as a factor didn't register with you, did it?'

James looked annoyed with himself as Chard continued. 'I suspect it was you who whistled to warn Schwartz and his confederates. There was no longer any point in involving them and any possible complications, because you thought you already had a perfect scapegoat.'

There was a bead of perspiration appearing on James's brow as he replied. 'All circumstantial.'

Chard leaned forward, ready to deliver the telling blow. 'Lady Annabelle has confessed to knowing of your intentions. Do I have a witness to you killing Sir Henry, or anyone else for that matter? No. However, I can confirm your stated intention to kill your father. In addition, I have strong circumstantial evidence indicating you had been in possession of the likely murder weapon and had planted it for us to find. Finally, you had the motive of securing a life together with your own child, your stepmother and her inherited fortune. The jury will be scandalised to hear of how you were caught in bed with your stepmother, whilst planning to leave for America the following day. Will it be enough to convict you? Yes, Mr Longville. Of that I have no doubt whatsoever. There will be no need to build a case around the other three victims, because we can only hang you once. It's a shame, because they didn't really need to die, did they?'

'You're talking nonsense.' The hatred was back in his eyes.

'Not nonsense. It was part of a brilliant, if rather over-elaborate plan. After recovering from the injuries inflicted by your father's hired ruffians, you wanted revenge. It took time to trace where he'd taken Lady Annabelle and your son, but that gave you time to think of a way around the main problem. In normal circumstances, if someone had murdered your father then the obvious thing would have been to look for a motive. That would initially have revealed absolutely nothing. With no other leads, whichever police force was investigating would have had to have done exactly what we did, and look closer into Sir Henry's family and background. Somehow you had to stop that happening, by creating an obvious suspect or group of suspects. Fortunately, you had become aware of a group of anarchists. A small cell of poor, deluded individuals who could be manipulated.'

Chard paused for a while, noticing the discomfort on James's features. 'The three other murders were just playing pieces in your little game. No connection between them other than the drawings of a black flag, a known anarchist symbol. Then, after Eddie Ward the printer had been disposed of, you played the part of the conscientious innocent young man, drawn into the world of anarchists, but now seeking redemption. You could have gone to the police in Cardiff, where the gang usually met, but no; you came and reported everything to me. Why? Because that way you could "help" by directing my investigation into Sir Henry's death towards your intended targets.'

Chard could tell from the look in the prisoner's eyes that he realised he was beaten. The expression now was that of a disappointed child. If an unknowing matron were to enter the room, she would undoubtedly want to put her comforting arms around him.

'My father wasn't there when my mother died. Did you know that? He stayed away from home during her entire illness. He was never worthy of us. When he remarried, I knew he would pass everything to Annabelle in his will, for he had no love of me. But the inheritance should be mine by right. Getting back at him by becoming Annabelle's lover was only fair, do you see?'

'Yet you also murdered him.'

'Only after he'd attempted to have me beaten to death...' the excuse faded into an uncomfortable silence, before the prisoner continued. 'What if I hadn't planted the garrotte at Wilson's? Would I have got away with it?'

'Possibly. It was the key mistake. However, I was suspicious of you before then. It was because you'd been too elaborate. Granted, you needed to find a way of not getting involved in a drawn-out conviction process for your minor involvement with the anarchists. That is understandable. But you went too far. Knowing what time your manager did his regular check of the Coal Exchange archives, you planted the bomb, arranging your meeting with me to coincide with the timing mechanism. The plan was to save the day and ensure your act of heroism would mean that any magistrate would deal leniently with your minor misdemeanours. The bomb, of course, would never have gone off. You'll have deliberately made sure that one of the connections was faulty and disguised the fact when you pulled the wires apart.'

'I thought...'

'Yes, you thought we were all fooled. I might have been had someone you loved been present. You see, in a case where there is a risk of imminent death but the chance to escape, most people will take it rather than almost certainly lose their life. The only exception might be to save someone you love: a wife, a child and so on. I couldn't believe you were prepared to risk your life for people you didn't know, who might have been able to escape anyway. From then on there were doubts in my mind. Not certainty, I grant you. At one point I did consider it might have been one of the others, and it did take some time to put all the pieces together. But as soon as Constable Morgan returned from Cumberland, it all fell into place.'

'Shit!' swore James, his face a mask of despair.

'Why did you pick the other three victims in particular? You needn't tell me, but as we are going to hang you for your father's murder anyway…?'

'I wanted to cause confusion, so picked Merthyr Tydfil and then Barry as places that are far apart but still under the County Constabulary, knowing that I would come to Pontypridd police station after my father's death and point you in the wrong direction. The old man in Merthyr was unlucky. I'd gone into a pub looking for a victim and there he was, buying drinks and proclaiming how important he was. As for the constable, I just felt like killing a copper,' said James with a cold smile on his lips.

Chard wanted to strike him, but held his temper.

'As for Eddie,' continued the prisoner, 'I needed an excuse to come to you for help and so one of my fellow anarchists had to die as part of my story. Because the gang met in Cardiff it made sense to direct your enquiries there. I didn't like the little bastard anyway. Is that all you want from me?'

'I'm curious. You haven't asked one question about what will happen to Lady Annabelle or your son.'

James shrugged. 'I wanted revenge and her inheritance. Her body was just a bonus. As for George, he was an accident. I would have sent him away in any case.'

Chard felt an icy shiver down his spine at the presence of such pure evil. Still smarting from the callous comment about murdering a fellow policeman, he couldn't resist a final barb. 'It's ironic, isn't it?'

'What is?'

'You could have had it all. The inheritance, Lady Annabelle, a new life and freedom. If only you had received the letter she'd sent you, explaining that your father was dying soon anyway. But it's easy to work out what happened. It was in the evening mail, and as Mr Meredith set fire to it, you were there – watching it, and your future, burn!'

EPILOGUE

I haven't had the opportunity to thank you until now,' said Farrington to the man standing in front of his desk. 'Once again you have given excellent service, but this time it was obviously a matter of the highest importance.'

Dr Thatch, appointed as medical examiner by Farrington after the Archbishop's demise, shrugged. 'I welcome your thanks, but I did nothing.'

'Your modesty is admirable, but if the truth about the archbishop's death had come out—'

'But it did,' interrupted the doctor. 'He had a heart attack.'

'Yes, obviously; but I mean if the cause had come out...'

'That's what I mean. He had a weak heart. There was no, how can I say... outside influence.'

'What? No puncture wound? No pinprick?'

The doctor shook his head. 'Nothing. I can assure you. There was no foul play.'

Farrington sighed. 'Thank you anyway, Doctor. My clerk will see you out. I have important matters to consider.'

Once alone, Farrington groaned. Lucheni must have noticed he was in danger and abandoned the attempt on the archbishop's life. If only they had known, the successful elimination of the assassin could have been trumpeted as a major triumph.

'Damn!' Since they had arranged to have the body 'found' miles away in Birmingham, any such attempt at claiming a coup would throw suspicion on the original account. The possible inference would be that someone had indeed killed the archbishop and that this was now a cover story. No, better to leave things as they stood, he told himself. The sooner everybody forgot about the whole incident the better.

He picked up the newspaper and read the article that he'd been looking at earlier and read the headline aloud. 'Incest and Murder in South Wales.' He barked a sarcastic laugh. It appeared that Lucheni had nothing to do with the strangulations and Chard had fooled him into providing a reward. At least the inspector had managed to keep his mouth shut about what happened at Hawarden, so some form of recompense was due. Interestingly though, not many men would have asked for something so public-spirited. He would be a man to keep an eye on in the future.

***

'Any news on Victor Blandford?' Chard asked Morgan, once the constable had finished being given his duties by Sergeant Morris.

'None, I'm afraid, sir, nor of Charlie Janssen.'

'I'm not bothered about Janssen, he's probably gone to sea, nor any of the others for that matter. The only one likely to cause future problems is Blandford. Schwartz told me he'd had ideas about derailing a train, so he's a dangerous young man. I dare say he was also Frank Edwards's accomplice in the attempted payroll robbery. If he ever returns to these parts, I'm going to nail his hide to the wall,' vowed Chard, his emotion barely hidden as he recalled that it had been Blandford who had recruited Dai Books and preyed on his state of mind.

'At least we got Longville,' Morgan reminded him.

'Yes, though I feel the jury were more influenced by the incest than the murders. That was why it was so important to catch him with Lady Annabelle. Without her evidence of knowing about his intentions, he could have wheedled out of it.'

'I'm surprised she did give in and tell you.'

'What option did she have? It was either co-operate or face a worse sentence. They might even have hanged her as well. As it was, they accepted that she knew nothing other than his stated intention, and that she had tried to stop him. Her guilt was in not warning her husband in the first place. Unfortunately for her, the judge was so scandalised by her relationship that she got ten years anyway. At least she keeps her inheritance and her lawyers will appoint a guardian for the child, rather than leave the poor thing in an orphanage. Besides all that, I get the feeling she didn't really love her stepson. Once the deed had been done, she probably felt joining him for a new life was a reasonable option. He was the father of her child after all, and if she'd refused, he might have killed her.'

Morgan looked thoughtful. 'When May gets back from Bristol, I might pay her a visit and tell her all about it.'

'Regretting your decision not to ask for her hand?' asked Chard, raising an eyebrow.

Morgan shrugged. 'I'm not sure, to be honest. Perhaps I was a little hasty.'

'She's also been on my mind,' said Chard. 'I doubt I can get her job back at the infirmary, but I hear they're short-handed at the orphanage in Treforest. With luck I can put in a good word for her.'

'I dare say she'll be back soon, and then—'

'Thomas! I hope you don't mind me interrupting.'

Chard looked around in astonishment. It was Superintendent Jones who appeared in the doorway. Never, under any circumstances, was he that familiar.

'Please come into my office, will you?' he continued, face beaming with happiness.

Chard followed his superior and closed the door behind them.

'Yes, sir?'

'I'm sure you'd like a whisky. Ten-year-old single malt. I keep it for special occasions,' said the superintendent, taking two glasses from a drawer and pouring from a bottle of Scotch that was on his desk.

The inspector was feeling disorientated by the turn of events. Drinking on duty? What's going on, he wondered? Taking a glass and bracing himself (for Chard loved Irish whiskey, but abhorred Scotch whisky), he followed Jones's example and drank it in one swallow.

'May I ask what we are celebrating, sir?' asked the inspector, trying to hide his dislike of the fiery spirit.

'I've just been notified by the Chief Constable of some wonderful news. The Home Office, in conjunction with the Central Inspectorate of Constabulary, have taken an interest in our county. Given the importance of maintaining stability in this area on which, due to the coal industry, our High Seas Fleet depends, they feel there needs to be more investment in law and order. Consequently, the government is supplying direct financial support, with instructions to our local authorities to provide additional assistance in the form of extra funding over the next five years. In short, our constabulary's budget is nearly doubled with immediate effect. Additionally, your report on setting up a network of detectives in the county has been highly commended. We may need perhaps a few months to get everything properly in place, but it will happen.'

Chard allowed himself a smile. Farrington had kept his promise after all. 'I'm very pleased, sir.'

Jones patted him on the shoulder. 'And so you should be, Inspector Chard... or should I say, Detective Inspector Chard?'

AUTHOR'S NOTES

The plot to kill the Czar

My dramatization of Tynan's capture is reasonably accurate, though I have taken some literary licence with it. The quote about wanting to blow up Marlborough House, for example, was attributed to a conversation he had in New York. The Czar and Czarina did leave Britain safely and continued their European tour unmolested. There was of course an international row of major proportions when the French refused to allow Tynan's extradition. After celebrating his release with champagne, he returned to America where he wrote a book about his exploits. The whole plot from its initial discovery in America, the surveillance of the 'dynamitards' (the Victorian term for bombers) across America, Great Britain, Italy, Germany, France and Belgium involving international police co-operation, the adoption of disguises and false names by Tynan's gang, etc. is far too involved to explain fully here. Farrington is of course my own invention.

'Willy'

He is of course fictional, but influenced by a number of different sources. With regard to his name(s):

Rabinovitz was a surname used to buy one of Tynan's travel tickets;

Lucheni was the surname of a real anarchist who, two years after the setting of this novel, assassinated the Empress Elisabeth of Austria.

Willy mentions he was born in Ukraine and his father worked for the Hughes mining company. It was whilst writing this novel that I came across the origin of the Ukrainian city of Donetsk. In 1869 the Hughes Mining Company set up a steel works and several coal mines here and in fact the town's name was changed to Hughesovka (Yuzovka) and it remained so until the 1920s.

Willy's physical description might sound unlikely, but from a contemporary newspaper report I give you the description of another real-life anarchist from the same period, one Giuseppe Farnard who was active in Whitechapel:

'He was scarce above four feet in stature, thin as a rake, dirty, unkempt, and dressed in the shabbiest of shabby suits.'

Edward White Benson, Archbishop of Canterbury

There was of course no attempt on the archbishop's life, but the much-revered gentleman did pass away at Hawarden in October 1896, exactly as portrayed in the novel. When the local constable notified the authorities, the coroner telegraphed that there was to be no post-mortem.

Potential Targets for an anarchist attack

a) The Privy Council did meet at Balmoral soon after the Czar's visit and the Prince of Wales (Albert Edward) often visited Wynard Park.

b) Postboxes remained targets for political protest, with the suffragette movement using fire and acid in the early 1900s. In terms of its practical rather than symbolic effects, the modern equivalent would perhaps be the interception and permanent deletion of random e-mails and attachments including financial instruments.

Lord Penrhyn

Frank Edwards mentions his grievance with Lord Penrhyn. At the time the novel is set, there was an ongoing industrial dispute in North Wales at the slate quarries owned by the second Baron Penrhyn. It was to develop into a full strike the following year. Lord Penrhyn closed the quarries in response, putting the men out of work and forcing them to eventually capitulate.

The Coal Exchange

It is difficult to overstate the importance of this building in Mount Stuart Square. Trading at the Exchange determined the world price for coal and literally thousands of people would use the building each day. It is rumoured that the first recorded million-pound business deal was made there in 1904.

Pontypridd Post Office

The post office in the 1890s was in Taff Street.

Would there have been much post in the postboxes overnight? Hypo-thetically, yes. For those of us old enough to remember the days before e-mail and mobile phone apps, missing the last post collection was not unfamiliar.

St Deiniol's Library

This had been donated by Gladstone, but the building in the story is not the one that exists today. After his death in 1898, the magnificent Gladstone's Library was rebuilt and opened in 1902. I had the pleasure of visiting it whilst conducting my research.

Glamorganshire County Constabulary

One of the difficult challenges when writing historical fiction that has been deeply researched is knowing what not to include and what needs to be tweaked to the benefit of the story.

In this novel Chard undertakes a review of some of the county's police stations, mainly to allow the flexibility to search for Lucheni. I needed to present it as a difficult task for him, but for the flow of the story I've tried hard not to make it more involved than necessary.

In 1894 the county had 370 police including 6 superintendents, of which one was the deputy chief constable (Pontypridd's Evan Jones, a policeman of excellent repute). That's one man per 1,325 of the population at the time. The constabulary's administrative headquarters were located in Canton on the outskirts of Cardiff.

In terms of geography, the divisional commands could be very different in size. Those with concentrated populations such as Aberdare and Pontypridd covered a smaller area than, for example, Bridgend and Barry. The latter also covered the area surrounding Cardiff and into the Rhymney Valley, although the novel focuses on the docks and the town. There were many substations in the county, some fully manned but others occupied by just one or two constables. Incidentally, the Neath division excluded the town itself as the latter had a very small borough force, which I have left out of the narrative.

In terms of 1890s Pontypridd, the only substations worthy of featuring on an Ordnance Survey map in the immediate area were those at Treforest and Church Village (the latter hasn't been mentioned in the series so far, but may appear at some point). However, by 1898 there was also one at Ynysybwl.

By 1911 there had been enormous changes influenced by the industrial unrest and the deployment of troops in 1898 and 1910. There were eight divisions at that time, not including Merthyr Tydfil, which had split off to become an independent borough police force like Swansea and Cardiff. The number of officers had increased well beyond the levels of the previous century and each division had on average over 20 stations.

I would heartily recommend the wonderful Facebook page of the 'Virtual Museum of the Police in Wales' run by ex-policeman Ross Mather, who has been most helpful. Any incorrect interpretation of the structure of the constabulary is down to myself, either accidentally or as artistic licence to assist the narrative.

And Finally

My profound thanks to the Authors' Foundation, without whose assistance much of the research needed for this book would not have been possible. Thanks also to my wife Janet, for proofreading my initial draft, and of course to the team at Seren for their wonderful work in getting this to publication.

THE AUTHOR

Leslie Scase is a former Customs and Excise officer, born and educated in south Wales but now living in Shropshire. He is a member of the Crime Writers Association and of the Crime Cymru writers collective. He regularly gives talks on crime in the late Victorian period, has appeared at many literary festivals and been interviewed on BBC radio. His interests include military history, fly fishing, cooking, real ale, football and rugby. This is his fourth novel in the Inspector Chard Mysteries series.